PRAISE FOR SUSAN STINSON AND *VENUS OF CHALK*

"Venus of Chalk *satisfies like that first long breath after a good cry; like a thorough spring cleaning; like a warm, clothing-optional hug. If they ever conduct a census of fictional characters, the category of unapologetic fat woman will be nearly empty—a criminal lack—but for Carline, who courageously pursues her sense of self across continents, back to childhood, and into the mysteries of her own body. We can all benefit from her travel tips.*"

Marilyn Wann, author, *FAT!SO?*

"*Susan Stinson is at her best in* Venus of Chalk. *In characteristically gracious Stinson-style, she gives voice to detail with incredible delicacy and finesse, even in the most pedestrian moments. By so doing, she exposes the contours of an otherwise unseen and elusive world.* Venus of Chalk *is an engaging journey of discovery brimming with imagery and adventure, passion and politics. This book is going places—hop on board for a great ride!*"

Sondra Solovay, Esq., author, *Tipping the Scales of Justice: Fighting Weight-Based Discrimination*

"*This neatly-stitched tale of a latter-day home economist's 'glaring departures from sensible living' is a religious experience. Under Susan Stinson's microscopic needlework, the fabric of the phenomenal world shimmers with sublime beauty. A can of baking soda, a traffic pylon, a city bus—these things will never look the same again. Stinson lavishes the same minute reverence on her human subjects, discovering rich, sacramental meaning in their most banal small talk. This book unravels what you think you know about women and men, the freakish and the normal, shame and salvation—then mends it anew into a most surprising story.*"

Alison Bechdel, creator, *Dykes To Watch Out For*

"*Carline is brave, strong and beautiful, just like Susan Stinson's writing. As a reader, I was fascinated by Carline's journey; as a writer I was dazzled by the language in which it was told.*"

Lesléa Newman, author, *Heather Has Two Mommies*

VENUS OF CHALK

a novel by Susan Stinson

Firebrand Books

Cover Design by Jonathan Bruns
Cover photo © Getty Images
Book design by Jonathan Bruns

Printed in the United States

10 9 8 7 6 5 4 3 2 1

An application for cataloging has been filed with the Library of Congress.
Stinson, Susan

Venus of Chalk by Susan Stinson p.cm.
ISBN 1-56341-137-7

To my parents, Bill and Mollie Stinson,
in honor of practical, rock-solid love

Sections of the novel have been previously published in modified forms in the following:

"Bus Trips," http://www.blithe.com/bhq5.1/5.1.04.html, *Blithe House Quarterly*, Aldo Alvarez, Tisa Bryant and Jarrett Walker, editors. Winter 2001 / Volume 5, Number 1.

"Visiting," p 124 – 132, *The Mammoth Book of Lesbian Erotica*, Rose Collis, editor. Carroll &Graf, New York, NY: 2000. First published in the UK by Robinson, an imprint of Constable &Robinson Ltd, London: 2000.

"Heat," p 42-44, *Diva*, Gillian Rodgerson, editor. January 2000 issue, London, UK.

"Crease," p 52-55, *Diva*, Gillian Rodgerson, editor. December 2002 issue, London, UK

"Crease," p 343-346, *Groundswell: The Diva Book of Short Stories 2*, Helen Sandler, editor. Diva Books, London: 2002.

"Lake," http://www.lodestarquarterly.com/, *Lodestar Quarterly*, Patrick Ryan and Aaron Jason, editors. Winter 2003 Issue 8.

ACKNOWLEDGEMENTS

I am so grateful to the people named below, who did things like respond to drafts of the manuscript again and again over the course of years, or drive me halfway across the country so I could take notes through the window of a moving vehicle, or offer a fresh perspective when I needed it most. Some made me beautiful meals. Some made sure I got to a conference or that I had the things I needed to write (time, groceries, a computer, a teapot, a tutu). Some have done most of the above. Some love this book passionately. Many have inspired me. Almost all have sustained me with friendship. Their generosity stuns me.

Thanks especially to: Sally Bellerose, Lynne Gerber, Hilary Sloin and Don Stinson. Karen Oosterhous of Firebrand welcomed the book with energy and excitement. I'm way past grateful to Elaine Keach.

Thanks, also, to Max Airborne; Rene Andersen; The BBBB Fund; Angela Barth; Miriam Berg; Mary Bombardier; Elissa Braunstein; Phil Brocklesby; Cate Carulli; Carolyn Cushing; Elana Dykewomon; Vahram Elagöz; Jerry Epstein; Valija Evalds; The Fairy Foundation; Nancy Folbre; John Ford; Judy Freespirit and the Feminist Caucus of NAAFA; James Heintz; Tryna Hope; Beth Klemer; Meridith Lawrence; Evie Leder and the women of the Curve board; Kelly Link; Elizabeth McCracken; Lynn Minnick; Lisa Nelson; Lesléa Newman; Nolose; Elaine Pourinski; Martha Richards; Marci Riseman; Evan Sagerman; Alice Sebold; Alison Smith; Sondra Solovay; Judith Stein; Barbara, Garrett, Marissa and Emmett Stinson; Mike, Eva, Candace and Parker Stinson; Karen Stinson; Linda Stout; Nancy Summer; Cynthia Suopis; Barbara Tobias; Dot Turnier-Nelson, Sarah Van Arsdale; Marilyn Wann, Becca Widom. And with strong memories of my radiant grandparents, Emmett and Nan Jordan.

I'd also like to honor the three generations of home economists in my family: Mollie Stinson, Inez Stinson, Corinne Stinson, Mary Dale Forbus, and Shelley Fillipp.

PROLOGUE

In the middle of Maryland, I shoved the bus window open as far as it would go, knelt on the seat and stuck my head and shoulders out the window. Wind crackled in my ears and nested in my hair. I held my mouth in an O, inhaling rings of fast-moving air until I had to laugh, giddy with mist and speed.

I was in a valley far from home, passing white barns and big houses as I leaned into emptiness, heavy breasts bouncing in my high compression nylon/lycra motion control bra, one of two passengers on a corroded city bus with loud exhaust and soft brakes rattling south to Texas to be sold for salvage. As we left behind a sign that said, "Pick your own pumpkins," I tried to think of recipes. Instead, pressed into the sharp edge of the window frame, I looked down past the shivering flank of the bus to the jittery road streaming beneath me, and grabbed hard onto another kind of joy: Lilian.

Lilian, in a crinoline and a beaded body suit, is reading aloud to our friends. Jen, Sarah, everyone is here. We've already had homemade crackers, waldorf salad and wine. We've all been sitting in the living room, eating and flirting in a neighborly way, talking about pellet versus wood burning stoves and the threat of Wal-Mart coming to town. It's a party in honor of Emily Dickinson's birthday. Lilian is reading:

If your Nerve deny you –
Go above your Nerve –
He can lean against the Grave,
If he fear to swerve –

I'm lingering in the kitchen, putting a cherry pie in the oven. I set the timer and watch through the doorway. Lilian's big thighs are visible under the audacious slip she's wearing as a skirt. I made it for her.

Technically, crinoline refers to petticoats stiffened with horsehair thread, but, for Lilian, I didn't even use starch. Her slip is all soft fullness: three yards of blue tulle, nylon thread. I wrapped her bare waist with the tape measure and marked the correct quarter inch with my thumb. The slip had to fit tightly, or it would sag under its own weight. I folded a strip of organza between two layers of cotton, and sewed three rows of stitches to guide me in attaching the translucent skirts. I felt tender as I gathered and pinned the tulle, which made a tiny ruffle along the inside of the waistband that only she would feel. The balls of my fingers became pricked and tender from bunching the fabric, but then hummed with vibration as I fed my work under the needle of the Singer. I loved the motorized stitches streaming over bumps of gathered tulle.

She's finishing the Dickinson:

If your Soul seesaw
Lift the Flesh door –

She has asked my permission to read the piece she's been working on about me. I looked it over last night at the kitchen table, and felt distinctly nervous. "What does this have to do with Emily Dickinson?"

Lilian chewed on a fingernail. "Adrienne Rich called Dickinson 'Vesuvius at home.' She has that in common with you."

I didn't try to deny my volcanic qualities, but fiddled with my earrings, thinking about times I'd seen her pause in writing to reach under her t-shirt and take both breasts in her hands. She would hold them for a moment or two, then pick up her Dr. Grip pen and go on. Picturing that, I said, "Okay."

Everything Lilian writes matters, even if it makes me want to fill the sink with water and put my head under until it is over. She offered to change my name, but I chose notoriety. That may surprise those who know me, but I am more proud of my lover than afraid of anything, even the truth. So now she lifts the page and reads:

When compelled by a persuasive idea at a meeting, Carline fingers her belly. Once I volunteered for the finance committee of a food bank about to go bankrupt just so I could watch across the table for that gesture, strangely invisible to others. She loves to chair and take notes, both; refuses to do one without the other. She's not always popular, but she's effective. When she shows me a brochure she has written, she puts it down and opens to the middle, smoothing the pages back, creasing the binding to give me the heart of it before she'll let me wander. She built our bed.

I used to try to get Carline to show a little flesh at the monthly tea dance on a Sunday afternoon. I bought her a camisole to wear under the double-breasted butterscotch jacket she uses for big presentations, but she never wanted to flaunt anything, not even for a staid bunch of lesbians still doing the macarena. I gave her a rhinestone evening bag, but she said it wasn't practical enough to be her serious purse.

People see me, but Carline gets missed. She puts on one of her pantsuits in a durable fabric, and becomes a fat lady waiting for a bus, a woman whose inner life is of interest only to the truly adventurous. Of course, my friends, I count you among them. I tried to get her to be Elvis one Halloween, could imagine the shrieks of delight if she greased her hair, wore a leather jacket and baggy trousers, offering her hips in performance. I knew she had the concentration to pull it off, but she rolled her eyes, mildly offended, and went as Marie Curie, instead.

I've been asked what I see in her. It's a question beneath the dignity of an answer, but in this company, I will say that Carline is present in the sweetness of her body, in its pain and its raunch. She would never speak of this, but sometimes she falls backwards off the edge of the bed until her shoulders rest on the floor. Her heels try to hook the far rim of the mattress while her hips hold their ground. She's stretched, belly suspended above the warm split where I press with one hand, using the other to keep a thigh on the bed. She gives up noise, modest apartment cries that open to bigger rooms. She groans. Her neck bends at a difficult angle, but she takes more weight on her shoulders, arches her back. Four fingers in, I watch the underside of her belly ripple, curving lewdly, fat with abandon. I kiss the crease at its base.

Lilian puts the sheet of paper down. Our friends are hushed, gathering breath to praise and tease. Before I can recover, Lil takes my hand and pulls me into the room. "Your turn, Carline. Tell us about your trip."

Without letting myself stop to think, I begin:

In the middle of Maryland, I shoved the bus window open as far as it would go, knelt on the seat and stuck my head and shoulders out the window…

BUS TIP

Avoid sharing personal revelations with your traveling companions, as tempted by tedium as you may be.

I CUT BRISKLY THROUGH THE CEMETERY ON MY WAY home from work. The route took me out of my way, but I was happier off the street. In summer, teenagers gathered on the corner to insult pedestrians. They must have been waiting for other things, too: the early movie, sexual confidence, cars.

I wasn't interested in owning a car, myself, although Lilian let me use her Toyota in emergencies. She drove with an assurance I found seductive. On weekend trips, she would rise to eloquence about big topics like childhood, taxes and Shakespeare, punctuating stories with lucid changes of lane. She thought that in choosing not to drive, I was neglecting one of the basic pleasures of life.

But as much as I loved to watch her behind the wheel, I also loved to navigate, especially with a map. Lilian was not possessive of my talents, and I shared them as freely as my friends shared rides with me. It was a beautiful thing to support a driver in making the leap from the abstraction of an address to street signs with literal arrows marking turns that led on roads—generous as roads always are—to the desired place.

I liked riding the bus, too. With no need to help with directions, I could work on a project. Even on a moving bus, I stitched a tight seam.

The cemetery road started with asphalt then shifted to packed brown dirt. I had been at the office late, getting a little too lyrical about shades and blinds on a tight deadline. Waiting for me at home was a set of rod-pocket curtains that I had been making out of a beautiful piece of rose-colored tulle. Working with the same fabric I had used to make Lil's crinoline added to my pleasure in sewing. Eager to finish the curtains, I tucked my purse under one arm and hurried through the dusk. The kids were sure to have collected into a crowd, so this was a strategic detour through the quiet cemetery.

A breeze loosened the heat. I slowed a little, letting my eyes trace names and skull angels on Puritan headstones. Early settlers, I had read, believed that God's chosen would rise with their bodies on Judgment Day. I was a mature woman who was proud that I could still do a backbend. I sensed a link between these two attitudes toward the temple of the flesh, but it seemed too ill-defined to develop into a pamphlet. As the editor of a respected series called *The Modern Homemaker*, I was always on the alert for ideas. Looking at a spreading oak, I thought I could lean back and walk my hands down the trunk to the ground.

I didn't try it. Maples moved above the graves. The rustling of the leaves built and fell. Watching them illustrate suppleness, I thought that maybe I should try to get a pamphlet on *Body Image from Puritan Times to Today* past my board, after all.

I believed in pamphlets; anything could be shown and understood.

I had, in fact, suggested that my office create educational materials about the destructive effects of heckling on adolescent development. The kids waiting to yell at me on street corners were afraid of their own hips. I had gone so far as to submit a grant proposal to the state, but the response had been that, as a home economist, I was out of my field. Such decisions were political, of course. People who thought home economics was just pie crusts and vacuuming occupied every station in life; they outnumbered, perhaps, those who believed home economists no longer existed. I stopped to pick up a plastic bag that was littering the fence, then strode out of the graveyard.

A package for me was waiting on the stairs to our apartment.

It was from my Aunt Frankie, addressed, as always, in firm magic marker. I carried the box inside, pleased to hear from her. I set it on the kitchen table, and called, "Minnaloushe! Hello, beautiful."

Our careful cat hid until he was sure I was someone whose legs he wanted to rub. The sound of my voice alone was not proof enough. I took pleasure in the moment Minnaloushe crawled out from beneath the clawfoot tub, threaded between my legs, and purred.

The cat and I were the only ones home. Lilian, who usually filled the apartment with taped chanting from various religious traditions and the smell of grilled humus sandwiches, had been away at a poetry slam that was part of a queer writers conference. It was in Boston at a fancy hotel. She was due back in two days. I thought I might make a cinnamon supper cake in her honor. Lil was my size. Her body flooded my hands with softness. It pleased me to make her desserts.

She came home from slams agitated, exhausted and hoarse, with scraps of paper covered with email addresses and phone numbers of the other contenders. She would climb into the bathtub and lie there, too tired to lift her arms. While I washed her hair and combed it out with crème rinse, she told me what had happened in great cascades of talk.

I would fill a plastic pitcher with water and gently lift her breasts and belly to rinse underneath. Lately, I soaped each beloved fold with a bar shaped like the Venus of Willendorf. Scented with lemongrass, the soap was all sumptuous torso; the head dissolved against Lil's skin early on. She had brought a few bars back from the women's festival in Michigan one year, along with a ceramic Venus of Willendorf ashtray with a hollow where her belly should be. Lil told me that the original sculpture was the oldest known representation of a human figure, more than twenty thousand years old. The echoes of our bodies, Lil's and mine, in the fat goddess theme made me laugh. We kept the ashtray on the table next to the salt and pepper shakers.

Lil always brought me home a t-shirt if they had one that would fit, but most of the time it was souvenir pens and staple-bound books. She read to me in bed. I loved tracing the curves of her back under the sound of her roughened voice. She could feel when she had me, and edited based on the pressure of my strokes.

Now I set a bowl of Friskies and half a can of tuna select out for Minnaloushe. I threw the plastic bag from the cemetery into the trash, then put on a t-shirt and a pair of Lilian's drawstring pants. Wearing her clothes gave me a lift, despite the stain on one thigh. I propped my leg up next to the sink and rubbed detergent into the spot, humming an old disco tune, fingers slippery with effort. It sponged clean.

I dried my hands and stood at the table to cut through the tape on Frankie's box. Opening the flap, I found old *National Geographics* and kitchen utensils wrapped in the *Dallas Morning News*. There was no note. She rarely enclosed one.

I had spent most summers of my childhood with Frankie, but I hadn't seen her for years. Still, she regularly sent packages that, in a different way from Lilian's presents, made me feel well-prepared and loved. Every now and then, she went into flurries of clippings about weight loss. These phases of Frankie's never lasted long. I replied with thank you notes and occasional batches of fudge or prune bread, packed to mail with waxed paper inside a decorative tin. When I was pressed for time, I might just send a thoughtful recipe, such as Chinese Chicken for One, clipped from the *Living* section of the paper. Lilian said we were competing for a Betty Crocker award in the Spinsters category. Pushing me to be a little more forthcoming with my aunt, she had given me Venus of Willendorf soap to send to Frankie, too. Frankie had thanked us for the gift and said it smelled good. Manners ran in the family.

I imagined what Frankie looked like, holding onto the counter and bending stiff knees to kneel on the linoleum and clean out her cupboards in her chilled Texas kitchen. When I was a girl, she used to send rolls of LifeSavers, plastic tortoise shell barrettes, once a copy of *Our Bodies/Ourselves*, and once a subscription to *Young Miss*. For a decade, it had been note cards and holiday ten dollar bills, but over the past year she had been sending me small household goods. I was happy that this time she was passing on to me dish towels, cookie sheets, a liquid measuring cup and magazines full of pictures from all over the world.

I lugged the box into the living room, then put water on to boil and shucked some of Lilian's corn. She had brought home a bag full of vegetables from her plot at the community gardens for me to eat while she was gone: Swiss chard with bright yellow stems, three kinds of tomatoes, bell peppers, hot peppers, broccoli, squash, chives. I mixed garlic, basil and toasted walnuts with silken tofu to make a dip, put crackers on a plate, poured myself a glass of Dr. Pepper, and fished the corn from the pot. The pop was a throwback to my childhood. Lil was always offering me cranberry juice, but it just didn't have the right kick.

We shaped each other's tastes. Lil fed me raw parsley, and I taught her my mother's recipe for cornbread. She loved watching me work in the house, said that I put more focused energy into sponging off counters than some people put into whole years of their lives. Lil had written an erotic poem about my passion in dusting, the way my shoulders and breasts got involved. When she read it in public, I was embarrassed, but not displeased.

Feeling her absence, I took the plate into the living room, and sat down next to the box. The corn was steamy and sweet. Smelling basil on my fingers was almost like touching Lilian. She had so much basil that she brought home whole plants, pulled up by the roots, to strip for our meals.

I ate slowly and dug through the magazines. When I opened one from the year 1969 with a rocket on the cover, I found the map of the moon.

I spread it out on the wooden floor. It was titled, "The Earth's Moon," which I loved for its suggestion of many moons, as if I were "The Earth's Carline" to distinguish me from Carlines in other planetary systems. I could remember Frankie getting me out of bed to watch an eclipse when I was a little girl. I had stood on the sparse grass in pajamas and tennis shoes as the moon went from silver to coppery dark. I let my head loll back on my shoulders, full of limber wonder. On ordinary nights, Frankie and I would sit on the porch eating ice cream with chocolate sauce, listening to insects humming like a loud pulse, and watching the moon shine.

I had room to maneuver in the drawstring pants, so I got on my hands and knees to study the map. The floor was smooth under my palms. Two years ago, Lilian and I had persuaded the landlord to rent a sander so we could varnish the hardwood slats.

I pored over giant topological close ups of the near side and the far side, which were backed with dark blue. Hunched as I was, I cast a shadow that trailed behind me as I read the captions on the craters and seas. There was a crater named Billy, and a dark, flat place called Lake of Dreams. The dense names of dust seas rose from the surface in lyrical type: Serenitatis, Fecunditatis, Nectaris, Nubium.

I dusted crumbs from the map and read about the metonic cycle, the fact that every nineteen years the moon's phases occurred on the same day of the month. I felt I couldn't afford to miss the phase tonight. I jumped up and grabbed the scrap bucket to take the cobs and stalks down to the big compost bin that Lilian had installed next to the dumpster. At the same time, I could get a look at the moon.

I used the back door to the parking lot. There was a streetlight for security. The compost was only mildly ripe when I emptied the bucket. Lilian took it to the garden often. Some of our neighbors used the bin, and some threw their garbage into the dumpster to rot. Lilian told me not to judge people by how they handled their trash, but I thought it was a better way to judge people than most.

It was a faint quarter moon. I couldn't see many stars, but I wasn't sure if the sky was cloudy or if all the light around me bleached them out. The lot was full of cars as familiar as my neighbors' faces. The air had a warm, swollen feeling. All wind was gone.

I couldn't identify anything on the moon. It was slightly smudged white. I thought maybe it was waxing towards full, but I wasn't sure. I wanted to try to pick out the Sea of Tranquility. I crossed the asphalt to the sidewalk, looking for a better view.

A group of boys were gathered on the corner, away from the light. They were talking loudly and smoking, surging forward and jumping back from each other.

I couldn't have been more than a silhouette to them, but they spotted me right away.

"Look at that," said one of them.

"Oh my god," said another voice.

They all turned, cigarettes flashing. I backed off. I wasn't far from the apartment door, but I was scared, and I knew I was slow. Somebody yelled, "Sooee," as if calling a pig. Somebody else started repeating the word, "fat."

The first cigarette landed in my hair. I knocked it to the ground. The lit end glowed red. Another one bounced off the scrap bucket. I turned and ran for the door, showered by stubs of light.

None of the cigarettes burned me. Only a couple hit me at all. But fear caught in my gut and stayed there when I was safe in my apartment with the door locked. I didn't approve of self-hatred, but that was no help as I leaned over the kitchen sink, wheezing with pain as if I had inhaled a burning world. Fat. It always came back to that. I knocked a dead butt out of the collar of my shirt. It skittered near the drain. Vicious comments on the street, carefully worded references to "professional appearance" in job reviews, suddenly masked looks on the faces of friends; at this moment, hatred was all I could see, all I could breathe, all I was. I opened the tap of cold water over my wrists, trying to calm.

After a while, my breathing eased up. I shut off the water and switched on the light. The map of the moon was still flat on the floor with tofu dip drizzling onto the crackers beside it. It made my head ache. I sat on the bed with my eyes closed, hating those boys. I heard something like footsteps on the stairs, but no one came to the door. I started shaking. Minnaloushe crawled out from under the bed to curl at my hip.

I had a number for Lilian, but couldn't get my brain to form anything to say. I didn't think that I could stand to be touched, but wanted her near. The plate on the floor bothered me. It would attract ants. I took it into the kitchen.

The half-smoked cigarette was swollen in the sink. It smelled of wet ash. I scooped it out with a paper towel and threw it in the trash. I put the dip into a bowl, threw out the damp crackers and rinsed the plate. I didn't want my body, not any part of it. In the back of my mind, I gave myself good advice: pick up your sewing, make a list, sleep. I was in the grip of shame, though. I took a match from the box next to the stove, lit it, and held it to my wrist.

It hurt. Moving the flame in a tight circle, I watched the spot turn red. I was suspended and impersonal. I didn't live in the sparse hairs, the dry layers of skin that had risen to the surface to be sloughed off. It was a feeling I remembered from high school, when I was the age of those cigarette boys. I used to hack my arm in the girls' room in a small way. I had a tiny tool kit with a screwdriver for my eyeglasses and a pick with a blunted tip that I used for etching pits and scratches in my arms. Physical pain had been a focus, almost a relief.

The match made a burn the size of a penny. I imagined something called the blowtorch diet, a surefire way to lose weight. I blew out the match when the skin in the center began to turn gray. Numb, I was nowhere near my skin. I dropped the charred stick into the Venus ashtray.

I put my wrist under the water a while, then went to sleep on the quilt. I forgot to shut off the light. Minnaloushe slept near me, warm against my leg.

I lay in a drowse of anxiety almost all night. I twisted and sweated under the fan's machine breath. Finally, I took off my clothes and put on my sleeveless nightgown. I kept touching the burn, then getting up to go to the bathroom and wash it with anti-bacterial Dial. I covered Lil's soap with a washcloth. My crying disturbed Minnaloushe, who left me for the red chair in the living room.

Around two in the morning, I got up and took the *Joy of Cooking* down from its shelf by the stove. I turned to the section on burns for a review. I was instructed not to throw water on a grease fire, and to choose flat-bottomed, well-balanced pans. For extensive or painful burns, I was to lie down, remain calm and keep warm until skilled help was available. I was to submerge smaller burns in cold water, wrap with sterile gauze or clean linen, and refrain from using butter or other home remedies.

I sat in the bright light of the kitchen with the book in my lap, unsteadily braced by having followed the proper steps. I picked up a pen to make a list of what to do next, but my concentration kept slipping away. I wrote nothing. The burn was throbbing. I flipped cookbook pages at random until the idea of sauerkraut dressing made me feel ill. I closed the book and put it away next to Lil's ancient paperback copy of *Diet for a Small Planet*.

Back in the bathroom, I wiped my eyes and nose on a tissue, rinsed the burn again, and tried to survey the situation as if consulting a helpful index. Burning my wrist was a bad way to express pain because it caused more. I knew this. I figured the burn for a lapse into youthful weakness, unlikely to disrupt the patterns of my life, which I loved. That calculation proved wrong. Even at the time, though, being afraid to step outside to put out the trash was unthinkable. I had to go out again.

I pulled on an old ERA YES t-shirt and tied the string of my sweat pants tight to my belly. My hands were shaking. I sat on the bed to put my shoes on, then lay back. Minnaloushe jumped up to rub my hand with the side of his face. I lifted my finger to make an edge for him to press against.

Minnaloushe soon got bored, and jumped from the bed. I was reluctant to move, but unwilling to take off the t-shirt I had just put on, now threaded with cat hair. Finally, I went into the kitchen. I opened a cabinet and found the baking soda in its gold cardboard box. The cookbook had mentioned soda for putting out fires, but it had an impressive range of household uses. It would help cookies rise, stomachs settle and sponges scrub. It also absorbed smells. Comforting traces of daily life clung to the box, giving it power.

Reaching for the baking soda diminished my distress. In the weeks to come, I harnessed myself repeatedly to such small comforts. I could appear to be in utter control, but part of me was constantly wrestling with the awareness of being despised for my body, and, worse, the moments of despising it myself.

Now, frightened but well armed, I seized the garbage bag with its lump of paper and ashes, unlocked the door and climbed down the stairs. I stood there and cried for five minutes before I opened the outside door.

Wiping my face on my arm, I stepped onto the asphalt. I jumped when a truck went past, then the street was still. I lifted the lid, disposed of the bag, and emptied the box of soda over all of the trash. It fell in clumps and fine powder, like white dust rain.

The decaying smell stayed thick above the dumpster, but I felt as if I were breathing something cleaner. I tossed in the box and lowered the lid of the dumpster with a soft, considerate clank. Taking my time, I leaned against the brick of my building and looked up.

Stars shimmered faintly above the haze of street light. The outside air had cooled. There was no longer a moon.

I WAS STIRRING, REACHING FOR MY ASTHMA SPRAY, when the phone rang in the morning. I took a puff and jumped out of bed, thinking, "Lilian."

I ran into the front room and picked up the receiver, tugging my twisted nightgown down over my hips. "Hello."

"Did I get you out of bed?" Frankie's accent was unmistakable, sunk in my brain like a handprint in concrete. This morning, though, she sounded faint.

I was reacting slowly, exhausted after my long night, but my aunt's voice startled me. She sent lots of packages, but rarely called.

"Hi, Frankie." I picked up the pen attached to the phone, and started smoothing the kinks out of its cord. "I was just rushing around a little to get ready for work." The burn on my wrist had swollen into a tight blister. I poked it. The pain was sharp.

Something rustled on Frankie's end. I was having a hard time concentrating, but the pause seemed awkward, too long. I pushed myself to imagine her sitting at the kitchen table, leaning rough elbows on the morning paper's crossword, already filled in with ink. The room would smell of Jimmy Dean sausage and dark toast. I knew her habits from childhood. We didn't visit. She lived in Chalk, Texas —a long way from me.

"Oh, you're in a rush." She sounded so sweet that I was sure something was wrong. Frankie's natural ways were blunt and high-key, but she fell back on graciousness in periods of stress.

It surprised me, as weary and far from her as I was, to be having this insight into Frankie's character. I couldn't come up with a way to respond. It was as if something inside me were stunned or asleep. Getting over the night before was harder than I had thought it would be. The best I could do was more small talk. "Lilian's out of town."

Frankie, after a pause, said in a shaky voice, "I bet you miss her."

I missed her more than I could summon the breath to say, but whatever was causing that quaver, I didn't think it was the mention of my lover. The fact of Lilian was not news. I made a stab at getting the reason for the call. "How's your health?"

"Fine." There was pressure behind every word she said, but I couldn't guess the source. I had learned to read Frankie even before I could read the backs of cereal boxes, so now I felt dumb. It was frustrating. Also, I needed to use the bathroom. Minnaloushe strolled in and started batting at the pen on its dangling cord.

I was about to tell Frankie that I had to run when I remembered her package. "Oh, thanks for sending me that box of things. I had been wanting a four-quart cup." Mentioning the measuring cup made me feel practical, always a boost. I didn't mention the map of the moon.

She said, "Well, good. I've been clearing things out. I hoped you'd find a use for that stuff." She sighed again, and then she told me. "Ida died Saturday. I wanted you to know."

"Oh, Frankie, I'm so sorry to hear that." It took a moment, but I knew who Ida was. She was a close friend of Frankie's. I remembered her driving a big boat of a car to take Frankie and me to the beauty parlor one summer. All three of us had our hair done. That was the night we made crystallized peanuts for the Chalk Library Guild award reception. Ida's certificate of merit stuck to her fingers at the podium. It was a hoot. "Had she been ill?"

"No." Frankie was breathing loudly. "It was sudden. She had a stroke. They already had the funeral, yesterday."

"That's terrible." I ran a finger around the edge of the burn, trying to make myself present for my aunt. "Ida was a nice woman.

Where can I send a card?"

Frankie's voice kept its shake, but got higher, with another jolt of protective cheeriness. "There are two boys. Kyle and MJ, you might remember them, but why don't you send the card right to me?"

That didn't seem efficient, but I thought there might be special small town etiquette involved; maybe she wanted to hand deliver it. It didn't matter, whatever the reason, because it was what Frankie was asking me to do, and she was the one grieving her friend. I was starting to be more alert. "Of course."

Frankie was suddenly in a hurry to get off the phone. "I won't keep you, Carline. Just wanted to let you know."

I rushed through my preparations for work, trying to get back in stride. In the shower, I washed briskly with Dial, holding my wrist up to the nozzle to flood it with cold. It ached in a way that could pass for ordinary. My feelings were still flat. Patting the burn dry with a washcloth, I urged myself to get a grip. The death of a friend was a real problem. Petty harassment and mental lapses were not. I felt unsettled in myself and worried about Frankie, but, after I toweled off and dressed, I added a necklace of glass beads to my outfit. By the time I took up my purse to leave the house, I had a positive attitude in place. Ignoring the depth of my confusion and distress seemed like the practical thing to do.

Waiting for the bus, I pressed my fingers together in little steeples and played air piano, doing exercises to stave off carpal tunnel syndrome. I kept a polite distance from the gray-haired guy with big jowls and a pot belly who was bouncing a superball on the sidewalk. They were long bounces. He was tall. He wore a suit, and had a radio tuned to a polka show on the ground near his feet. He was a regular at this stop. I'd heard him chatting on the bus, but we rarely even nodded at each other. While I was doing my wrist sweeps, he caught the ball in the air and shoved it in his pocket. I looked up to see the bus rounding the corner, tilting toward the curb. My spirits lifted. They always did when the bus arrived. I loved the way it barreled toward me with its panoramic windshield, the driver distinctive in the high seat behind the dark glass. I smiled when I recognized Tucker. He caught my eye, even in profile when a bus sped past. He drove recklessly fast, but he was always courteous and on schedule.

The tall guy shut off his radio and flashed a pass at the driver, who said, "Morning, Mel. How's tricks?"

Mel claimed a seat that faced sideways, propped an ankle on a broad knee, and said, "Fine, Tucker. You?"

Tucker touched finger to thumb to signal a-okay, and watched me drop my money in the box: quarter, quarter, nickel, dime. He was the most helpful driver, with a case full of schedules for all the other routes. Sometimes he carried a camera and took snaps out the window. I wondered how he stayed interested, doing loop after loop of the same route. Now, he hit a switch that made the coins rattle and drop out of sight. "Hi, Carline."

I usually said hi quickly to the drivers so as not to insist on friendliness in somebody's working day, but Tucker was always ready to engage in conversation. He made smooth transitions from sociable to professional, raising his resonant voice to call out the stops. This morning, though, he seemed agitated. When I paused to check his face, he glanced at the burn on my wrist. I hurried to an empty seat a few rows back before he could comment. I noticed variations in mood of the people I saw on the bus every day, but the key to a good commute was balance between familiarity and privacy. I trusted that the driver felt the same.

He put the bus into gear. His hair was combed back in its usual voluptuous sweep, but stray strands drifted across his forehead and rose in a shivering tuft above his ear. His mouth dipped at the corners, and his eyes engaged everything. As he drove, he talked.

"You know," he said to Mel, who looked up from turning the dial of his silent radio, "even when I was a little kid I wanted to drive a bus. I used to race friends on my Stingray with the banana seat, but I liked it better if they lined up in two rows behind me, pedaling as hard as they could down the canal road in the park, past the supermarket, and behind the high school, then home. I've still got some jittery pictures I took over my shoulder. We called that a trip around the world."

Mel's face was somber at rest, but he had a brazen smile. "Kids."

I traced the alphabet in the air with my feet to loosen my ankles, wondering what was bringing up the bus driver's memories this morning. I had left my curtain project at home. It might have been a good time to consider grief, death or questions raised by the bitter events of the previous night, but instead I listened for clues in Tucker's voice and made a mental list of supplies needed to weatherproof windows. The list would be a nice appendix for the window treatments pamphlet I was finishing.

Tucker said, "There's going to be a sub driving for the next few days. I'm not going to be around."

Mel slid the antenna on his radio all the way out. "Going AWOL?"

Tucker looked over his shoulder at Mel's deadpan, then back out the windshield. "It's an extra thing. The company thinks this bus is about worn out, so I'm getting paid to drive it to Dallas to auction. Probably, it'll end up in Mexico."

Suddenly, the fact that my aunt had called me about a death this morning was on the tip of my tongue. It was all I could do to keep from blurting everything out: Frankie was grieving near Dallas. I had burned myself last night. A trip to Texas sounded good.

As we crossed the bridge, the bus squeaked and shook. I looked down at the water. The newest buses had ads for doughnuts and body shops painted over their windows. They gave a blurry surface to the view. This bus was old, so it had clear glass. I could see the car buried up to its steering wheel in sand that formed part of the far bank.

For a moment, I got the feeling of standing on the back steps at Frankie's place, looking across the scrubby grass past the water tower and on through the sloping tin roof of the open shed, past the dark outline of Frankie's tractor to more sky on the other side.

Once we were over the bridge, someone pulled the cord. Tucker stopped. A small, wrinkled guy with a feather in his hat went out the back door. Tucker turned in his seat as if to call after him, but didn't speak.

The bus stayed at the stop with its door open, although

there was no one getting on. I looked at Tucker. He was watching the departing passenger, who hovered at the edge of the crosswalk, hesitating before the onslaught of cars. The man danced with indecision as he bent and shifted, peering for an opening while the feather ruffled above the brim.

When my gaze met Tucker's in the rearview mirror, his heavy-lidded eyes were full of regret. His distress was so blatant that I had to speak. "Tucker, what's wrong?"

He looked startled at the sound of my voice, but he answered. "That would have been a good picture."

"You love your passengers." This had been obvious to me for a long time.

He nodded, and pulled away from the curb in the wake of a bread truck. The windows rattled, as always. I moved up to the seat behind him to make it easier to listen.

He hesitated, his expressive face reddening above his uniform collar. "It's a lot more interesting to drive with people on the bus." He lifted his arms in a dangerous gesture that included me as part of a great crowd. Mel and his radio came under the sweep of it, too. "Keeps me awake."

Tucker's attitude made me feel like one of many live ripples in the rhythm of blue seats. This was oddly compelling. I said the impractical thing I was thinking. "Take us with you. Why drive all the way to Texas alone?"

Mel's antenna was cutting the air, annoying a woman who always got off at the post office. She sighed dramatically, but he paid her no mind. He called out, "How about the Bahamas?"

Tucker laughed. He'd heard fantasies from passengers before.

It was simple. I said, "If you contract with the passengers individually, you'd be liable, not the company. You could check with a lawyer, but I'm pretty sure that's right."

The post office lady made a *tching* sound and yanked the cord. Evidently, she didn't approve. Mel set his radio on the seat she vacated, eyeing me speculatively.

A strip of Tucker's ankles showed above his socks. "I'm leaving first thing tomorrow. There's no time to set up a trip."

I settled back in my seat. I wasn't going to try to talk Tucker into bringing passengers along, as he obviously wanted, no matter how much sense it made to me. It was his job, his bus and his trip.

The bus pulled in at the big horseshoe drive at the university. Before he opened the doors, Tucker pushed the button to make the sign flash his new destination, which was where we had all just been.

When I reached the door, he swiveled toward me with decisive grace. The edge of a modest t-shirt was just visible under the open collar of his blue uniform. "I'm leaving tomorrow. I'll drive the route an hour earlier than usual, starting at five AM. If you want to come, wait at your regular stop. Payment at the time of boarding. Cash only, please."

Mel was standing too close behind me, eager for the door. My heart pounded at getting the invitation I wanted, but I smiled politely and smoothed my skirt, which had hiked up in back. "I'm supposed to work." I stepped down.

He gazed at me a moment longer, then shrugged. As people poured out the door, I called over their heads, "How much?"

He raised an eyebrow and made up a price. "Seventy-five dollars."

It was such a bargain that Mel turned to stare as Tucker shut the door.

I waited until the bus was out of sight, then opened my bag and began to rummage for my note pad. I touched my keys on their hook near the rim, then travel packs of Kleenex and the bottle of aspirin, the little box of cereal for when I finally felt like breakfast, and the folding spoon. Further down, I found my umbrella, a paperback murder mystery and my pocketbook. I could get in and out of secured places, I had money and painkillers, I could sneeze with discretion. These were comforts on a work day scale. I found them calming.

Finally, I pulled out my pad, sat on the concrete bench and wrote, "Windex, paper towels, caulking, plastic, X-acto knife, measuring tape, pencil, blow dryer, tape. Hammer and tacks, optional." Weatherproofing supplies. It was the opposite of the list I would write if I were going somewhere.

I got off the elevator and hurried down the familiar hall. I called hello through a couple of doorways, then went into my office and shut the door. That made me feel guilty. Crystal had been asking me to brainstorm with her about what to wear at a briefing for congressional staffers on some policy proposals about gender and nutrition. I thought she'd be most comfortable in a serious suit and (to keep things in perspective) frivolous underwear. Odds were, Crystal had some, unlike me. Also, I wanted to check with Lou in computer support about how her ultrasound had gone. She had been suffering with the preparatory water drinking yesterday afternoon.

Instead, I took off my shoes and hung them on the coat rack to air out. This extended the life of the leather. I had learned that years ago as a student in Home Living. Now an administrator in a home extension program, I taught an occasional course myself.

The true love of my professional life was the pamphlet series. I liked to think of women in Hawaii and Oklahoma running more efficient households because of our efforts. The sad truth, though, was that the glory days of home extension clubs were gone.

Women no longer gathered in large numbers to eat luncheons and learn to make their own mattresses. Most wanted independence and needed to generate income, and that meant less time to devote to the art and science of living. A celebrity homemaker like Martha Stewart was no substitute for a committed grassroots movement. Despite outreach efforts, our programs had never interested men at all. The pamphlet series had subscribers on five continents, but I found it harder every time I tried to pull together a good potluck.

I sat at my desk, sharpening pencils and waiting for my computer to boot. The writing was already on the wall when I had chosen home economics as my vocation in the late seventies, but I had spent my first year of college in a co-ed dorm, wading to the showers through piles of cans and plastic cups heaped on the floor. I needed a haven. The mixture of pragmatism and idealism in home economics—with its all-female faculty, its commitment to hands-on demonstrations, its mission in sharing ideas for the improvement of home and community life—soothed me like a bath in a clean tub. The discipline of home economics wasn't fashionable, but it was a fount of traditional women's skills, and I was an ardent feminist. Plus, I had crushes on three of the faculty. My parents made mild suggestions about law school or dating, but didn't interfere. I became even more engrossed in the ideal practices of the home after my mother, Frankie's quick-tempered older sister, died of unexpected complications from a hernia operation during my junior year.

My idealism had long been tempered by infighting and bureaucracy. I still threw myself into pamphlets, of course. I loved my work, liked my job, and respected the board and my colleagues —ardently, most of them—despite the recurring arguments about whether the apron logo on our letterhead was funny or obscene. They were a rare gang of twenty-first century home economists, full of ideas and thriving in an indifferent world. The ones I admired most showed up on time for meetings and remembered how to sew.

Now I browsed through some figures and drafted a memo about federal cutbacks. I moved from the computer to the filing cabinet in a wash of unease. This wasn't the discomfort of spending time on an unpleasant task. That feeling was much like my chair; not comfortable, but functional enough. This morning, the uneasiness hurt.

After about a half-hour, I changed the dressing on the burn and ate my box of cereal without milk. I put it down on my desk to pick out the candy charms. They squeaked under my teeth. I collected four of them in my folding spoon—heart, star, clover, moon. Crude symbols of dreams and luck, they tasted like sponges, only too sweet.

I licked my fingertip to pick up the little moon. It was a crescent. I thought about myself running from those boys last night without even yelling at them to stop. The fact that I was bigger than every one of them had been useless. I never considered defending myself. Burning my own arm had seemed inevitable. I struggled to hold the thought that perhaps it was not.

I should have gotten down to work on the windows pamphlet, but instead I propped my elbow on the desk and twinkled the moon back and forth. I thought of Lilian pulling red fishnets over black tights. I thought of her hand gripping my belly. I remembered the way Frankie's fields cut a generous line of horizon against low sky. I needed to go to Texas, where Frankie was feeling sad among her dish towels; where I last turned violence on my body's failures twenty years ago.

The phone rang. I lifted the moon off my finger with my tongue and swallowed it. I took the call, canceling a meeting, then got on the Internet and priced flights to Dallas. Everything leaving the next day was more than a thousand dollars. Besides, I hated to fly even more than I disliked driving. The seats were much too small to be comfortable. The train was expensive, too. I called several rental car agencies, but the rates were exorbitant for one way trips, and I had no idea how long I would be gone. Even if I had wanted to do it, my driving skills were rusty, so safety was a factor, too.

I had a fleeting moment of regret that I had never owned a car.

Every commercial bus schedule involved layovers in the late hours of the night in Cleveland, Ohio or Birmingham, Alabama or arriving at Dallas between one and five in the morning. The shortest trip was one day, seventeen hours and 33 minutes. Every fare was twice Tucker's, or more. I would be much better off with a cheap trip from a known driver whose only destination was Dallas.

When I signed off, my fingers were shivering on the keys. The next logical step would be to check my vacation days and ask Lou and Crystal to cover for me. Instead, I turned on my voice mail and spent the rest of the morning writing up a guide to my files, keeping giddiness in check with the need for clarity. I typed the weatherproofing appendix. The only things that the windows pamphlet still needed were copy editing and layout. I did a brisk timeline for the next three months, which I placed in the center of my desk. When I finished, I bounced in my chair a few times. It strained and creaked. Then I called my supervisor and left a message. "I'm sorry, but I quit."

There was a gasp in my voice as I said it. The shock of loss hit me even before I hung up. I was leaving friends stranded in half-finished work and abandoning years of fiercely defended procedures on the strength of bearable pain and an invitation to take a ride. Steadying my hands on the edge of the desk, I reminded myself of the dip I had created from peanut butter and salsa. Succumbing to impulse sometimes yielded good results. I knew I had to go. Neither Velcro nor the zipper would have been invented if someone hadn't turned from the fine-stitched slit of the buttonhole.

ON THE RIDE HOME, I HAD AN UNFAMILIAR DRIVER. It was a new bus, with a surveillance camera and a sheet of bulletproof plastic behind the driver's head. I sat in the long last seat, the one usually staked out by impassive boys who held their legs wide apart to claim extra space. I plopped down smack in the middle and put my bag on the seat next to me, as if I were one of them. Jostled by potholes, I felt reckless, and scared. I pulled a notepad out of my purse with a mild flourish, then leaned it against my knee to begin a new list.

I needed to buy food for the trip: oranges, bananas, carrots, pretzels, mustard, a loaf of bread. I could bring cheese in a can. Peanut butter. Knives, cups, a package of napkins. I should call Frankie and tell her I was coming to see her.

I drew an asterisk, then continued, urgently. Aspirin, toothpaste, asthma spray. A canteen? I was planning so hard that I almost missed the stop for the Big Y.

At the store, I lingered among the produce, falling in love with both the oranges I chose and those I left behind. I bought a sympathy card and stood next to the mailbox in front of the store to address it. As I tried to think of the right words, it occurred to me that I should have bought two cards: one for Frankie, who had lost a friend, and one for Ida's boys. In the end, I wrote to Frankie, because she was the one I loved. I said that I was sorry about Ida's death, and that I remembered her scarf fluttering boldly as she drove her big car up the lane. I wished Frankie strength, rest, everything she needed to get through her grief. I added that I was on my way for a visit, which I hoped would not inconvenience her.

I must have been reluctant to give her the chance to say that it would.

Dropping the card in the mailbox was a relief. I might get to Texas before the card did, but at least it would be on its way. I crossed both "card" and "tell Frankie" off my list.

When I got to our apartment, I left the groceries on the table in the Big Y bag. Minnaloushe almost knocked it over, but he calmed down after I put out some canned food. I stroked his back while he crouched over the bowl. Suddenly, with a shock like touching an electric fence, I thought of Lilian. I had to let her know that by the time she got home tomorrow, I would be gone.

I had been about to go into full packing mode, but, instead, I moved away from Minnaloushe and sat down at the table. He looked over his shoulder at me, then went back to eating. I fingered the tablecloth and took a slow breath. Lilian.

If I left a message at the hotel in Boston where she was staying, there was no telling when she would call me back. Lilian was slamming. She would be filled with poetry and adrenaline, distracted. I needed to be looking in her eyes when I told her that I had quit my job so I could leave tomorrow to go spend time with Frankie.

Lilian had never met my aunt, but she had watched the stream of packages bring serving spoons, Tupperware and sofa sleeves to our door. She said my aunt's gifts seemed materialistic, which made me bristle. Once she came across some Aunt Jemima potholders from Frankie that I had shoved in the back of a drawer. I had been keeping them hidden but available to use when I was alone with something hot to lift.

When Lilian found the potholders, she slapped them down on top of my plateful of toast. We had to talk. Later, I threw them in the dumpster. It was wrong to use racial stereotypes to sell pancakes, but the folds that Frankie had worn into those potholders fit my hands like nothing else. It was hard to give them up.

Lilian used dish towels to take pans out of the oven. She could be lazy in the kitchen, but she was full of moral energy. I embraced her influence as much as I resisted it.

Now I found the Boston schedule in my files under "B," and followed my finger down the shaded column of departure times. The next bus left at two fifteen and got into Boston at five. If I hurried, I might make it.

I rubbed Minnaloushe on the side of his mouth, grabbed my purse, and rushed out the door. I could hear him complaining all of the way down the stairs. Minnaloushe expected to be combed and toyed with after he ate.

As it was, I got to the bus station out of breath and bought my round-trip ticket with just minutes to spare. Usually when I traveled, I made careful preparations, but this time I hadn't eaten lunch, and I didn't even have water for the trip.

I tucked my ticket into the zippered compartment of my purse, then checked my watch. I thought of the packing I should be doing, and of the late night I was going to have when I got back from Boston. Tucker had said to be at the regular stop at five in the morning. I went to the counter of the doughnut shop, and ordered a cup of tea with milk. I didn't buy a doughnut. To risk the agitation of sugar on an empty stomach seemed unwise. The man at the cash register had an unlit cigar in his mouth. My bus was announced as he took a drag of air and handed me my change.

The bus was half empty, so I had a seat to myself. The seats were padded and comfortable, designed for long trips, a fact I took for granted at the time. I waited with the cup in my hands until we were on the highway, then opened the lid. Heat rose in a soft column through the cooled air. I leaned my face into the steam and took a sip.

It tasted milky, with a mild edge. I held it in my mouth, shivered, swallowed. The cup bent in my hand. I took another sip. As the bus moved along the highway, I drank the tea and left bite marks around the circle of the waxed rim. When the cup was empty, I traced its lines and worried the paper seam with my nails. Tea, heat, milk, and cup brought me back to the nights when I first met Lilian: Tuesdays at seven, I would sit on a folding chair in her used clothes store to drink Earl Grey with cream from a paper cup and let Lilian give me lessons in expression.

I had copied her number off a flyer in the Laundromat, and was part of a small class of earnest adults. I wanted to be more effective when I spoke up at work.

Lilian taught expression by standing in the clearing at the front of her store and listening with motions of her head and body while students read aloud. She checked us for varied tone and nervous habits. She was a big-hipped woman whose clothes made soft sounds as she moved. She was a little smaller than me, or maybe a little larger. I was a bad judge of that.

I wore a corduroy jumper to the first class. Lilian let her fingers brush it and said, "This is nice." I was pretty sure she was a lesbian. She wore nail polish. When I asked, she said the color was plum.

Inspired by Lil's teaching, I offered to organize a class reading. On the last night of the eight week session, we all gathered at the Methodist church. I had rallied everyone to put up flyers and invite friends to hear us. I felt awful beforehand, full of clarity as I read from "The Lottery" by Shirley Jackson, and simply happy afterward. I wasn't sure of the practical applications, but getting listened to was a pleasure and a relief. Then Lilian got up to read for us.

She wore a short silk dress with boots and patterned stockings. The pews swept out in front of her in waves of varnished pine with cushions on the seats. There were only twelve in the class, with maybe twice as many guests, but Lilian filled the room. Her fingers flew with drama. I loved her glamour. She wore eyeliner and read from Yeats.

Who will go drive with Fergus now,
And pierce the deep wood's woven shade,
And dance upon the level shore?

Lilian had something conscious in her voice, and also something asleep. I leaned forward to listen, propping my elbows on the back of the next pew, and put both hands over my face. I wasn't getting the full sense of the words, but my body was fluttering. I ran my tongue in circles across my knuckles. My skin tasted of soap. Everyone else was watching Lilian. I bit one knuckle, lightly. I felt a small jolt pass like a breeze up my arms to my elbows, then wash over my breasts and shoulders to my face. Lilian's voice flowed over my head.

And no more turn aside and brood
Upon love's bitter mystery;
For Fergus rules the brazen cars,
And rules the shadows of the wood,
And the white breast of the dim sea
And all dishevelled wandering stars.

She finished. That was unexpected. It took a minute before I could lower my hands to clap. Lilian gathered the applause for a moment, then directed it toward the class. We basked in it until it faded away. Before we left, Lilian passed out class evaluation forms.

I picked up a hymnal and ruffled its pages with damp fingers, then I pulled a pencil from a small hole in the hymnal rack, and wrote on the form under Any Further Comments: "Can I see you again?"

Now I looked out the window and let my fingers play with the cold edges of the air conditioning vents, thinking about how well I remembered that poem, with its mythic road trip arriving at the dim sea and dishevelled stars. It was about moving toward death, or away from it into mystery. I thought of looking it up in one of Lilian's books to copy for Frankie, but I wasn't sure she would have the patience to make it yield a meaning. She was a long-time subscriber to *Readers Digest*, where articles got right to the point. We passed a deserted factory with the ace of spades painted across a bricked-up window. I was still moved by the sound of Lilian's voice under a poem, even when I didn't follow the words. We'd been together seven years.

The traffic was heavy. We were approaching the city. I had torn the cup into bits of paper, shedding wax, and rehearsed the liquid measure volume equivalents. Sixty drops equal one teaspoon. All of the other passengers were facing forward or leaning against windows. Murmurs drifted through the quiet bus.

The driver slowed at a toll booth. I thought of Lilian practicing for the poetry slam the night before she left. She had been sitting on the edge of our bed, saying her poem over and over. I had stroked my palm across her surfaces, listening. Her back had two folds: one where her belly met her thighs, and one under the shoulder blades with a swell where her breasts began. Her hips were textured. When she read her work in public, I found it hard to concentrate. I was distracted by the waves of her body under her clothes, and by wondering if others saw them, if so much motion were safe.

Lilian teased me about underwear. I believed in firm support.

By the time the bus pulled into South Station, I had been thinking of Lilian for hours, but I was no closer to what I wanted to say to her than I had been in the kitchen. All I knew was that I had to see her before I left for Texas. I stood for a moment in the bus port breathing thick exhaust, then went looking for a pay phone to find out how to get to the conference hotel on the T.

Once I was out of the rank smell of the subway station and settled into my seat, I studied the map on the opposite wall of the train. Around me, varied people stared relentlessly inward, except for those who read. The map was so easy to grasp that I found it to be a thing of beauty. I was in a middle car, clattering along without a driver. Tracing the line I was on to its furthest limits, I tried to imagine how I would feel if a voice came over the crackling intercom and began to tell us that this train was switching tracks and heading above ground, away from the ocean, across state lines and geographic regions, into another part of the country. Surely there would be a final stop on the regular route where we could all get off, inconvenienced and grumbling, but free to make transfers or emerge to take cabs to ordinary destinations. I couldn't imagine keeping my seat while everyone left, letting the doors slide closed to strand me on a runaway train.

Perhaps, though, if I had fallen asleep—if, for reasons beyond my control, I had been exhausted and unable to resist the urge to nestle my head on my purse, neglecting my own strict rules for public conduct—I might miss warnings and explanations to wake on a subway train hurtling along other tracks, maybe beside a full river, passing through small towns with their names written on station walls. The names would tell me nothing about where I was unless I gathered the courage to stagger between the cars to search for other passengers, a conductor, or the T driver who had made it out of the tunnel, dragging along a burden of cars painted to match the Red Line on an elegant, well-conceived map that would no longer matter. The idea was frightening but romantic, like hopping a freight, something that yesterday I would have said was not in my repertoire of credible dreams.

I didn't miss my stop.

I hesitated on the sidewalk outside the hotel, watching a series of calm families carry luggage through the automated glass doors. Two tastefully dressed men came out holding hands and wearing name tags. I wished I had taken time to change from my blouse and slacks into my butterscotch suit. I surveyed my hair with my fingers and fished chapstick out of my purse to give my lips protection. I was intimidated by the controlled lushness of the guests, but, more than that, I was nervous about facing Lilian.

I stood there a moment longer, shifting my weight from hip to hip, missing the enclosed starkness of the subway. I considered making use of my time by doing Kegel exercises, but, instead, my pressing need to find a bathroom propelled me through the big glass doors.

An impeccable toilet in a wide stall steadied me. After washing, I helped myself to hand lotion and a free sewing kit shaped like a matchbook. I took a deep breath, nodded at my dependable haircut, tucked in my blouse, and strode back into the lobby.

I found Lilian sitting in Au Bon Pain, leaning across a croissant toward a husky, brown-haired woman, who was speaking eagerly. Lilian—visibly tired, radiant and engaged—was stroking a paper napkin with the blunt end of a pen. I hurried towards them, dodging tables.

Neither of them noticed my approach, so I touched the strap of Lilian's dress where it had fallen to the soft top of her arm. "Lilian."

She glanced at me casually, a little bit irritated, as if I had interrupted her conversation at our kitchen table, then she gave a start. "Carline. What's wrong?"

I lifted the strap back to her shoulder and put my purse down on the table. "Everything's okay. I just need to speak to you."

Lilian leaned toward me so that her shoulder touched my side. The strap stayed put. Nodding at her friend, she said, "Judith, this is Carline."

"Oh, Carline. Pleased to meet you." The woman smiled, alert and friendly. "I know from Lilian's poems how important you are to her."

"Carline is a terrific editor. She has her own pamphlet series." Lilian thrummed the table. Coffee trembled in the cups. Her poems made people feel that they knew us, but she was always quick to point out that I had a life outside of her work. As she spoke now, it hit me that I wasn't the editor of *The Modern Homemaker* anymore.

Lilian turned to me. "Judith is a fine poet."

Judith laughed, touched her own cheeks. "From you, that means a lot."

I liked her, but needed her to be gone. I pulled my billfold out of my purse. "I'll get something to eat."

I bought roast beef and brie on a roll, with an orange juice. By the time I got back to the table, Judith was standing beside Lilian's chair, handing her a skinny yellow book. "See you in the semifinals," she said.

Lilian dropped the book into her bag. I sat down. She looked at me and opened her hands in the air, available. "What's going on?"

I picked up my fork, then put it down. "How's the slam? Did I hear Judith say you made the semis?"

She sat up straighter. Her hips curved over the sides of the small chair. Her voice got sharp. "Carline, right now I need to know, why are you here?"

I stuck my hand in my pants pockets and stared at my plate. She waited, fingering her cheap plastic pen, trying to sheathe her impatience.

Still, I gazed at the sandwich, gathering my thoughts. My fingers closed around the sewing kit. I pulled it out of my pocket and opened it, as if I were doing a small, hard chunk of work. "I quit my job. I'm going to Texas to see Frankie. I'm leaving first thing tomorrow. I had to tell you."

Lilian's expression was flat, with uncertainty swelling underneath. "What?" she said. "Huh?"

The sewing kit had two white buttons, a brass safety pin, and a needle bound to a piece of cardboard by rows of threads in common colors: white, pink, brown, black. I folded the cardboard down and slid the needle back and forth beneath the threads. "Don't worry, I'll still pay the rent."

Lilian shoved the table away from her. A little coffee spilled.

I was ashamed. Money would be a big problem, but I was using it as a smokescreen for the fact that I had made my decisions without her. Besides, it was insulting to suggest that money was Lil's first concern. I didn't believe that for a moment. "I'm sorry."

Her voice shook. "Are you leaving me?"

I pushed the needle free and balanced it between my thumb and index finger, with the point against my thumbnail, near the quick. "No, love," I said. "I'm not leaving. It's just a change. A trip. I got the offer of a cheap bus trip to Texas, but I have to go at five in the morning. Tomorrow. That's the only time. I've been frustrated at my job. You know that. I'll be back soon. A few weeks. I haven't seen Frankie in so long. I'm worried about her. She didn't sound right on the phone last time we talked. She just lost one of her friends. I'm sorry, Lilian. I love you. It's only a couple of weeks."

The strap of her dress fell off her shoulder again. "This doesn't make any sense. Who's driving you to Texas?"

I reached out to stroke her arm. I held the needle flat against my fingers in my other hand. She let me touch her, but I couldn't feel her presence in her skin. "It's nobody. Just the driver from my regular bus. He has to go for his job, needs the cash, and wants company. It's nothing, Lilian. That's not it." The guy at the register rang somebody up.

Lilian separated herself from my hand, straightened her strap, and rubbed her eyes. "Carline, you have the money to buy yourself an airline ticket. You've got vacation time. You didn't have to quit. And I don't understand why you have to go tomorrow. Tell me what's happening."

I sat back and ran the point of the needle lightly across the grooves of my fingerprints. This trip didn't have anything to do with her, except that my leaving so abruptly would affect her whole life, if only for a while. I hadn't let myself consider how that might feel to her. My thoughts flicked away from it even now.

Maybe I could help Lilian with her strap, attach it to the other one across her back, so neither would slide around. It wouldn't be good when she took the dress off or put it on again, but just for today, for the semis, it might work. Some kind of tie would do the trick, but a stitched thread would be more stable and more discreet. I could do it in about three minutes, in the women's room.

I didn't suggest it. Instead, I gazed at my lover with her puddle of coffee and her puffed up eyes, and thought of watching her at a reading, how she stood in front of people and let words pull things up from her deep places. I'm going to a deep place, I thought, but I'm a literal woman. I believe I'm going to get there on a bus.

I put the needle down on the rim of my plate and mopped up the coffee with the napkin. Lilian reached across the table, picked up the needle, and inserted it carefully in the paper that had wrapped her croissant. I was surprised she had noticed it. I considered taking a bite of my sandwich, but that seemed indecent. Instead, I rested my fingers on the damp spot left by the coffee, and said, "I'm trying to tell you what's happening, Lilian, but I'm not sure I know."

She took a breath and used her knuckle to draw a wide circle around the blistered burn on my wrist. "Start with this."

I closed my eyes for a moment, then opened them. I had come with a plan. I had decided to say, "kitchen accident," to anyone who asked about the burn. Just those two words, which were almost true. I had thought that no one needed to know anything more, but now I could see that Lilian did. I nodded at her. "Some boys threw cigarettes at me. In the parking lot by the dumpster last night, when I stepped out to see the moon. They were yelling 'fatso' and calling me like a pig."

"Baby, that's awful." She leaned toward me.

For a moment, I pretended that we would crush the little table between us, then I squeezed coffee out of the napkin onto her saucer, and said the next thing. "I went upstairs and burned myself. With a match."

Lilian settled back. I let my eyes stay on her arms. A group of women sat down next to us. She picked up her pen. Finally she said, "Why?"

I twisted strands of my hair into curls with my fingers. This was not good behavior for any table. I reminded myself that we were in public, and put my hands in my lap. "God, Lilian, I don't know. I've been trying not to think about it. Maybe because a burn is a conversation piece, a mark of feelings I don't have words for. I don't think I can make anyone understand, not even you."

Lilian's face was still, with just a tremor around her mouth. She kept looking at me, so I kept talking. "I just can't do it any more. I'm sick of cutting through the cemetery because I get insulted on the street."

Lilian rolled her pen between her fingers, shaking her head. "If you think you're going to get away from that shit in Texas, of all places, you're in one silly dream. If it's not fat, it's something else. Don't you know that much about the world, Carline?"

I did, in fact, know a few things. Lilian had taught me to look people in the face and speak when they stared on the street. I had, in my time, moved close to surly men to mention that they were being impolite. I had stopped tasteful women in the midst of stares to speak of food. Most would look away if I said something like, "I eat tuna fish sandwiches." Lilian moved down a sidewalk with a firm stride that reminded me of Frankie. I tended to step briskly, too, but now I found myself exhausted. I ached with the desire to take a very long ride, but there was something else, too. The thought of the white rock at Frankie's was as raw as the burn on my arm. I felt not only empathy for my aunt's grief, but also the grate and pull of my body's private history. It was nothing I had words for, but I knew I had to go.

I rested my eyes on Lil's strained face. "I can't explain it. I'll miss you every day."

She winced as if she'd been hit. She tapped the eye end of the needle with her pen. "Do you want me to lance that blister for you?"

We both started crying when I told her no.

By the time I got back to the apartment, it was ten-thirty at night. Minnaloushe was crouched low at the door, staring past my feet and down the stairs, as if considering making a run for it. I scratched his head and he let out a yowl. He hated disrupted routine.

I used the last of the milk, eggs, cheese and cooked rice to make a frittata for supper. I emptied the refrigerator, washed it out, and left it unplugged to defrost. I had an old-fashioned refrigerator that had to be tended. It reminded me of the one Frankie had when I was a girl. Often when Lilian came home from a slam, I would have lemon mousse chilling in our most beautiful bowl. She would have to do some shopping when she got home this time, but she wouldn't have to face my leftovers rotting in margarine tubs.

I often daydreamed, as I did housework, of long stretches of Bermuda grass pulling wind and light across flat land until it was hard up against Frankie's picture windows, but that night I was riveted, instead, by the immediate details of each task. The oven glowed when I scrubbed faint spatters from its door. There was much that I loved about my home.

Lilian had walked me to the T stop, even though she needed time to gather herself and look over poems before the next round of the slam. We both wanted to be in each other's company a little longer. She told me that she was planning to wear, not the sun dress with its problem straps, but her dazzling blue jacket and velvet tights. I was sorry to miss her in that.

The subway had been so crowded that my whole attention went to hanging onto the pole and keeping physical contact with sweating strangers to neutral areas like shoulders and unavoidable hips. I had no room to dream this time underground, maybe because I had just made my departure from Lil or because the subway had quickly come to seem too fixed in its orbits to surface and stray from the route.

On the bus ride home, though, I got a sudden memory of the time Lilian and I had sat in a wading pool with the hose running. It was at her mother's house. When Lilian stood to get out, the pool tipped like an open shell. I caught a glimpse of her wet face as

I spilled with the water onto the lawn. On the bus, I saw it again—Lil's shining face, grass, blue pool. She had laughed and fetched dry towels. My pleasure in looking at Lilian was more nuanced and complete than any dream of escape. Still, the urge to go was insistent. I hoped I wasn't tempting loss by traveling alone.

Now I packed my clothes in my old Amelia Earhart brand suitcase, which used to belong to my mother. My father had given it to me when he remarried and moved into an impeccable condominium with sweet, gaunt Nanette, a librarian of suitable age for him. She inserted screws into the soles of her athletic shoes so she could continue her recreational runs throughout the snows of winter. We were affectionate, but not close.

I tied down a pile of pants and sturdy skirts, and tucked socks and underwear into the salmon silk pockets of the Amelia Earhart. I crawled under the bed and pulled out the bulky wooden box Frankie had made for camping. As with everything Frankie constructed, the camp box was way too strong for its purpose. I lifted it by the handles onto the kitchen table, and unlatched the door to survey its compartments. There were plates, flatware, plastic cups, a pan with a burned bottom, and a skillet hung from a hook. I took everything out to rinse and repacked with fresh food and supplies. With a vague sense of ritual, I dumped the burned match from the Venus of Willendorf ashtray, wrapped her in a napkin, and slid her into a shallow drawer in the camp box. Even though I wedged the matchbox into her hollow place, she fit.

Minnaloushe jumped on top of the camp box, and curled up. I had to remember to write a note to Lilian about Minnaloushe. He didn't like turkey and giblets or the so-called mixed platter she bought for him sometimes; he only liked tuna. She had named him after a cat in a Yeats poem whose eyes were like the changing moon, but I was the one who took care of him.

It was late, but I couldn't sleep. I didn't want to think about Lilian and the cat left alone, so I got out my atlas. I opened to the map of the United States to scan for routes among its reduced towns and prominent roads. I wouldn't be making the decisions, but I liked to have an informed opinion, just in case. I reviewed the legend on the highway map of the United States. Even numbers are east-west routes. Three-digit signs that start with an odd number are spurs into a city; those that start with even numbers are routes around. Toll roads are green. Interstates, major rivers of commerce and pleasure, are blue.

We could swing north, I saw, and stay on I-90 through Albany and along Lake Ontario and Lake Erie. Syracuse, Rochester, Buffalo, and Erie all sounded cold to me, like cities spilling against each other because they couldn't build on the Great Lakes. We could cut south on 71 at Cleveland. Or we could take I-95 down the Atlantic coast, risking traffic snarls in Hartford, New Haven, and New York City, before braving the New Jersey Turnpike.

I got dizzy looking at the tangles of thick blue lines we'd have to follow and intersect with throughout the East, all pulling in so many urban directions. But, as I decided to suggest a route using 90, 87, 84, and 81 to stay well west of New York City before heading south, I surprised myself with a sense of blatant anticipation. Despite the strain with Lilian, Frankie's loss and my turmoil, I was pleased to be taking a trip.

The west route looked calmer and sparser. I-81 through the Appalachian Mountains to Knoxville, Tennessee. 40 west to Little Rock. 30 through Texarkana to Dallas. I thought of the raised pits on my map of the moon, and was caught in a strong wish for something simple and distant. Chalk could be it.

Far north in the Texas panhandle, I saw Dalhart in small dark type. The word looked as beautiful as it had on maps in my childhood, when it had meant a stop at the Dairy Queen on family trips. I flipped the pages of the atlas, looking for the state of Texas. I struggled with confusion between maps of Texas/Western and Texas/Eastern, then found the string of towns I had loved most on the cut between the two.

Dalhart and Dumas in the north, yes, but then rolling in rhythm like a car hitting raised yellow dots as it heads too much toward the shoulder, I found Clarendon, Memphis, Childress, Chillicothe, Vernon. These were not towns I knew, but places that, as a child, I always loved passing through. They weren't on the way to Mexico or Chalk from here, but they raised the ghost of myself as a child humming in the back of a station wagon as I watched a white moon. After a long stretch of feeling absorbed and alone, I heard Mama say my name softly to Daddy, something about Carline being awake still. Across the chasm of the middle seat full of my sleeping brothers, in a quick flush of joy at being spoken of, I had felt that my parents were happy, too.

Now I said, "Memphis, Childress, Chillicothe," right out loud. I got a red pen and bore down on my chosen route to Dallas, in case I was asked.

I was agitated, and barely slept. I got up several times to mop the melted ice water from the floor beneath the refrigerator. Each time I got back into bed, I was circled with worries about walking out on Lilian, my job, Minnaloushe, the window treatment pamphlet, not saying goodbye to Crystal or Jen or any of my friends and that I had forgotten to ask the office to forward my last check. The whole income thing was too frightening to linger over, despite my savings.

At two forty-five, I turned on my desk lamp and got out the map of the moon. I stared at it with a half-focused intensity, reading that Shroter's Valley was a prominent cleft easily visible with a small telescope. Prinz was an incomplete semi-ghost ring in the Harbinger Mountains. Mairan, twenty-five miles across, had exceptionally precipitous walls.

I shut off the light and lay back down. My mind wouldn't stop rolling thoughts around like dusty oranges. Dazed, I compared the underside of my breast to the moon's northwestern crescent limb. Both had shadows and pores.

I had read on the map that nature's favorite shape was a sphere. People saw the world that way, I decided, because our eyes were orbs. True crescents, the map claimed, were almost never found. I touched my belly, and thought it could be either a crescent or a globe. In the middle of listing our sun's planets, I finally slept.

WHEN I AWOKE, IT WAS FOUR IN THE MORNING. I hit the alarm, then stared at the meetings the ceiling made with the walls. It was too early for the usual rasp of traffic and voices to come up off the street.

I got up and staggered to the bathroom. I took a shower and washed my hair, then pulled on jeans and a loose t-shirt that I had cut the neck out of to let me breathe. I had finished the cut edge with rickrack. Sitting on the bed to towel my hair, I thought bleakly about going to work to see if I still had a job. I looked at the camp box and the Amelia Earhart suitcase waiting for me by the door. They were so contained and orderly that I got an inspiration: the trip could be, not a hasty departure, but a How To project about taking the bus.

It was timely (for me, at least), modest and practical: perfect. Maybe my old department would hire me to do a freelance series, a spin-off from *The Modern Homemaker* called something like *Modern Homemaker On the Go*, or, for a fun attention-grabber, *Go Home*. I could pull in some favors and give bus workshops as an in-service to home demonstration agents working with zero-car households. On fire with practicality, I found my purse and pulled out my notebook to make a quick list of possible titles: *Planning the Long Distance Bus Trip*; or *Bussing It: A Guide*. Maybe just *Bus*. No, the obvious was best: *How To Ride A Bus*.

I thought about the cover: a parked bus, perhaps, shot from the side, with its curbside doors opened invitingly, bright sun on the sidewalk, and the back of a woman who has just climbed into the interior. The head of the driver would be a charismatic silhouette against the slice of light from his window. The passenger's calves would be sturdy on the shallow steps. I saw a white bus with a bold red stripe, like the ones I entered mornings and evenings, paused for its passenger on a pleasant street. Speed and distance could be suggested in the font for the title, wind-swept letters leaning toward the unknown.

The lit numbers on the clock radio were at 4:40. I reset the alarm for seven so Lilian wouldn't get a rude shock the next morning. I knew I had burned my bridges with the department. Even if I were still the model employee I had been yesterday morning, the case for a bus pamphlet would have been difficult to make with the editorial board, who were going through a collective obsession with feng shui. Yet, I felt an instant commitment to the idea of *How To Ride a Bus*. It gave me a sense of purpose, which I needed even more than asthma spray. I took two puffs, then got up to secure the spray in my purse.

I mopped the final pool of freezer water and propped open the refrigerator door with a kitchen chair to prevent mildew. Lilian didn't get the same pleasure I did out of clean appliances, but she relished a strong image. I hoped the gleaming refrigerator would speak of love to her.

Still, its emptiness made me uneasy in the morning light. Minnaloushe was rubbing against my legs, pleased to be joined on his early rounds of the apartment. I worried he might jump into the refrigerator and leave paw prints on the shelves, but that could not be helped. I didn't see any way he could dislodge the chair and shut the door on himself to suffocate.

I gathered the curtains I had been making into a shopping bag, along with scissors, thread, tape measure, needles, pin cushion, and a ripper. I could supplement the How To pamphlet with the curtains. It was always good to have at least two projects going, in case one didn't work out. The curtains were almost finished. After I had double-hemmed the sides and lower edges, I had turned the top edge and topstitched it to make the rod pocket. Then, feeling playful, I had sewn pockets of the same sheer tulle material in a scattered pattern over the curtains. I had been planning to fill the pockets with squares to match our quilt, and hang the curtains in the bedroom as a surprise for Lilian. Light would come through everywhere except the pockets, and the color scheme could change. I hadn't started the squares, though, and I didn't have time to gather fabric scraps. I got another inspiration. I took the picture album from the shelf next to the television and stuffed it into the sewing bag. I could fill the pockets with pictures: friends, birthdays, vacations. It would be like making Lilian a present of our lives.

I sat down at the kitchen table to write her.

"Lilian. I love you. Frankie's number is in the Rolodex under 'F.' Minnaloushe prefers tuna cat food, one-third of a can every evening, and as much dry as he wants. I hope your poetry went over big. I borrowed the picture album. Don't worry. I'll miss your voice, your face and your touch. Carline."

When I read it, the words seemed flat, but it was the best I could do. I counted on Lilian to catch suggestions of unspoken passion, especially mine. I clipped the note to the middle refrigerator rack with a clothespin, gave Minnaloushe fresh water, and checked to be sure the oven wasn't on. I unlatched the camp box one more time and put in two Dr. Pepper bottles full of tap water, then scratched the last item off my list and stuffed the notebook in my purse.

It took me two trips to get the camp box, the sewing bag and the Amelia Earhart suitcase down the block to the bus stop. The camp box was very heavy. I could have carried food in grocery bags, but the fact that Frankie had built the camp box made it feel essential. It would be a stable surface, hard to find on a bus. I hefted it and staggered down the sidewalk. There was a morning haze holding down the heat. I caught the smell of toast drifting from the open-early Silver Plate on the corner. It was the smell of morning, urging me to go.

When I climbed the stairs for the last trip, Minnaloushe was standing on the threshold, staring at me as I opened the door. He jumped onto the suitcase before I could pick it up, so I squatted to give him my undivided attention. I combed his dark fur with my fingers, and rubbed his face every place that he offered me. I scratched behind both ears. I told him that I would be back. When I stood up and tilted the suitcase a little, he jumped off.

I was sweaty and out of breath as I stood in front of my stuff with my purse strap over my shoulder, waiting for the bus. As soon as my breathing quieted, I became impatient.

I thought about how I always eased myself to the curb while I was waiting with a crowd of commuters. I improved my chances for good positioning by trying to look the driver in the face. Full eye contact usually brought the bus right to me. That was how I had first noticed Tucker's responsive eyes.

As I dug in my purse to note my strategies for the How To project, the bus came around the corner. I watched the rear swing wide, blunt and boxy and comforting. The bike rack was gone from between the squinted headlights. It was a shock to see that the bouncy initials of the transit authority had been painted over with hasty streaks of red paint, to match the stripe. The cartoon of a bus bent with speed, trailing light like a meteor was gone, too. Of course, the company took no responsibility once the bus was out of its territory. The sign read, "Out of Service." Tucker pulled up so close that I was brushed with a motion of air.

Tucker opened the door with a hydraulic hiss. He was wearing cut-off jean shorts instead of his uniform. When I saw bare legs where I had expected his usual pants, I stepped back from the curb and turned as if toward home. As I bent to grab the handle of my Amelia Earhart, Tucker sprang out of the bus.

"Morning," he said with genuine courtesy. "Let me help you with those." Long-distance coaches had low compartments for baggage, but this was a small-town vehicle on its way to be junked. He hoisted the camp box casually, as if taking a date by the elbow, and climbed the steps.

I hesitated, then said, "Thanks." I could smell exhaust fumes, and, faintly, toast. Seizing purpose from the thought that I must urge my How To people to pack lightly, I took a tight grip on my suitcase, squashed the sewing bag under my arm and stepped onto the bus.

There was no one else on board. I slid my suitcase out of the aisle, pushed the sewing bag under my seat and sat down, close enough to the front to be polite. I tucked my purse in beside me. Tucker stowed the camp box in the back of the bus, then came up the aisle with a couple of jitterbug moves I was sure he hadn't learned from lessons at Arthur Murray. He skidded to a stop beside me. Unnerved but entertained, I unsnapped my purse and pulled out three twenties, a ten, and a five.

"Exact change." He took the money, made a clicking sound in his cheek, and pointed his finger at me. "I knew I liked you," he said as he hurried up the aisle.

I wanted to go home. Maybe, if I asked, Tucker would drop my stuff off at the bottom of the stairs, but instead he sat down behind the wheel, checked his watch, brushed back his hair, took off the brake, and said, "Let's shake, rattle and roll."

He glanced back to grin at me, but the atmosphere in the empty bus was too intimate, already. I didn't smile back.

"Is it safe, do you think?" My voice seemed shrill. "Cross-country travel in a defective bus?"

He patted the fare box. "In my opinion, the bus could last another ten years. There's some corrosion in the body. The air conditioning's shot. The brakes are a little soft, but I'm used to them. It's got a nice, powerful diesel." He raised his eyebrows in the mirror. "The company has to get rid of old vehicles to buy new. I love this bus. We'll get there."

"Good," I made an effort. "That's what I wanted to hear." I wondered where the engine was. There didn't seem to be room for it in the snub-nosed front. I thought it must be in the rear, like a Volkswagen, but it wasn't necessary to get into all that. I turned my face to the window.

The haze was starting to burn off. I got a clear look down Union Street, full of closed businesses and the ordinary paths of my life. The street stretched generously in another direction, to the lights at the pond. As I ran my eyes along the edges of parked cars and slight trees in ambitious barrels placed by the Chamber of Commerce, I wanted to sit at the table eating corn flakes with soymilk and watching through the doorway as Lilian did stretches on the bedroom floor. I could see her clutching knee to belly as her thigh bloomed out of ripped sweatpants.

I felt reckless leaving my sleeping town, with its one percent rental vacancy rates, the downtown blocks of brick buildings filled on the upper levels with student apartments, and on street level with florists, shoe stores and tolerant or historic churches. I felt a pang, as we passed, for the absent Woolworth's, but it was much too late for that. I kept looking. My mouth seemed to taste of ground chalk.

Tucker was talking. "The new buses are great, but I don't care about them. I wish that a lot of the retired buses would come back, like the 1981 GMC RTS 11/8000." He sang out the zeros, making a tender little tune out of them as he drove smoothly around the deserted route, pausing almost imperceptibly at each stop. I pulled out my notebook and wrote the numbers down. It was too technical for my audience, not to mention out of date, but I needed to get into the habit of capturing things. "The engines could be totally rebuilt, with new windows, a good cooling system. That would make it enjoyable to go places again."

I sat sideways in my seat, leaning against the window, making a list: diesel, corrosion, brakes. He didn't pause. "Not that I don't enjoy myself." He looked over his shoulder, squinted. "Most mornings on this run, I get to the first stop early and run across the street for a cup of coffee from the Silver Plate. I told Ruby yesterday not to look for me."

"They make nice toast," I said, watching him as he talked. The way his dark hair rippled on top reminded me faintly of Minnaloushe. His chin was definite. His arms tended to muscles. His legs were pale. I still felt they should be limited to a white strip between the top of his socks and his cuffed pants. He had a knapsack and a camera case tucked beside his seat.

I got up and shuffled along the blue-grooved floor to unlatch the camp box and pour water from one of my Dr. Pepper bottles into two spillproof cups.

"Thanks," he said, raising his in salute.

"Feel free to help yourself." I read a notice pasted to the dashboard: *Danger: 35 foot vehicle*. I went back to my seat, uneasy. It was unwise to ignore official warnings, so I copied it down.

Tucker grinned and pulled up in front of the Post Office. A tall figure stood stiffly in the flat, soft light. "Look, it's Mel."

Mel, who must have been in his late fifties, took the steps with vigor, as if a talk show announcer had just called his name. He burst in with his suit coat flying. He had a duffel bag, and his radio was tucked under one arm.

"Hey, how are you, buddy?" he said to Tucker. He paid up, then tossed his bag into an empty seat and looked at me. "Hi, miss."

"Hi," I said, friendly but clipped. I hadn't been planning on more than one man. Also, I was not thrilled about the radio. I knew from the bus stop that Mel's taste ran to polkas.

Tucker, driving, looked back. "You two know each other, don't you? Carline, this is Mel. Mel, Carline."

Mel took off his coat and stretched his arm across the back of his seat. "Oh, yeah, sure, I've seen Carline a lot. We usually wait at the same stop, but this one's closer to my house. I walk down there to get my exercise." He patted the buttons of his shirt over a minor-league belly and winked at me. "Glad to have you along."

I smiled very slightly, sipping. The spillproof cup failed as we hit a bump. A little water splashed on my wrist, where the burn kept up a small ache. Mel faced forward in his seat.

My seat had duct tape over a rip in the upholstery, even though it was nothing but industrial carpeting, with no stuffing to leak. The windows could be shoved forward to open, and there was a cord to yank for the bell. Tucker had a broom stashed behind the side-facing seat. He asked Mel to pick it up and use the handle to push open the emergency hatch in the roof, for the sake of a breeze.

When we took the bridge over the river, I looked, as I always did, down the long stretch of water, catching a glint of metal from the buried sedan on the bank. I unlaced my Rockports and pushed them off with my toes, making myself at home.

Tucker pulled onto the highway with practiced calm, but his voice smoldered with excitement. "Okay, folks. We're on our way to Dallas. I figure it will take us two-and-a-half days or so. A little more with breaks, but I'm trying to make good time."

Mel rubbed his hand across his face, jostling the folds. "If you need any help driving, buddy, I'm happy to take a shift."

Tucker turned around to make eye contact without the mirror, acknowledging good manners, then he looked back at the road and said, "Thanks, Mel, but I'll do the driving. You're not licensed for this vehicle. I appreciate the company, though. You'll keep me awake."

I slung my heels up on the seat, putting on a show of being at ease. "I'm going to Chalk, Texas, to see my aunt. If you take me to Dallas, I can catch a shuttle van to Chalk." It didn't sound quite right. I sat up straight and put both feet on the floor, remembering my manners. "Thank you very much, Tucker, for including us on your trip. It's a bargain." Tucker touched his fingers to the bill of his cap in a stylish salute. Warming, crossing my ankles, I said, "There are cups and water and food in the camp box for anyone who wants it." I felt an urge to hoard for the uncertainties ahead, but that would have been wrong.

Mel nodded cordially, unbuttoning the sleeves of his crisp shirt and leaning back in his seat. "Yeah, I'm going to Dallas, too. I've never seen that old cow town."

Tucker waved his cup of water, and said, "Thanks." I'd commuted behind Tucker long enough to know that he was a talker. There was a sign posted near the fare box asking passengers to refrain from unnecessary conversation with the driver when the vehicle was in motion, but either he ignored it altogether or figured that "unnecessary" was open to interpretation. Of course, there were slashed circles over pictures of cups and hamburgers, forbidding food and drink. I wasn't about to inquire further into the details of company policies on carrying passengers on cross country trips to bus auctions.

Now he started a story about how as a kid he had walked the shoulder of the old state highway looking for anything fallen off a car. He found hub caps and mufflers and black chunks of rubber from blow-outs, but his favorite finds were tires that had kept their shape. He had painted a truck tire and filled it up with a wheelbarrow full of sand from a pond to make a sandbox for his sister's kids. His dad had hauled the whole collection to the landfill after a visit from the health inspector about the state of their yard, but Tucker said he still had an album full of Polaroids of each item he had found, captioned with road and date of discovery.

Mel leaned back expansively. "Where was that? One of those vowel states, maybe? The Midwest?"

Tucker pushed his sunglasses down from the top of his cap, shook his head. "No, I grew up around here. Not far from North Adams. My folks had a lunch stand on Route 2 called the Twin Kiss. They had maple soft serve. My uncles tapped the trees. Big plastic sculpture of a twist cone on the roof. It shattered in my hands when I was trying to take it down one year after an early freeze."

Mel was being chummy. "Ironic."

I imagined Tucker as a courtly fourteen-year old behind the counter, keeping up banter with the leaf-peepers as they streamed up the Mohawk Trail to see the colors. He would have been liberal with chocolate jimmies, sizing up the tourist cars through screens that he slid back to take an order. A bus meant a flood of orders. No wonder he started to picture himself in the driver's seat.

"Even that young, what I loved was the circle of a tire without the weight of a car pressing it to the pavement, flattening the curve. It's a pure shape, beautiful. Rainwater would spin inside an old Firestone, but never spill out, not even if I bounced it on concrete. I tried pounding them against the roads in off season, even throwing them from trees. They never lost that water." He continued, lit up with the conversational pleasure of getting something across. "I've seen a field full of tires. Torn, split, twisted and whole, with flowering weeds and ferns punching up from underneath. I used an entire roll of film, taking pictures of that." He glanced back to check our reactions. I kept quiet about the risk of fire and the cost to the earth, because riding so far in an empty bus was tantamount to slinging another tire into the field. Besides, I was interested in what all the pictures he kept mentioning meant to him.

Mel shook his head. "My favorite vehicle of all time is the 1933 Pontiac Economy Straight Eight sport coupe. Good enough horsepower, nice lines, good gas mileage for that time. I have a feeling for the past. But tires, I want to depend on them. I prefer new."

Tucker shifted lanes and said, "I still love to see gravel jammed in worn tread gone slick and gray from all that contact with the surface of the road." Last night's dream about curves and spheres teased at the back of my mind. I was surprised to hear how free he was with the word "love."

Mel loosened his beaded belt a notch, looking grave. "You can't trust a tire company." They began to rehash the news.

Watching the outlines of athletes flash by on huge orange slats outside the Basketball Hall of Fame as we drove through Springfield, I felt a rise of heart. We were already away from home, even though it would only be a six-dollar fare back from here on a Peter Pan bus.

Tucker was saying, "Bus conversion is a whole movement. I thought about going to their convention in Nevada last year. They'll teach you how to pick one of those old motor coaches, forty-footers, and strip out the seats and the luggage racks, raise the roof. Some of them square it off with a ceiling to get rid of the rounded feel, then they start sketching out floor plans with tape. They always have to overhaul the mechanics, of course, update the headlights, taillights, fenders, not to mention the engine, brakes, bushings, shocks, the works."

Mel laughed, cracked his knuckles. "Sounds ambitious." We were boxed in on both sides by gray sound barriers.

Tucker took a handful of cheese curls from a bag beside him. I hadn't noticed when he got that out. My attention was fading in and out of the conversation, but I found the idea of turning buses into homes oddly appealing. They'd need custom curtains, of course, and an inspired use of storage space.

Tucker was drinking Coke, too. He must have brought his own supplies. He offered the cheese curls to Mel. "I'm telling you. They end up with luxury homes. They install 100-gallon tanks in the luggage bays and start putting in furnaces, bedrooms, tiled bathrooms. They have armchairs and microwaves and a VCR above the windshield."

Mel took a handful of curls, knocked a knee into the back of a seat. "Yeah, but you have to find a place to hook up all those utilities every night. Not to mention parking space." He wiggled the bag on the back of his seat. "Carline?"

"No, thank you." A maroon vehicle merged in from a ramp. Possibly for the first time in my life, I read the make and model as it careened past. Isuzu Trooper. The driver had bleached hair, major fingernails, a chandelier-style dream-catcher hanging off the mirror and a gold framed license plate. She crossed two lanes with no signal, but Tucker adjusted his speed. We were safe.

Tucker rolled the top of the bag and shut it with an alligator clip. "The thing is not to ignore opportunities. Some people look at an old bus and see junk. Some people see a steel skin that can be stretched. They add on pop-out rooms."

I finished my water and stopped listening. The sun was shining through dust on the window. The sky was colored like milk in an iron skillet, shading from slate to white behind the tree limbs and wires. I rubbed the window with a Kleenex, but the dust was on the outside. Pieces of light broke into color through imperfections in the glass. The men talked.

Tucker showed more of a feel for buses than I could ever muster, exotica like nouveau bus mansions and all. He was obviously not the target audience for *How to Ride a Bus*. Expertise could be intimidating, but I had confidence in the value of the passenger perspective. His interest in taking pictures was mysterious, though. I realized that I had watched him pointing a camera out the window on the regular route for years, but had never seen a single photo. He had mentioned pictures of old auto parts and tires. I saw the automotive theme, but wondered if there might be something more. If he took any trip pictures, I'd have to ask him to make copies for me.

TUCKER DIDN'T ASK FOR ROUTE SUGGESTIONS, but plowed down I-95 with fierce nonchalance. "I had a route from Western Massachusetts to Penn Station when I first got my commercial license. Talk about trial by fire." He passed a pickup with a load of wooden chairs strapped in the back, a beefy, tattooed arm hooked out of the driver's window. "I learned the hard way."

I stared at a car tilted on a roof as it flashed by just before a building painted with the words ZAP THE FAT. I didn't catch what was being sold. We passed a dome tiled with blue stars, sudden stone bridges, railroad tracks, other expressways, and more lanes than I could count. Mel lay flat on his back as we crossed the George Washington Bridge. "I used to do this when I was a kid. Watching the girders makes you feel like you're on a Ferris wheel." Leaning out the window to look up at the cross-hatched metal arching against a cloud-inflated sky, I let my mouth hang open, giving up all pretext of professional demeanor. I didn't realize until I stuck my head out that I had been trying to keep that up.

"That's dangerous," Tucker sounded like a person in charge.

I ignored him recklessly, but kept a hand on my glasses. A gnat hit my teeth before I pulled back in.

Traffic was backed up before the toll booths on the New Jersey

Turnpike, so Tucker pulled off into a rest area. "Vince Lombardi spent all those years coaching at Green Bay, and they name a rest stop after him in New Jersey." Mel twisted in his seat to get a longer look at the sign. "The man never had a losing season. He deserves a rest stop in every state in the Union."

There were baskets of artificial flowers on each sink in the restroom, and plenty of toilet paper and seat covers in the stalls. Both the doughnut place and the McDonald's at the rest stop were mobbed with teenagers. I jumped the beverage line to get hot water in styrofoam cups. Outside, a middle-aged couple in McDonald's uniforms were necking at one of the concrete picnic tables. It was oddly affecting. Mel paused at the next table over, giving them a hungry glance, but I carried our food to the back. The picnic area was edged with cracked pylons faded from orange to dusty pink, held together with reflector tape. I put the water on the table and handed out packets of instant oatmeal and plastic spoons. I had plain, which was suspiciously buttery. It was only 9:30 in the morning, but Tucker opened another can of Coke.

"I worked in one of those tollbooths right out of high school," said Mel, scraping oatmeal from the bottom of his cup. "Between Teaneck and Paterson. I grew up in Lodi."

"Pure products of America go crazy." I could hear Lilian's voice reading William Carlos Williams as I rubbed oil into the calluses on her feet. "I think that's from a poem about Paterson."

Mel bumped the concrete table leg with the tip of his well polished shoe, then rubbed the scuff mark. "I wouldn't know. I met the love of my life on that job."

"Those are good jobs," said Tucker, offering Mel the bag.

Mel took the last handful of cheese curls with a little shiver, then squared his shoulders. "Sure. State payroll." He ate a curl.

Tucker dropped the oatmeal packets into the curls bag and carried it to the trash. He glanced at the cars scattered throughout the parking lot, then stretched his arms above his head. His camera case hung off his neck.

"I'm going for a walk, folks. I need to move a little before I start driving again." There was no invitation in his voice. He stepped quickly over a pylon and followed a small footpath behind the building.

I suspected that Mel would take the opportunity to tell me more about the love of his life, but he poured a little water from the Dr. Pepper bottle onto a napkin and wiped his face. "Mm," he said. "That feels good. Maybe I'll go to those restrooms and really wash up." He picked up the bottle and the spoons. "I'll get more water, too."

I carried the leftovers to the camp box, glad to see the men making helpful gestures after eating my food. I stepped over a pylon to climb a small rise behind the picnic tables, then sat on the grass. I watched a toddler stagger between the cart selling sunglasses and the front of the building, near the slamming glass doors. A man calling in a New Jersey accent became a better destination. The surges of sound from the highway lulled me. It reminded me of noise rising from the street to our bedroom at home.

I prodded the burn. It oozed. I waved my wrist to dry it in the sweltering air, then picked a green penny out of the dirt with my fingernail, remembering how my father would pull off the highway on those long trips back to Texas. He knew a stretch of road somewhere in New Mexico that was full of dips and hills like a rollercoaster. He would make the station wagon fly over the dips, and my mother would say, "Dwight," while my brothers and I bounced and screamed. The whole family visited Frankie, but I was the only one who stayed all summer long.

An Airstream trailer idled near the bus. Mel crossed the parking lot toward it, leading with his chin in a staunch way that reminded me of my aunt, only Frankie led with her breasts, hiked up by a powernet bra.

Frankie. I spun the penny. I had to call her. It reeked of poor planning to be on the way to visit without a word to her except a PS in a sympathy card, a mistake too obvious to even mention to potential bus pamphlet readers. It was bad manners, too.

I dropped the coin into my pocket, and sighed. The glaring departures from sensible living I had been making in the last couple of days gave me pause. I wondered if I were going through some rite of passage, perhaps related to aging and estrogen cycles. Lilian had recently gotten into a fight that involved actual shouting with a woman who cut in front of her in line at the post office. She had been so overwrought that she stormed out without mailing the manila envelope containing her immaculate but hopeless submission of six poems to *The New Yorker*. I had to take it to work to meter on the office machine.

Lilian and I had speculated that the incident was biochemical. She had been trying to change her body chemistry by drinking boxes and boxes of vanilla soy milk. Maybe I should have tried adjusting my nutritional balance before I packed up and climbed onto the bus.

None of that mattered now, though. I got up to find a pay phone.

"Hello." Frankie sounded faint and irritable when she answered. I felt a wave of relief. I had been scared to call her and hear more hints of grief.

"Frankie, it's Carline. How are you doing?" I played with the cover of the coin return, pushing it back and forth with my fingers, checking for more forgotten change. It was empty.

"Oh, Carline. What a nice surprise." There was that formal sweetness, again, poured over Frankie's familiar edge. "Can I call you back? The ladies from the Library Guild are here, and we're just about to take a vote. We've had a disagreement about the historical importance of keeping back issues of the *Chalk Weekly Bugle* with the new librarian."

I remembered the staunch women of the Guild from my childhood. They worked together ferociously, with high feelings and without pay. Every one of them had sent me a high school graduation present. Kimmie Griggs had given me a silver thermos; Gwen Watson had bought me a dictionary; and Mrs. Poll had presented me with a cherry red Samsonite overnight bag. Mrs. Poll always had flash. Ida had been thick with them. I looked at my watch again. It was seven-thirty in Texas. I hoped that such an early meeting was a sign that Frankie was getting extra attention in her time of grief. A vote was serious business, but the news of my impending arrival couldn't wait. "Frankie, you can't reach me. I'm calling from a pay phone."

She caught her breath. "What's wrong?"

I stuck the green penny in the coin return slot, as if it were a little present for the next person checking for dimes. "I'm taking a bus to see you. I'll be there in a couple of days. I'm already on the road."

"Land's sake." I could hear voices in the background. Frankie rattled something. I pictured her leaning forward to pick up a glass of iced tea, ice cubes shaking with her effort. I imagined the living room full of opinionated women, looking out the picture window to the farm-to-market road, picking at their nail polish, itching to get back to the stalled debate. I got a little nervous as Frankie's silence stretched out, but I was also yearning to sit on the long couch to sip tea and watch down the lane for red birds in the midst of Frankie and her friends.

Finally, I said, "I hope it's okay that I'm coming. You can always put me to work."

Frankie took a drink. It was audible. She swallowed, sighed, and said, "Sure, come on. You can sleep in the back bedroom."

The phone clicked, and a recorded message came on. If we kept talking, I would owe more. She said, "Sounds like we better hang up."

I opened the slot again, took the penny out, and scraped the top with my fingernail. "It will be good to see you."

I turned from the phone to see Mel leaning in the shade of the bus, watching me with his arms folded. His sharp blue eyes made me uneasy, and it must have showed, because as I stood there fidgeting with the penny, he uncrossed his arms and pulled a small red plastic jar from his shirt pocket. He unscrewed the lid, lifted it, and blew a stream of bubbles through a yellow circle stuck to the lid by a plastic stem.

The bubbles drifted toward me, popping on antennas, hoods, grass or nothing. Mel nodded when I laughed.

"Breaks the ice," he said, screwing the lid back on with a pleased spin.

"With who?" I was a little put off, but couldn't stop giggling.

"Ladies and kids." Mel grinned, showing nerve. "People who inspire me."

Wanting to back him off, I brushed empty air from my shoulders. "I'm not a lady or a kid. You carry bubbles just in case, huh?"

Mel looked at his feet, still pleased. Tucker came briskly into the parking lot from the foot path. Zipping his camera case, he walked into the last bubble without noticing. "Hi, folks. Ready to go?"

The bus was hot. I slid all the windows open on my side. Mel sat across from me, toward the back. He was crowding me a little, but I didn't mind the company. Tucker ruffled his thick hair with his palm, murmuring, "Okay." He set a dusty cassette player in the aisle and stuck in Hank Williams. He kept it low, but I got snatches of the lonesome blues as he pulled the bus back onto the highway. My dad had always liked that music. The traffic had thinned considerably. We got through the toll booth without much trouble.

I pulled the sewing bag out from under my seat, ready to settle in for some work. I pulled one of the curtains out, spilling sheer material on the seat next to me. Tulle does better heaped than folded, but I was careful to keep it away from the floor.

Mel reached out to rub a corner of the fabric gently between his fingers. "Pretty. What are you making?"

"Curtains." I was busy digging through the bag for the photo album, pin cushion, needles and thread.

Mel let go of the fabric, looking down the length of the bus to Tucker's shoulders, which were shifting with the music, then asked me, "Were you calling home?"

"No, calling ahead." I felt a slice of worry, as if it were Lilian I should have been calling instead of Frankie, but I spread the curtain over my lap to count the pockets, trying to get grounded at seventy miles per hour. Lilian might not even be home from the slam yet. A couple of highway signs leaning against each other by the side of the road made me think about the poem where everything depends on the red wheelbarrow glazed with rain water beside the white chickens. The connection in my flickering brain was something about dependence. The horizon edge of the sky was the color of clean concrete, but it pulled up into clouds and dim blue. No rain. It was much too soon to be making phone calls to Lilian, even if highway signs needled me with poetry.

Six pockets, so I needed six pictures for this curtain. I figured I would baste the pockets shut to hold the pictures in place. The backs of the photos might not be attractive from outside the house, but I'd hang a blind behind them, anyway, for the times when I really wanted to block light.

Mel unbuttoned his shirt collar and settled back with an expansive stretch of his arms that I already recognized. "Me, my wife, we never call. It costs too much and it doesn't feel that good. Say the dog is lost. What can I do? Say I'm stuck somewhere. What can she do?"

Threading a needle, I thought about his bubbles. "Do you have kids?"

Mel tugged one bushy eyebrow. "Grandkids. They think I walk on water. My wife brags on me to them for months at a time, when I'm gone."

I stuck the needle into the pin cushion, considering how much I wanted to know about Mel, then went ahead and asked. "What keeps you away from home for so long?"

He shrugged. "I'm retired. I was a foreman, and had too many people answering to me all the time. Now, I like to travel, with nobody to take care of but me. I meet people, of course. I always do."

I smoothed the curtain over my thighs. He had already mentioned both a love and a wife. I started to flip the pages of the photo album while he told me that his wife, Simone, stayed home. She had another sphere. She loved the sky and the garden. She hammered coins and made them into refrigerator magnets and musical instruments. Lately, she'd been making musical magnets. They chimed. She used superglue, although he disliked the fumes. She baked. She studied the human condition. Mel admired her energy. He loved her whether he was right up close to her or on a trip to see the battle sites of the Civil War. Or anywhere. She knew about his desire to keep moving.

I was looking at snapshots while he described his relationship with his wife. Every now and then, I slipped my fingers between the plastic sleeves and pulled out a photo to consider for Lilian's curtains.

Mel said that the first time he took off, they had talked about how to stay in touch. He used to promise to call, which she hated. It meant being tied to a time that either of them might miss, waiting for a distant voice. So he wrote her letters, almost every day, in a loose blue hand. He didn't have a fixed address, so she couldn't write back, but she prepared things to mark her thoughts of him in absence. She dried flowers and filled the freezer with ground basil and a salsa he liked.

Although my hands were busy, I made a few mental notes for a section of my pamphlet called, "Maintaining a Relationship While On the Road." I liked the idea of herbs in ice cube trays. It would be so handy to drop them into a soup pot when a loved one returned. I turned the page to a picture of Minnaloushe, eyes yellow with the flash, staring up at the camera. Lilian's thumb covered a quarter of the picture, and the shelf of her breasts in a favorite sweater blocked his paws and tail. She must have been pointing the camera down to catch Minnaloushe sitting at her feet. I pulled it out, despite the problems with composition, because it was the only one of Minnaloushe. He was a camera-shy cat.

One time, Mel said, he came home to find that Simone had made a crazy quilt out of his ties. His favorite was safe in his duffel bag. The quilt was loud and warm. He cried and hugged her when he saw it. He had been aching cold for a week under thin motel blankets. I didn't tell him that I'd made my love a quilt, too.

"I'm always with Simone for the winter. We miss each other, and she needs help with the shoveling." Mel threw me a wink. "I'd never miss a free trip to Dallas, though. I hear it's a wild town."

He was rubbing his hand and watching my face, so I gave my head a little shake. Lilian would have snatched that wink, balled it in her fist and thrown it out the window. I settled for a strained smile.

Mel smiled back. An office building unfolded with multiple corners, like an accordion. A half-hearted windsock rose above the roof. There wasn't much to see.

I reached into my pocket for the penny I had found, then leaned across the aisle to hand it to him. "A present for your wife. For her handicrafts."

Mel flipped the coin into the air and caught it with a practiced flourish, like a magician pulling an egg out of an ear. He held it close to one eye, then made a big show of polishing it on his shirt sleeve before he tucked it into a balled pair of socks in his bag. "Very nice. She'll appreciate it. She likes them moldy." He slapped his side a couple of times, an example of what she liked.

I laughed, watched Tucker change a tape. He picked some bluesy rock that I didn't know, head bobbing in time. The sound barriers here were studded with stones and hung over with vines in the flat light. Cars were thick around us. We had spent all morning heading south and were near the sea.

It was a good moment to tell Mel that I was a lesbian. I came out to people when they mentioned wives, husbands, girlfriends, boyfriends or dates. The curtain in my lap was another chance for a declaration of sexual orientation. I usually said it firmly, the way I said brand names like Tampax. It was my policy.

I opened my mouth to say I missed my lover, too, then shut it without speaking. Mel could peg me as anything he had the imagination to picture: old maid, divorcée, widow, dyke or runaway wife. Even if he got the category right, he wouldn't know much more than what he could observe across the distance between two bus seats. I had no desire to give anything away. Let him guess. Suddenly wishing I were alone in the closed world of a car, I glanced out the window at a trailer full of wrecks.

Mel pulled a news magazine from his bag, but kept it rolled in his hand. He looked at me, ready to keep talking, ready to stop. I had never been drawn to speak to the man in all the years we had been waiting at the same bus stop, but now I found that I had acquired an opinion of him. I considered him old-fashioned, probably helpless to name his own feelings. I made him nervous to about the same degree that he put me on guard. I closed the album and ruffled briskly through the stack of pictures. "Excuse me," I said, "I need to concentrate."

Mel raised his hands in the air apologetically. "I'll stop talking your ear off." He took his magazine and moved to the front seat facing Tucker.

I chose a picture of Lil and her friend Sarah on the front porch of Sarah's old house, slipped it into a pocket and picked up the pincushion.

Tucker looked over his shoulder. "Be careful if you sew while I'm driving, Carline."

I pinned the material tightly over the picture. "I always am."

The men started talking, softly but passionately, about property values. When the tape ran out again, they found a fifties music station on Mel's radio. Tucker, looking back and forth from the road to Mel's face, quoted a real estate seminar. His cheeks were flushed. Mel, waving his hands, described opportunities in Alaska. His shirt showed sweat. Their deep voices and sturdy shapes were surprisingly comforting. When he turned, I could see one of Tucker's bare knees. Over the long hours in the bus, it had become familiar, almost touching.

The tulle cast its faint net across the picture. Within it, Sarah, grinning in sunglasses, shorts and a sports bra, leaned on Lilian's shoulder. Her knees had a marked resemblance to Tucker's. Lil held a glass of iced tea, had spilled a little on her tank top. She pressed her cheek against the top of her friend's head with a beautiful smile. A mobile of flying birds looked real against the yellow clapboard of a neighbor's house. Lil's face was flushed. Her sister had taken the picture. Sarah's cleavage echoed the long dimple in her cheek and lines on the bridge of her nose above her glasses. Lil's shirt wrinkled softly over her belly, and her hair stood up a little at the back. They both had big thighs. That house had been within walking distance to our apartment. Lil and I missed it when Sarah moved closer to her job.

Feeling as if I were tucking the two of them into a safe niche, I basted the pocket closed. It was a small job, soon done. The engine droned loudly beneath the ribbed floor. I sewed the picture of Minnaloushe into a low pocket, so he would have the chance to admire himself.

I put the needle down, flipped through a few more photos. I was relaxed, but my shoulders were stiff. I stretched my feet out under the seat in front of me. Great waves of lethargy and reverie rose through me, like emanations rising from the engine through the heels of my socks. I rubbed the ball of my thumb over the smooth heads of the pins stuck in the cushion. Their sharp ends poked out the bottom when I squeezed. The curtain, with its one full pocket, enfolded me and the seat in an extravagance of rose.

The bus bumped along. The men kept talking. Every now and then Tucker snapped a picture of an old building for no scenic reason I could see. Mel cast a few inscrutable looks at the curtain and me.

I stopped on a picture of Frankie in a pair of overalls behind the shed, reaching to scratch her dog, Tartar. Tartar had her nose in the air, her neck fully exposed, ready to receive attention.

I felt filled with memories, but reluctant to string them into thoughts. I saw Frankie walking down the lane during the summer of a diet, wearing stretch pants the color of a cigarette filter, moving her arms vigorously to burn more calories. She was smaller than usual, temporarily. The back of her neck blazed red.

Frankie's dog ran through the field on the other side of the barbed wire, glancing back now and then to be sure Frankie was maintaining her pace. I was a moody thirteen-year-old watching from the picture window in the living room while I was supposed to be in the kitchen peeling skin off chicken and spreading diet margarine on half-slices of bread. Instead, I was eating something extra that I could get away with: a hard gingersnap from a loose bag.

I was impressed by Frankie's successful reduction. I lost thirty pounds myself that summer. I enjoyed the glow of moral purpose. We were both shamefaced and sheepish when we saw each other fat again the following spring. We didn't speak of it, and we didn't strip the chicken that year.

Years later, Lilian and I sat on the couch in my living room and swapped diet stories. It was an early move toward intimacy. By then, I wasn't a dieter, but a careful cook who knew affection toward my bulk, rippled with flashes of loathing and fear. Lilian leaned across the stiff cushions to cup the softest part of my arm with her palm, murmuring, "If starving yourself were a virtue, women would get rewarded for it with places on their bodies that feel as good as this."

I had already heard the old girlfriend stories, so I knew Lilian had lines for thin women, too. She had eyes for all kinds of beauty. By the time Lilian and I moved in together, I had once or twice seen her flick those eyes over her body and mine in judgment, weakness, and doubt. We both struggled sometimes, but her mouth always felt true when she sucked on my arms. It had scared me to face her after I burned myself.

My wrist ached as I sewed the picture of Frankie and Tartar into its pocket. The fabric made the white dirt in Frankie's picture look pink. Lilian was going to love how the photos blushed and shimmered in the windows.

I felt a brief longing for the distracting demands of a day at work. I tried to think more about Lilian, but I had left abruptly over her protests. She wasn't about to be a simple dream to help me while away my time. I pictured her at the used-clothes store, digging through recently consigned heaps, lifting the best pieces to size them up. I saw her sureness in sorting, her tired eyes, and then I left her, again, to her work.

We crossed another bridge. The sign said, "Welcome to Delaware. Small Wonder."

The next picture I basted in was of our friend Jen at her place up in Chesterfield, standing in tromped snow in her big boots, cap with flaps and lined jacket, hugging one of her goats, the delicate one with a creamy belly and dark socks and hooves, up on her rear legs as if about to butt heads, while the oldest nanny foraged in the snow behind them. The photo-developing process left a chemical burn on the cold thicket of bare trees beyond the fence that Jen had been working on for years. The goats made gaps by walking through the fence, and she filled them in with gathered brush, a broom handle, chicken wire, anything that worked. In the picture, both Jen and the goat looked mildly pleased. Jen had come over to give Lilian foot massages three times a week when Lil had pneumonia.

My mind was getting heavy, pressing from inside as the window frame pressed my cheek. I was in flight from an ordinary, beautiful life. The flight wasn't special, but as I fitted my spirit to match my container, the shape of it was. I was short and boxy in a renegade city bus on the sleek drift of the road. My pulse ricocheted off the roof. My breasts were—what else?—headlights and the windows were eyes; any two of them mine, the rest available for other sensibilities, peering in or out. The amazing thing was: I was rolling. I was going places. I had a seat to myself with tulle rising around me like smoke from a diesel.

Tucker took I-70 west outside Baltimore, where the highway islands were planted with wildflowers. We drove through air low with mist past big white houses and a billboard for a corporate campus. I heard him say something about HUD. Sewing a picture of the Shelburne Falls bridge of flowers in full summer bloom, I smelled my own sweat, and possibly the sea. I was kneeling on the fluttering curtain when I stuck my head and shoulders out the window into a moment of ecstasy. The whole world whipped through me like a rush of highway wind. I said my lover's name: Lilian.

Mel came down the aisle to bring Tucker more Coke. He clamped his hands over his head like a prizefighter. I gave him a joke salute, but there was no reason to speak. Two school buses slumped together, parked with their rears to the interstate. It seemed that every building was white, even the barns. The bulldozers left piles of red dirt, digging for condos. Tucker whistled, made a sign for money by rubbing his thumb against his fingers.

I put the curtain aside to make avocado sandwiches with mustard and sharp cheese, working on a paper towel spread on the surface of the camp box. Tucker was a smooth driver. The washed baby carrots were still cold. Tucker ate large, one-handed bites.

We stopped in Hagerstown to gas up and pee. Mel climbed down and said, "This was a Civil War battlefield." There was a rank smell from the toilet. Tucked invitingly behind the toilet paper dispenser was a small pamphlet. *How To Be SAVED And Know It* was printed across the front over a wavy pink road. Wondering if there were blue roads in the men's room, I flipped it over and saw that it was tract no. 185 from a fellowship league in Idaho. Skimming the back, I stopped at: "All tracts are free, as the Lord provides." They had to be doing something right, to pull that off. It was a golden opportunity to check out the How To pamphlet competition. I slipped it into my purse, then gave my teeth a quick brush.

Tucker linked his fingers and pretended to crack them backwards as I climbed on. "The pause that refreshes," he said cheerily. His good attitude was holding up.

I put the sewing back into its bag under the seat and pored over the tract as we drove. It had a sweet design, just a single sheet six-and-a-half by five-and-three-quarters, folded in half. I checked the dimensions with my tape measure. It made good use of bold headings, italics for Bible verses, and red ink reserved for quotes credited directly to Jesus. I realized that all the red quotes were on the same side of the sheet as the pink road, printed from a single ink. Cheaper that way. I liked it. The whole thing was too brief for what I had in mind for *How To Ride A Bus*, but it made me think about the impact of an effective summary. I was taken with the challenge of writing a pamphlet that a reader loved enough to distribute in roadside restrooms, for the edification of others.

I didn't have sweeping themes like sin, repentance and salvation for content, but there were lessons to be learned on a bus. If inclined to motion sickness, sit near the front. Take Dramamine or chew mints. Ask the driver about transfers on boarding, not disembarking. Make conversation selectively. I was mixing strategies for city buses and long-distance trips, but editing would come later. The practice of making small choices deliberately was a comfort in many situations. After my mother died, I had polished all her silver and wrapped it in Saran wrap. There had been no need to polish it since.

My eye caught on a bold heading in the tract: **There is nothing you can do to save yourself.** I had something different to say to bus passengers. "Bring supplies of water, " I urged on my pad. "If you don't know your stop, ask."

As we made our passage through the Appalachians and intersected with US 40, I remembered a nineteenth-century painting of Daniel Boone and other angelic, muscular settlers crossing Cumberland Gap. I wasn't sure how to warn my How To people not to repeat the mistakes of the past.

"That's the start of it," said Tucker. "Forty was the first highway built with federal funds." I copied it down.

Mel snorted, and said, "Figures."

"I read about it in a guidebook back at the gas station." Tucker's voice carried as if he were using a microphone. "The old C&O Canal ran through here, too."

They began to talk, in a warm, discursive way, on the history and practice of commercial transportation. Once I summarized the topic to my satisfaction, I turned back to my notes. Their conversation could have been relevant to my pamphlet, except that I was inspired by *How To Be SAVED* to keep my focus narrow but deep.

"Everyone, look," called Tucker.

Glancing out the window, I saw three large crosses staggered on a hill with a sign that announced, "Noah's Ark being rebuilt here."

It was too much. Mel looked uncomfortable, too, but Tucker gave a forced smile and said, "Religion aside, I think it will pay off." I couldn't believe that Tucker cared quite that much about money, since Mel and I were getting such a deal. I returned the tract to my purse.

We took I-79 south at Morgantown. It was green, hilly country. Tucker drove another three hours straight, almost all the way through West Virginia. Small brown signs noted wildflowers planted in memory of the dead. We passed near Clay, Maysel, Procious, Clendenin, Elkview, Pinch, Big Chimney. Tucker kept rubbing his eyes after we swung west on I-64, and the traffic picked up in Charleston. Mel had stopped talking and closed his eyes. Tucker put on an old Bonnie Raitt tape, and sang poignant harmony to "Blowing Away."

I chose one more picture to finish the curtain I had been working on, although there was another with empty pockets still in the bag. This one was Lil's birthday party.

She was standing before the cake, hand to her mouth, while candles burned and our friends sang to her. Sarah had hands behind her back, her lips parted and a silver balloon tie trailing over her shoulder. Jen was leaning on the doorframe, not singing, but smiling. I was in the picture, too, eyes closed and head back, really belting it out.

As I finished the sewing, I looked up to read a sign advertising a place called Gravy's. Tucker said, "When in Rome."

He took the exit. I tied a knot and bit off the thread, hungry again, too.

MEL HELD THE DOOR TO GRAVY'S OPEN FOR ME. IT was against my policies to accept such gestures, but I flicked an errant grasshopper off my blouse and passed through. Tucker had gone to refuel.

The restaurant was bright, with Formica tables and maroon booths. Half of the tables were empty, but the rest were peopled with small groups: old men with white foreheads and weathered faces grinning across silver napkin holders, muscular young men with faint moustaches having coffee, the mother of a family telling her little girl to turn around and stop staring at us across the back of a booth. Mel laughed and handed her a superball. She took it gingerly and turned around. The mother exhorted her to say thank you. She said it bouncing the ball on the hard table, looking at me.

I blushed, ridiculously pleased, as if we were among friends. That was when I knew I was passing for straight.

The booths were wide and firm. We picked one on the far side of a wooden divider decorated with pots of plastic ivy. Through the big windows, I could read the sign out front: 24 hours cream gravy liver and onions now hiring. Gravy's was apparently a chain. I could smell onion rings. A television hung from the ceiling was playing a Star Trek episode from thirty years ago. It was the one where an old friend of Captain Kirk's gets cloudy eyes with no pupils and starts to think of himself as a god.

The very young waitress brought us menus. I told her we would be joined by one more. Mel sat across from me studying the menu like a husband or a father or an emissary from another world. I liked that he had put his suit coat back on and tightened his tie. I was glad the rickrack dressed up my shirt. I felt modestly festive and appropriate, a welcome traveler ready to dine from a beige plastic plate divided into compartments with courtesy and appetite.

I tapped my fingers on the table to the juke box music—a country swing instrumental of "Honeysuckle Rose" that tinkled along under the Star Trek dialogue. Tucker strode in, then slid into the booth next to Mel. He picked up the menu and said everything looked good. I noticed a stack of highchairs in one corner.

I chose something a little risky – a salmon croquette. It came with mashed potatoes, biscuit, green beans and gravy for 3.99. The waitress nodded politely. Both the men went with burgers and fries. I squeezed lemon juice into my ice tea, dropping the slice in, too. I was sparing with the caffeine consumption at home and didn't use table sugar at all. Now I ripped open a packet of sugar, poured it into my spoon, then stirred it in the glass, just as Frankie would do. Across the highway was a metal shed with a sign: "Have a hardcore day."

When the food came, I grabbed Mel's cuff, and said, "Grace." It was another gesture from my aunt's table. I was forcing the men into family conventions with me.

Mel let me grasp him. Tucker, tipping the catsup bottle, looked at us. He said, "I'm not a Christian."

Mel shrugged and offered his hand. "I'll try anything."

Tucker regarded Mel's hand for a moment as it hung in the air, then took it and said, "Now what?"

I leaned across the table to catch his wrist, careful not to get my breasts in the gravy. "Nothing denominational." I felt giddy, winging it. None of this was habit. I glanced around the room. People were looking at their plates or at the television, not at us. "I'll count to three and say 'amen.'"

"One." Their hands were warm. I tightened my grip. My family used to pray at meals on holidays and vacations, but I felt crazy, faking it with unwilling men. I never would have tried it if I had been traveling with Lilian.

"Two." Lilian wore slips as dresses and asked for meatless spaghetti sauce, but even when she wasn't doing anything else peculiar, she looked intently into my eyes when she was speaking to me. Two fat women relishing each other attracted attention. In the company of plain-faced men, even the fact that I was fat seemed to be coming across as normal.

I had been enjoying a reprieve from conspicuousness, but even if I were toying with passing for the duration of a meal, public prayer was hardly the best way to fit in. Perhaps the content of *How To Be SAVED* had affected me more than I had realized. That would be hard to explain back home.

"Three." Not that this could be strictly considered prayer. I wished Frankie and Lilian protection. That was no stretch. The Star Fleet captain turned alien lost a fight to the death full of zingy sound effects. Bobby Goldsboro doing "Honey" came on the jukebox. "Amen."

When I looked up, Mel unfolded a napkin and raised his eyebrows. Tucker had already opened his bun and was dressing it with mustard. He said, "We don't do that every meal, right?"

I picked up my glass, humbled, confused and embarrassed. "Right."

Tucker paused with burger in hand before he took a bite. Bobby was still crooning. "That's got to be the worst song ever written."

We ate. I relaxed.

Mel and Tucker were talking mileage over coffee when I went to the women's room. It was small and clean, with a low sink and a gritty bar of soap. I locked the door, then took off my shirt and hung it neatly on the knob. I was sticky after traveling all day in the heat, and there was no telling when we would stop again. Tucker was planning to drive most of the night. I unfastened my bra and draped it over my shirt. I needed to wash.

I inspected the burn on my wrist before I soaped up. The blister was coming down. For a moment, I felt as though I were seeing it through a bus window as I rode swiftly somewhere else. When I touched it to wash, though, it was part of me again, hurting. I couldn't drive away from the burn. It was coming along.

Pumping the dispenser, I rubbed myself with liquid soap, which was a long way from Lil's scented goddess. I looked closely at my skin. It was a muted cherry vanilla, rippled with stretch marks and veins, flecked with hairs. My breasts were reddened on the top. My nipples were edging toward erect. I flicked them with my fingers, wishing Lilian were with me. I was a lesbian, no way around that. Lil drew stares, but she knew me, body and mind. She could squeeze into this tight space to sit on the toilet and help me decide if there was meaning in my sensation that, damp under a bare bulb in this West Virginia restroom, I was whiter than I remembered.

I tried not to get water on the floor as I rinsed. I mopped away the small pool with paper towels once I was dressed again. I was lucky. Nobody knocked. I got my toothbrush out of my purse, and brushed my teeth.

The payphone was near the restrooms, but I didn't pause. I didn't feel like talking into the receiver to anyone, not even Lilian. I was willing to be immersed in the company of strangers and acquaintances. The restaurant was radiant after the dim hall. I heard a lyric about a man holding on to a woman letting go. A guy with a black t-shirt and vivid eyes buttered a roll. I dried my hands on my jeans.

Tucker was standing with the bill in his hand, ready for my money. Mel had stepped outside for a smoke. All I had were twenties, so Tucker went for change.

I slid back into the booth. The table had already been cleared of everything but its permanent huddle of condiments. I traced the loops in the salt and pepper holder, strangely reluctant to leave.

I glanced around. Tucker was in line to ring out behind a slow-talking lady who was fussing with her baby and trying to get into her purse. Polite as always, he stepped forward to help. The waitress was eyeing him appreciatively as she slid plates onto another table. I could see the cook through the opening to the kitchen, bent over the gleaming grill.

No one was paying attention to me. Suddenly, I was angry.

Holding my fingers still against the table top, I tried to tell myself that I was irritable from travel, that I could have been happy if I had eaten chef's salad instead of salmon croquette. But I was not suffering from stomach upset. I was suffering from the cumulative effect of everybody in Gravy's acting as if I looked ordinary. It was like what they said on nature shows about coming up from a deep sea dive too fast. I had the bends.

Being fat was not uncommon, but it marked me. People let me know that they hated my shape. Strangers might simply be cold or they might throw trash. If it didn't happen here, it would happen down the road. Passing or praying would not stop that.

I wanted to settle up, but my anger festered and burned. Reaching for my purse, I knocked over the salt and pepper. Both spilled across the clean table.

The waitress was there with her damp cloth. I must have looked upset. "Don't worry about it, sweetheart," she said before she hurried away, wiping pepper from her hands.

My rage subsided as quickly as it had come, leaving no trace except maybe the slow throb from my burn. It galled me to be grateful, but when Tucker brought my change, I slid two more dollars under the sugar, padding the tip.

When we crossed into Kentucky, oil refineries loomed all around us. "Valvoline," said Mel, reading the side of a huge tank. Tucker downshifted. We passed through them quickly, back into quieter hills. Everything out the window was starting to blur from my fatigue and the low angle of evening light. When I squinted, the clouds were the same color as the sky. Tucker put on a Jerry Lee Lewis tape, keeping his body in quiet motion.

I slept more deeply than I knew. When I woke, Tucker was off the Interstate, pulling up at the sign for Angler Courts, a stretch of stone cabins at a high place in the road. Beyond the sign, before a little store on a curve, I could see the word "liquors" already lit in the lingering sun. He parked beside the low fence that surrounded the pool, and looked over his shoulder. "I got tired. This will be cheaper than the chains."

"Where are we?" There was a sign in the office window that said, "Fish stories told here."

Tucker shrugged. "I think we crossed a river called the Little Sandy. We're a long way from Lexington, yet."

Tucker had driven hard. I thought better of quizzing him about exactly how far we had gotten. If I had wanted to know, I could have stayed awake myself. Plus, I could work the feeling of disorientation into a reassuring How To tip.

Tucker sauntered under the porte-cochere to talk to the man I could see through the window of the office. Mel got out for a smoke. Plants hung in white macramé holders next to a bug lamp. A very large American flag flew over the sign. The list of amenities ran down next to the word motel: pool, air cond., TV. The word CABLE had been added in block letters at the bottom. I thought macramé was a good sign.

A bell over the office door jingled, and Tucker came back out, looking a little flushed. We conferred at the bus steps. "We can get two queen-sized beds and a folding cot in one room, or two separate rooms without the cot," he said. "What do you want to do?"

Mel exhaled. "I'd be happy to share. Save some money."

Tucker nodded. They both looked at me. I felt as if we were a small flock of birds, barely enough to form a V. I could see a rifle on a rack behind the desk. I didn't want to break off for the night. It wasn't a matter of propriety or money. It was allegiance. "A three way split is the best bargain. If you don't mind."

Tucker nodded crisply. Mel, grinning, straightened his cuffs. Feeling a pang of regret for my lost privacy, I went to my seat to gather my things.

The cabins faced the highway and the pool, screen doors echoing each other under their abbreviated awnings. As soon as Tucker unlocked the door, I wanted to leave. There were faint, powdery traces of a carpet deodorizing tablet in the tracks the vacuum cleaner had left in the gray and pink rug. It left a sweet scent that mingled with old cigarettes and mildew. My very first breath made me wheeze.

I went into the bathroom to use my spray. I was discreet about asthma. A shared motel room was no place to let that slip. There was surprisingly good tile on the bathroom wall, and the state of the grout was reassuring. When I opened the door, Mel was hovering. I waved him in.

Tucker wasn't in the room. His knapsack leaned against the pillow on the stitched spread of one of the double beds. Mel had taken off his shoes. His oxblood wingtips were stowed in a corner next to his duffel bag, which was half unzipped. I caught a shimmer of pale fabric. Fancy dress shirt, I thought, for when Mel gets duded up. I sat down in a pine chair with a butterscotch vinyl seat and stared at a painting of a tiny cabin in big woods. I wasn't sure what to do with myself.

Mel came out of the bathroom with his face damp and a towel around his neck. He noticed the gaping bag, and quickly zipped it up. Winking at me, he started opening drawers in the big bureau.

"Here we go," he said, holding up a pad of paper with letterhead from Angler Courts. There was a convincing drawing of a fish along the bottom. "My wife appreciates local touches."

I sat looking at him long enough to see that he began his letter with a formal, "Dear Simone," then I picked up my purse, and said, "I'm taking a walk."

I gave the bus a pat as I strolled past it on the asphalt, thanking it for the boxy, businesslike way it had proceeded up and down these hills. This was a private moment, of course, not suitable to be written up. Perhaps a dedication on the front page of the pamphlet mentioning the bus by number would be nice, though. The evening mosquitoes were out.

There were only a couple of other cars parked in front of the cabins, but there was a cluster of sedans and pickups gathered near the office. Kids were splashing in the pool. The road had a broad shoulder to walk on, but when I looked up the hill, I saw Tucker with his cap slung around backwards and his feet pressed together, concentrating on taking a picture of an abandoned gas station pavilion beyond the liquor store. There were no longer pumps, just evenly spaced supports on stained concrete and the flat, sheltering roof. He was sockless and noticeably bowlegged. He ran across the road to get another angle, and his sunglasses fell off his cap onto the solid yellow line.

I watched until he had safely retrieved them, then turned away as a tractor trailer chugged between us up the hill. I headed toward some white posts with humped tops—small columns with nothing to bear—that kept people from driving on the motel lawn. My knee ached as I cut between them and walked past another sign for the motel and around the side of the last cabin, away from the road.

The first thing I saw was a dumpster, vivid with paint and gradations of rust. It was surprisingly full, with a box sticking out the top. It crossed my mind that the dumpster would make a good subject for Tucker's camera. I wondered if boys or drinkers came back here to smoke or otherwise ruin the sleep of travelers. I flinched and thought of turning back, but hadn't come halfway across the country to be intimidated by the sight of a dumpster. Behind the cabins, I could see that the hill dropped off sharply for a darkening view of tree-covered ridges. A swing set with board swings and a high, curving slide were outlined against the distant hills. There were pressed plastic chairs set out for people to enjoy the view, but I was dubious about their strength. A little further on, closer to the fenced yard behind the office, was a cinder block with an old seat cushion on top of it, next to an outdoor grill set in concrete, with metal flaking off the corners of the thick barred rack, and pine needles gathered underneath. I took a seat and pulled the pad out of my purse.

I scratched a bite on my neck, pulled off my shoes and socks, and picked up my pen, a reliable Bic that had escaped my job with me. I had to squint to write in the fading light.

"If a passenger plans to ride a bus through sunrise or sunset, she or he should choose a seat carefully, so as not to stare across the chests and faces of those on the most scenic side of the bus. If there are no such seats available, use good grace. The landscape out the opposite window will have its own rewards."

The chain of a swing clanked against a post. "Avoid sharing personal revelations with your traveling companions, as tempted by tedium as you may be. Bring plenty of water in large plastic bottles—never glass. Vary your seat selection to experience the view out the front window, from the side in each direction, and the metal wall at the back. Try everything."

I glanced up into the face of a turkey coming up over the edge of the hill, regarding me intently out of one eye. I screeched. The turkey took a step closer, feathers swelling. I jumped to my feet.

He was huge. His tail came all the way to my hip. His skin was blue around the eyes, bubbly peach down the neck, then hung in thick lobes of fire hydrant red. A flap fell over a fierce beak.

I backed away. He strutted sideways, paying close attention to me, making a big display of his fanned tail.

The scrutiny of a turkey was only a nuisance, but I found it intolerable. I was as furious as I had been at the restaurant. Clutching my pen, I flapped my hands at him.

He gobbled and shook his head. The beak flap bounced in his face. Dark feathers formed false eyes beside his real ones. A skin-covered bone swiveled his tail. High-stepping, he turned to make me face him.

I sucked on my pen. He was a fat, ugly bird. I pointed the pen at his real eye and threw it as hard as I could.

Even before it hit his neck, I was sorry. The turkey ran very fast. I heard his feathers ruffle as he disappeared into the brush. I felt like a bully.

I sat back down on the cushion, picked up my purse and hugged it to my chest. A list was forming in my head: matches, fingernail clippers, needles, safety pins. Anything could be a weapon.

I tried to hide my feet in the grass, but it was too sparse. I didn't want to live as if surrounded by enemies. After a while, I opened my purse and put away the pad. The light was gone. I had no way to write more advice.

WHEN I GOT BACK TO THE FRONT OF THE MOTEL, the curtains to our room were open. They had ruffled cuffs, but no lining. It would take someone with a sewing machine half an hour to add blackout lining and spray the pole with silicone so the rings would glide smoothly. Mel was clipping his fingernails and watching *Perry Mason* on a stately old set. I had noticed rabbit-ear antennas for it on the top shelf of the closet. Two butts were crushed in the ashtray. Determined to be tolerant, I tried to wheeze discreetly.

Mel didn't look up when I came in, but continued to pare his thumbnail in a contemplative way. The television music emphasized a point about justice. The air conditioner hummed almost as loud. Cold smoke motored across the room. I coughed.

Mel held a finger to his lips, nodding toward the bed. Tucker lay on his side under the spread, face turned to the wall.

The ice bucket was full, so I scooped some out with a glass. I sat down in a chair across from Mel, and whispered, "How come you don't smoke on the bus?"

Tucker sat up, rubbing his eyes. "It's not allowed."

I smiled at Tucker. He enforced good rules. He was wearing a different t-shirt in bed, plain and clean.

Mel got up to empty the ashtray. He wiped it out with a tissue, and said, "Anybody got a pack of cards?"

Tucker stuck his legs out from under the covers. "No, I wish I did. I'm in the mood for a little five-card draw."

I was happy to see that Tucker still had on his jean shorts. I questioned the wisdom of allowing outdoor clothing to come in contact with sheets, but these were unusual circumstances, and he had erred on the side of decency. I smiled at him again.

"I'll go ask at the office." I didn't know much about poker, but it seemed important to bond. Also, I wanted to check on the delivery of the cot.

The man in the motel office didn't have cards. In the rooms behind him, I could hear a child talking. He looked me up and down with magnified eyes behind thick glasses, then offered to lend us his dominoes. He kept them on a shelf beneath the counter. I picked up the box while he went to get the cot. They made a satisfying clank. Frankie played a domino game called Forty-two, and, with my visiting parents as opposing partners, she had taught me.

I rolled the cot back across the parking lot and left it outside the door. Mel and Tucker had pulled chairs around the little table and were eating cupcakes and drinking Cokes from the vending machine. Caffeine didn't seem like such a good idea when Tucker needed his rest, but I didn't make a remark. Instead, I opened the box and spilled the dominoes onto the pine surface with a dramatic crash. "The guy didn't have cards."

Tucker and Mel were disappointed, but they let me teach them to play Nel-O, a variation of Forty-two for three players. The point was to lose every hand.

After a couple of rounds, Mel was adept at shuffling. "This game goes against human nature," he said, sliding the dominoes in flashy patterns under his palms. "I don't like trying to score low."

Tucker set up his dominoes in loose rows in front of him. "It's good to try a new game every now and then." He peeled icing from the top of a cupcake. "Keeps you flexible."

I gave them pointers about bidding until Mel, who had his shirt sleeves pushed up his forearms, said irritably, "Are we going to talk or are we going to play?"

We were already playing, but, after that, I let them cut their own throats.

It was unnerving to sit in a motel room in an unfamiliar town and play a family game with two strange men. They really were strange: Mel, for all his bubbles, had an undercurrent of yearning. Tucker was private, but had invited us on this long ride. I knew Tucker from his attentiveness as a driver. I knew Mel from waiting silently beside him at the stop. Circumstances demanded that I trust them, and I found it surprisingly easy. I threw down double blank and won another hand. "Read 'em and weep."

Mel started flipping the dominoes over with thick, confident fingers. He shoved them to Tucker, who shuffled casually, with an air of detachment.

Mel took on a certain glamour as we played. I tried to figure out its source. Analysis of the other people at the table was an unspoken feature of the game. Part of Mel's magnetism was in the way his sad sack of a face would light up over silly repartee. Another part was sheer dexterity. He could handle the dominoes. He picked up on the fine points. He kept his shoulders square but unbuttoned his collar.

I was aware of being a woman, but none of us played that up. I felt wide and amiable in the padded motel chair. I tried, for a moment, to slouch like Tucker, then pulled myself erect like Mel. Imitating the men didn't bring me any kind of edge. I gave it up and fluffed my hair with my fingers.

Tucker was talking, again, about uses for tires. "You can shred them for rubber, if you've got the equipment. Or fill one with concrete and stick a pipe in it to make a tether ball. Or half bury them in a row across your lawn to make a decorative fence."

I played three-two. "You could write a pamphlet of hints for recycling tires. Or—this is a better idea—illustrate one with your photos. "

Tucker gave me a startled smile. I noticed how his lavish

hair was cut sharp over the ears. Nobody got under my three. The truth about Nel-O was that it was mostly luck. It would be a poor choice as a way to while away the time on the bus because of the need for multiple players and a flat surface. A notebook computer or a Gameboy were the ways to go if a passenger had the resources; solitaire, paperbacks and crossword puzzle books were good choices, if not. I scribbled a cryptic note on the score pad, keeping busy myself.

I thought about full-fledged Forty-two games with my family, all of us hooting and turning red in the face. My brothers sat on stools at the corners of the card table, peering over shoulders until they got their chance to play. Frankie and my father kept up a determined patter. I couldn't remember which of them first told me, "Read 'em and weep."

My mother would drift off into reveries that she broke with distracting comments about the length of my fingernails or Frankie's mice problems. She tended to underbid.

In that context, bluffing came easy. Each of us tried small fakeries and obvious ploys, minor variations on the root game that my grandfather had taught his daughters. Even as a child, it had been easy to read their faces, except for those baffling hands when, suddenly, I could not.

Mel snorted as he set Tucker with blank-one. Tucker balled up his fist and gave Mel a punch on the arm. For a moment, as they glared and snickered at each other, they looked like my distant brothers, come of age.

I accepted the offer of one of the beds, but still, I couldn't sleep. Like Tucker, I chose the better part of valor and kept my clothes on under the sheets. Tucker stretched and turned in the other bed. Mel snored from the cot by the bathroom.

It was a hard night. Every time I moved, the bed creaked. I worried about keeping the others awake, but the lumpy mattress made me shift. It was hot in the room. The sheets were dusty. I argued with myself about whether my itches were flea bites. Putting my face in the pillow to bury coughs made me anxious about breath.

Tucker had switched the air conditioner off. My mind kept catching on that fact with irritating repetition, then flashing to the restaurant—smell of hot onions, glance of a man as he buttered his roll, my fingers on the hard table—as if I had made nameless mistakes in going in for that meal. I remembered how the turkey squawked as I hit him. Hours strained through me. My wrist ached. I felt desperate.

Light from the porch shone in through the unlined curtains. I touched my wrist. Throbbing with worry and covered with sweat, I began to feel as if my body were one big blister. If that wasn't true, then people looked at me through blistered eyes.

I sat up, disturbed but unwilling to panic. No one was looking at me now.

Mel's snorts and whistles grated on my nerves. I thought of turning the TV to a dead channel for the white noise of static, but I was afraid it might wake them without helping me. I wished for Lilian, whose steady breath and warmth could lead me through a bad night.

Finally, I got up. I used Mel's duffel bag to prop open the door so I wouldn't get locked out. I made my way outside with shoes in my hands.

There was a single bulb lit over every cabin door. I stood for a moment with a conversational gathering of plastic chairs in our cone of rented light. It caught the forehead of the bus, but the rear was dim. The office was dark, except for the glow and hum of the bug lamp. A car passed. The sound stirred above the songs of frogs and peepers. I walked in its direction, toward the highway and the motel pool. Asphalt warmed the bottoms of my feet.

The pool was surrounded by a low chain-link fence. It was only waist high, and would have been easy to climb if I were the kind of person who would do such a thing. As it was, I didn't have to. The gate was unlocked.

When I stepped onto concrete from asphalt, my sticky feet were slow to pull free. Tall light posts stretched their necks over the water from each corner of the fence, but they were off. The scent of chlorine beckoned me toward the water. There were rules posted on the fence, but it was too dark to read them. The porch lights joined at the edge of the parking lot to form a common shine against the cabins.

I wanted to rinse my feet, but the cement lip of the pool was slippery. I was reluctant to sit down and get my jeans wet, since that would mean risking mildew in the suitcase. Besides, I was yearning to go all of the way into the water. I wanted to be soothed to the skin.

Finally too tired to stand on ceremony, I unzipped my pants, stepped out of them and hung them on the fence. I felt practical and profoundly alone, despite air conditioners whispering from some of the cabins. My belly brushed against the links with a metallic rattle. I held my palm to the fence to still it. The peepers were silent for a moment, then started up again. I unsnapped the shirt I had worn to bed, did half a shimmy with it down my back, then hung it next to my jeans. I took off my bra, tucked the straps into the cups, stepped out of my panties, and folded them neatly next to the bra.

A night bird flying low startled me. I looked back toward the cabins. Each door was crisp and clear in its bowl of light. They made a spectacle of welcome at a distance from where I stood naked at the edge of the enclosed pool. No one else was likely to be wandering around Angler Courts this late at night.

I climbed down the shaky metal ladder. The water hit above my knees. My thighs prickled with goosebumps. The bottom was gritty. I followed the gradual slope toward the center of the pool. My breasts floated. I dove.

I got close enough to touch the bottom, pocked and studded with gravel that floated between my fingers. It might have been the surface of the moon. I did a sprawling handstand, then rose like a cork, gasping and laughing as I broke the surface. The sky blurred like the view out a fast window. The bug lamp crackled. I was weightless.

I blinked my eyes clear, then poured back across the water, kicking, stroking, reaching for breath. Even tired, it was work my body loved. My legs, cramped from too much riding, freed themselves in water. I made clumsy turns, but in taking the lengths between them, I rippled like a curtain knowing wind.

Effort flooded my mind, and I stopped thinking, a pleasure very close to the release from gravity that let my breasts and belly float me near the surface as I pulled through the water with my arms. My will lapped against itself, smoothed out, lapped again, as if it were another muscle caught in the rhythm of use. If sweat dripped from my skin, it became water to carry me. Strain was the same as rest as I rose and sank like a wave lapping light reflected at the lip of the motel pool.

Finally, exhausted, I pulled myself from the water. I was so tired that I stretched out on the warm concrete, rimmed with shallow puddles. My mind moved sluggishly over the fact that I didn't have a towel. I didn't want to fall asleep, and told myself to get up, but all I managed to do was to lean my head on one hand, settling the other along my hip. Through half-closed eyes, I watched clouds mask the stars. Palm trees in barrels rustled on the highway side of the fence. My breasts and belly dripped, innocent as rocks.

I was almost drowsing when I saw a shadow cross the puckered water. I heard a click, and lifted my head to see Tucker between the palms, leaning over the fence with his camera. The lens was turned to me.

I sat up, swallowing a scream. His face was unreadable in the darkness. I reached for a shoe and threw it at him. It hit the fence. He held out a cautionary hand. "Wait," he said. "Just wait."

I rolled back into the water, shoulder deep, then got my footing quickly, so I could keep my eyes on him. "Lurker," I said, grit under my toes again. "Pervert."

He bent over the fence and picked up my shoe. He tossed it near the edge of the pool. It nearly skidded in. The camera was tucked under his arm. The case hung from a strap on his wrist. He started to hook his thumb in a belt loop on his shorts, then thought better of it. "I'm sorry, Carline. I should have asked."

I swung my arm hard through the water, raising an arc of spray, furious.

He stepped back, safe from the splash. "I'm sorry," he said. "The picture might not come out."

That made me unbearably angry. It was such a weak thing to offer after wrecking my peace. I pushed to the shallow end and stood up in the heavy air. I grabbed my belly with both hands and shook it at him. I was too mad to be ashamed. "Did you see this? Want a picture?"

Tucker looked down, jiggling the fence with his foot.

I punched the water. "Why did you point that camera at me?"

His voice was damp. "Because of how you looked."

I slid back under the water, suddenly queasy. "I am not a freak show."

Tucker wiped his forehead, tried again. "I look at every one of you."

I watched him walk around to the cabin side of the fence, with the lights behind him. The contrast between dark and light blanked out his face. "Who?"

He gave a vaguely formal wave of his arm. "The people on the bus."

I believed him when he said this, but I wanted to be clear. I drifted to the deep end. "Not the fat people?"

He touched his throat. I thought he was embarrassed. "Not just overweight people, no."

Moving my arms under the surface, I felt suspended and surrounded. "Not just women?"

He shook his head. When he spoke, his voice was very soft. "All the passengers. I get interested."

He had his hand on the locked gate. "I like being in the front, driving. I like people lined up in their seats, following me. I watch in the mirror. Sometimes I can see their whole lives."

A car passed, headlights blanching his skin and flashing on a faded Coca-Cola sandwich sign near the shoulder. The glare might have made me more naked. Tucker coughed. "Sometimes I imagine passengers living in an apartment building I plan to own. I know who would be good roommates. All I'd have to do would be to pass out flyers on the bus. People would rent from me."

I touched bottom and let him have it. "You're not interested in being a landlord, and even if you were, it would never be your job to say who lives with who. You think you see people's whole lives, but what you really see are surfaces." I was neck deep, holding onto the far edge. Home economists knew that the surface of things mattered immensely, but I wasn't about to give him that. "Anyway, why didn't you want my surface the way you know me best, in a nice outfit holding my purse in my lap and looking you right in the eye? If you're so interested in the human pageant, why don't you ever point the camera inside your own damn bus? You could ask permission or take pictures of the empty seats. They're interesting, naked. You didn't have to stalk me."

He backed up, shaken, zipping the camera into its case. "You're right. I should have asked."

I dunked my head, sick of being reasonable, but searching for a way to cut him slack. I heard honest apology in his voice. The truth was that I had no way to get away from this motel without Tucker. I needed to forgive him, so thought that I did.

When I came up for air, he was crouching, eye-level with me through the fence links. He gripped it for balance. "Friends?"

Kicking hard below the water, I stayed in place. "It's all right. Please go to the room and bring me a towel."

Tucker stood up and turned toward the cabins, then turned back. "What I came out to say was that I've rested enough. If you can sleep on the bus, I'd like to beat the traffic and get an early start."

I took a shower and changed into a sundress. I even remembered to go into the office to return the dominoes and help myself to hot water and a styrofoam cup for oatmeal. The men could take care of themselves.

The sleepy owner shambled in at the sound of the bells over the door to lean on the counter, and say, "'Preciate you, now."

Mel barely woke, but picked up his wingtips in one hand, slung his bag over his shoulder, and stumbled up the bus steps. He used his bag as a pillow and was snoring again before Tucker pulled out of the parking lot.

I was exhausted, too, but ate oatmeal dutifully, mixing a packet of raisin spice with apple and cinnamon. The bus shook. I brushed my teeth in my seat, spit into the cup, stuffed it with a napkin and threw it away. Everything was under control. Tucker drove. I fell asleep with my face on my arm, breathing scented motel soap and chlorine.

When I awoke, I was wheezing and my shoulder was stiff. A long barn full of hanging tobacco stretched out the window. I felt under my seat for my purse, found my asthma spray and took a couple of puffs.

The soft hills smeared with motion and heat. Sun beat in the window. Mel was sleeping stretched out in the aisle, his feet pointed toward me in black socks. Tucker had Mel's radio on, keeping it soft. The announcer said, "We just heard Johnny Cash doing 'Riders in the Sky.'"

When I stood up, Tucker glanced into the mirror and gave a little wave.

"Where are we?" I held onto the top of the seat with one hand and rolled my shoulders, trying to work out the kinks.

"Western Kentucky Parkway." As Tucker spoke, he turned to another station, a man talking urgently about snakes writhing before a brush fire, slithering into the water. The speakers shook with the force of his voice. He said, "Baptism can't save a sinner. Scrambling like a snake won't save you. No actions can save you, only true repentance."

Unwilling to entertain a sermon, I turned my back and sidled up to the camp box. There was no reason to be secretive, but I didn't feel like sharing. I palmed an orange, hiding it in the folds of my skirt.

When I turned around, Mel was sitting up, yawning. I squeezed around him, and went back to my seat. I wasn't in the mood to eat in front of him, so I slipped the orange in my purse.

He rubbed his face. "Lord, what a long night."

Tucker laughed, switched the radio off. "It's almost noon."

Mel moved up front, and they started telling each other stories about the worst places they had ever spent the night. Tucker's strongest entry was a trailer where he had lived with five other men when he worked on an oil rig. I started humming to myself when he described the sheets of the bed they had used in shifts. I was not in the mood to be interested or offended or to react to these guys at all. Mel was inaudible, but whatever he said caused them both to laugh and look over their shoulders at me.

I took out my pad to scrawl a note with an Angler Courts pen:

Always travel with ear plugs. I thought of getting my sewing out, but wasn't in the mood.

Tucker stopped at a rest area so we could use the toilets. Boy Scouts were handing out coffee, but I swerved away from their table. It called for too much social nicety. Locating a payphone beneath a large picture of the governor, I wiped the receiver with a Kleenex and called Lilian. She didn't answer at the store, or at home, either, so I told both machines that I was fine. I said "I love you" to the phone at home, and hung up feeling bereft.

When we were under way again, Tucker offered a bag of peanut M&Ms he had bought from the Scouts.

I shook my head. Mel took a few to go with his coffee and date muffin. "We're not that far from Graceland. I picked up a brochure."

He was reading aloud about the 1955 pink Cadillac in the Elvis Presley Auto Museum, when, suddenly, I knew what I wanted. I sat up straight and put both hands on my knees, trying to get a grip. Mel was droning on about a custom jet called the *Lisa Marie*, but I ignored him.

Tucker had said the photograph of me wouldn't come out. It had been dark. Had I seen a flash? I remembered the porch lights and the headlights from the road, but nothing from the camera. It didn't matter. Anger building in me, I pushed my skirt aside to pinch my thigh. I held on and twisted. It hurt. We passed a hand-painted sign for homegrown tomatoes. I moved my fingers back to rest on my knees, tired of self-inflicted pinches and burns. Jolting along, I wanted something different. I wanted the film.

Tucker wasn't a raw boy tossing out insults. He was a grown man, capable of being polite day after day to crowds of people sullen with the strictures of jobs and buses. He had asked me to come with him. He had lulled me with small courtesies, then reduced me to a spectacle the first chance he got. It was predictable, and possibly without malice, but I had had enough.

Mel, crooning "Marie's the name of his latest flame," was fashioning a guitar from a wire coat hanger he had taken from the motel. "We're going through Memphis, anyway. I really think we should make a stop."

"We'll see." Tucker murmured politely, steering with one hand while he dug in the back of his cassette case for a tape. He popped it in and turned up the volume.

It was some kind of bouncy rhythm and blues. "Carl Perkins," said Tucker, although nobody had asked. He kept time by tapping his fingers on the wheel. It made me so mad. He picked all the music. He thought he was some kind of leader because he was in the driver's seat. He thought he knew me because he knew my commute. He had an image of me. It was dangerous to let it go at that.

I put on my Rockports and tied the laces in careful bows. Carl Perkins was singing about his shoes. I picked up my purse and spoke sharply from my seat. "Tucker! I want that film."

He glanced in the mirror. "I'm sorry, Carline. There are other things on the roll."

I came down the aisle as if I were floating. My hips bumped the seats, but there was nobody to say "excuse me" to except Mel. I didn't say it to him.

I stopped at the line passengers are required to stay behind. I put my hand out so that it hovered just above Tucker's shoulder. "Give it to me."

Shrugging as if to brush my hand away, he kept his eyes on the road. "I'll make you a copy if it comes out."

I gripped his shoulder. He swerved a little, and said, "Carline, this is a moving vehicle." The bus rocked.

I crossed the line and spotted the camera on a little shelf to his left. I reached across him for it, saying, "You took something that belongs to me."

Tucker grabbed the camera and held on. He kept his other hand on the wheel. "For God's sake, I can't see."

Mel came up behind me. "Come on, Carline. Sit down and talk about this." He didn't touch me, but his voice had pull. He was a passenger, too.

I let go of the camera and stepped back. I looked at Mel. He was holding his guitar by its hanger, concerned. I let him in on the pertinent facts. "He took my picture at the swimming pool. I want it back."

Tucker pulled over onto the shoulder, and stopped the bus. He drew himself up like a security guard. I saw goosebumps on his legs. "I have to think of safety. This is company property. Either you sit down, or you'll have to get off the bus."

I made another grab for the camera, but he was gripping it tightly, so I went for the key. I pulled it out of the ignition, shoved open the door, and jumped off the bus.

I hit a wall of heat. I could hear Tucker right behind me. Cars were passing too fast. I jumped halfway up the far side of a ditch, kicked free of entangling wire and brush, and climbed out to run along a fence, breathing hard. Scattered trash was hidden in the grass. The tops of the fence posts were pink. The key jangled between my fingers. I dropped my purse. Mel was shouting from the door of the bus, "Watch out for snakes!"

My ankles were already scratched. Tucker caught me as I slid on an old paper plate. He yelled in my face. "Are you crazy? Are you completely devoid of common sense?" He wrestled the key out of my hand, then paced around me in a circle, waving it in my face. "What do you think you're doing?" He kicked the paper plate into the ditch.

He reminded me of the turkey. I didn't say anything, but turned back to find my purse. Squalls of grasshoppers jumped. Out of the corner of my eye, I saw Mel bending in the door of the bus.

Tucker watched me pick stickers off the purse strap and hang it over my arm, then he said, "Look, Carline. I'll drive you to the nearest town. I'll give you the picture and the negative when I have it developed, but there are other pictures on the roll that I want."

I barely listened. It was over. I was off the bus. I checked that the snap on my purse was secure, then threw it across the ditch. I slid down, stepping carefully between the strands of barbed wire of the downed fence that was sprawled along the bottom, and scrambled up the other side. I was sneezing and my eyes burned as allergies kicked in, but I had better footing on the mown grass near the road.

Tucker jumped the ditch. He followed alongside me as I picked up my purse and began to walk. "Come on, Carline. You're a reasonable lady. Don't make me leave you out here."

My nose started to run, but I was brisk and oblivious. Tucker might as well have been a chorus of boys yelling comments from the corner of my street.

Finally, he stopped. I think he watched me a while. I didn't turn to look, but stared down at the thicket of grass, dirt, thrown bottles and cigarette packs marking a path for me. I heard the bus start up behind me. It made a wind when they passed. Tucker honked lightly. I breathed the exhaust.

A sheet of paper flew out of one of the windows. It caught on the broken fence in the ditch. I kept walking until the bus was out of sight, then scrambled for the paper.

It was a note from Mel: "Beside the road for you." There was a phone number scrawled across the bottom, under which he wrote, "Simone, my wife. For help." I started crying then. The idea of help seemed impossible, but his attempt meant something.

I saw a bag sitting by the edge of the shoulder where the bus had been parked. I thought it was the sewing bag, with the curtain and our photos. My heart lifted with relief. When I looked inside, though, what I found was a jar of peanut butter and the last Dr. Pepper bottle full of water. Mel had been trying hard, but he couldn't have known how important the sewing bag was to me. I picked up the food bag, and, still crying, started to walk.

I had the choice between the littered grass or the coarse asphalt of the shoulder. The shoulder was easier walking, so I chose it at first, rehearsing the wrongs that Tucker had done as I walked. "He took my picture, naked. He didn't ask. He wouldn't give it back." My shoulders were shaking with messy sobs. Between sobs, heat, and the slant of the road, I found myself staggering. Cars leaned on their horns, veering abruptly into the far lane. Trucks blew past.

Corn fields stretched as far as I could see on both sides of the road. I wasn't much of an agriculturist, but there was no mistaking corn. There were small signs at the ends of some rows: Harness Xtra 6L, Pioneer 33. These had to be the names of either seeds or pesticides. I saw one for Roundup, which I knew killed weeds. After I trudged past the endless pink-tipped fence posts for a while, I decided that they were painted at the top to keep out rain water and prevent rot. At the corner of one field was a sign about four times as big as the row markers, but just as matter of fact. It listed the Ten Commandments. I thought it was unlikely that most interstate travelers took them in. I skipped them, too, but got a tube of sun screen out of my purse. I rubbed it on. My neck was burning more than my eyes. I had no idea how far it was to the next town.

I finally had to stop crying. It was pathetic, and I feared dehydration, so I wiped my nose on a Kleenex, took a long swallow of water, and struggled on. Weeds whisked my calves. I knew pedestrians were forbidden on the highway, and saw the sense in that. I was a distraction and a hazard to motorists moving with such speed. Many of the drivers stared. I could have tried to stop a car, but that might have been waving down trouble. I had read newspaper stories about good Samaritans hit as they got out of their vehicles. For the time being, it seemed best to walk.

I switched the bag from arm to arm as I strode along. My purse hung heavily on my shoulder, but my empty arm swung through the air. I wished the corn would hold me if I cast myself out into the field to swim. I could imagine pulling myself through the air by grasping ear after ear, immersed in heat and the tall rustle of the stiff, green leaves. I might leave a trail of broken stalks, but could save my ankles, which were aching, and cut away from the highway to find a body of fresh water, which would be a great help.

The thought of floating face down over so much dust and pollen made me sneeze. Slowly, through my blocked nose, a terrible smell crept in. Every step I took, it got stronger. I tried to ignore it.

I had lost the rhythm of accusation. I didn't know what it would mean if Tucker had caught my body in a picture, except that it would weigh me down with evidence of massive mistakes. It was brutal, for instance, to imagine Mel peering at it and saying, "Get a load of that."

I thought of the bus driving away with the only copies of Lil's favorite snapshots, her rose-colored curtains, the camp box and my mother's Amelia Earhart suitcase. Not to mention everything inside: slacks, skirts, clean underwear, cocoa mix, kitchen goods, and a Venus of Willendorf ashtray. Tucker would leave them in the back at the auction, and they would disappear into another country or be crushed at a Dallas junkyard. I couldn't imagine how I had come to put things I needed at such risk.

I itched to get to work on the curtain, to gather tulle in my lap and baste another rose pocket shut. I thought of a picture of Lilian, quizzical and shoeless in stockings and a short velour dress, trying to turn on the convection oven in our friend Karl's kitchen, while Karl—natty in a plaid shirt, hemmed shorts, and white socks—stood beside her on blond floor boards, looking on. That would be perfect to use next. I wanted to finish the curtains. I still couldn't believe they were lost.

It was a bitter irony that I had left on Tucker's bus a bagful of pictures of everyone I loved, absolutely not meant for him. Breathing through my mouth to evade the smell, I considered the worst things that could happen with the picture he had taken of me by the pool. He could use it for laughs or as pornography. He could show it to buddies, who would do the same. One of them might post it on a Web site as an example of ugly, naked women, and people in many countries could take a look. Or he might leave it in the bottom of a drawer until a public moment in my life—perhaps if my bus riding guide were a surprise bestseller—then cash in with the *National Enquirer.* They might run it as a centerfold, for comic effect, and the mainstream press might pick it up. Frankie, Lilian, my dad and Nanette, Jen, Sarah, Karl, prospective employers and everybody else would have a chance to see.

Such widespread exposure seemed unlikely. He had said his reason for taking the picture was innocent. He had ruptured our slight relationship and refused to rectify his mistake, but from some angles, this could be a misunderstanding, a lapse of courtesy. I had been guilty of such things myself in the past few days.

The smell was getting stronger.

A picture was just a stare, held down and slicked over. I had been suffering under stares, lately; feeling them like touches, like cuts. As I ran my tongue over my dry lips, I thought about what it might have been like to look at the picture, to see what Tucker saw. Trying so hard to empathize with him left me feeling a little sick. I couldn't quite pull it off.

The smell was on me, making my hair heavy and my throat close. I sniffed my hands and looked at the bottoms of my shoes. Nothing. I took another look at the strap of my purse. It didn't smell, but the air did, with a pervasive stench that made me cover my face and breath through a Kleenex as if it were a veil.

Suddenly a tanker with mustang mud flaps shot past me much too close. I stumbled back from the road, and stepped on the bare tail of a dead possum. Flies rose to a low height, then settled back on the stinking belly, matted and shining with blood.

"Oh god." I jumped away, gagging. I was not ready for this rank body. The truck might have hit me. I felt gut fear of my own death, on this road or closer to home, as Frankie's friend Ida had died. The possum's face was very small, gray and still on the cracked asphalt. Covering my mouth with my hand, I wished I had a shovel to move it off the road, but the smell was overpowering. It followed me as I hurried away, leaving the shoulder for grass to get a little farther from the road.

I stumbled along trembling, hoping that Minnaloushe was okay. I had forgotten to ask after him on the phone machine. I thought of Minnaloushe arching his back under Lilian's hand, but my mind slipped, with misplaced intimacy, to the blur of Mel's big fingers throwing a superball.

Some distance ahead, an arm appeared through the slot of a Buick's window to toss a cigarette to the ground. I fought off fears of being chased, ridiculed, burned. The impassive car shrank from sight.

I stopped walking when I spotted the butt, tip still red against the asphalt. The smell of smoke mixed with rotting possum. As I coughed, I could hear Lil saying a poem about plums in an icebox, "so sweet and so cold." It all folded together—faint smoke, dead body, Lil's voice, relentless cars. Everything I had feared, wanted or lost seemed to be rising along this stretch of road.

I ground the cigarette out with the sole of my shoe. My ankles were sore, but the twisting felt good. I rested a moment, retied my shoelaces, took a drink, and began to move forward again. As I walked, I faced the glaring fact that I had been behaving with disregard for my responsibilities. I had abandoned my job. I had walked out on Lilian. I had given no more thought to my cat than the briefest of feeding instructions. Tired and sorry, I wheezed as if breath were ashes. I had made reckless decisions that brought me to this endless shoulder. The question was why.

Sucking my lip, I concentrated on describing the nature of the emergency I was in. "Stranded bus passenger" sounded crazy. I had to do better than that. It had started, I believed, with the shouts of boys who were calling me something I was. Fat. The small flames they had thrown were nothing, but I had caught like dry brush. I had burned myself, slightly. On purpose. There was no denying that.

When I looked to myself like a flaw in the perfectible world, I became inconsiderate, or worse. I was ready to give up worrying about how Tucker's lens had seen me. The shoulder was empty except for the remains of animals, trash, weeds and me. Nothing turned on size or sexuality here except my state of mind.

Moving past tarred telephone poles, I cut my thoughts loose. I watched the asphalt flicker with the faint center stripe. The edge of the road blurred with heat. Time was measured by each drag of my aching feet. I had no idea how many hours had passed.

I stepped over a stiff frog, belly up with its bowed legs stretched. I wasn't going to get away from bodies by the side of this road, especially not my own.

What I felt for my body was identification with its animal urgencies: the sustenance of water, the need for shelter and rest. The pain in my feet led my thoughts away from the fading burn on my wrist, but the situation as a whole took me back to it. I was walking toward Chalk, toward Frankie in mourning, trying to place my reactions to being taunted about being fat on a map that located my tender-skinned childhood, aspiring maturity and displaced immediate present on a grid drawn to scale with the lives, desires, bodies, fights and deaths of road kill, family friends, intrusive bus drivers and everyone else. Underneath were things I couldn't name or chart, pressing up through me until my spirit was raw as my feet. I noticed a feeling of shame that self-harm and fat had brought me to this sloping shoulder, but as I walked, the shame fell away. I was groping and clumsy, unlikely to find the patterns I was straining to see, but something in me was white-hot to try.

The smell faded. Coming off a curve, I saw the low stretch of an overpass, with its rhythmic guardrail outlined against the frayed edge of a cloud. At first, I thought only of resting in its shade. Then, with a sharp lift of hope, I saw that I could walk someplace where the cars would go more slowly. It would be legal and probably safer. A small road might take me to a town.

Panting with exhaustion, I climbed to the girders on a slanted concrete slab that reminded me of a suburban driveway with weeds in its cracks. I liked the dimmed, sheltered feeling, and stopped to take a drink. I opened my purse and dug out the orange. Peeling it, I ate a couple of sections. I kept the rind in case things got desperate.

For a few moments, I stood there, dank with heat, every muscle in my legs throbbing as if earth stepped toward night only by my effort, then I straightened the straps of my sundress, clenched my fists, and pushed into the brush that covered the steep hill.

I swung purse and bag at the weeds in front of me, trying to scare off snakes and thrash out a path. Thorns scratched my arms. I scrabbled up the hill, breathing fiercely, slapping weeds, kicking hard into the shifting dirt. Bursting over the top, I was red-faced and gleaming. I stumbled over a low cable onto a cement two-lane with trees tight on each side. Leaning hands on my thighs, I gulped air in the middle of the new road.

BUS TIP

Try to make eye contact with the driver as he or she nears the stop

FRANKIE CAME OUT OF THE GARAGE IN THE RELATIVE cool of the morning with a wasp's nest stuck on her broom. She held the broomstick high, fists in latex gloves to prevent stings.

I watched from the picture window as she marched down the lane. Frankie looked stalwart in her blue pantsuit. I couldn't tell how much she might be suffering. Ever since I'd seen the red-winged horse on the giant oil company sign as the train pulled in to Dallas, I had been wondering what kind of help I could be to my aunt in her time of grief.

A gregarious family in an ancient station wagon had picked me up on the road. They were on their way to see Bobby Vinton at the Blue Velvet Theater in Branson, but had been kind enough to drop me off at the Amtrak station in Poplar Bluff. Since the station was locked, I had to wait outside half the night for the train, slapping mosquitoes and worrying in the buzzing dark.

When the *Texas Eagle* finally pulled in, I paid my money and turned myself over to the bumps and shivers of moving along a track. I slept while it sped me all the way to Dallas, whose Mobil Oil flying horse sign had been a landmark in my childhood. My father, buoyed by making good time on the highway, once saluted it in honor of fuel. My mother would get out her comb when she saw it, as if we were almost to her sister Frankie's house. Grooming the boys and me didn't take seventy miles, but we liked to be ready in plenty of time.

After my mother's funeral, Frankie had taken me to Padre Island for a week. We had cried on the beach with t-shirts and shorts over our swimsuits among drunken college students on spring break. Frankie had told me the name of every horse my mother had loved as a girl. She wrote them down on the inside cover of my paperback mystery.

Last night, riding toward Chalk in a van called the Waco Bullet, I had been thinking about keeping my aunt company in that kind of unstructured mourning. Pressing my face to the window to watch familiar fence posts with no sign of pink paint, I had prepared to be of use. Tucker and Mel passed through my thoughts in random patterns, like newspaper blowing across the highway. I had burned most of my anger at Tucker for fuel during my endless walk. I wasn't happy to have lost the curtains and the pictures—all of them—but I saw no choice except to let it all go. The men had probably made it to Dallas before I did. If I decided to find Tucker once I got back home, I certainly knew his route.

When I stepped off the van in the white dirt lane, Frankie had hurried out the door. We leaned into our hug. She still smelled of talcum powder and OFF.

I pulled back and looked at her. "I'm so sorry about Ida."

She squeezed my arms. "Where is your suitcase?"

"I lost it." Frankie had bags under her eyes. I had no desire to tell her the story of how I had been separated from my things. It seemed unconvincing and a little indecent. I squatted to greet Frankie's border collie, Tartar, who stretched her neck for me to rub as if we knew each other. I had never seen her, except in pictures. I had loved her grandmother, though.

As we walked to the house, Frankie said, "I'll call the bus company for you." Her voice had tremors. "How's your father?"

"I doubt the company can do anything, but I'll take care of it myself." I kicked my toes against the front steps to shake off the dust. Speaking more of Ida could wait. "Dad and Nanette were doing fine, last time I called them. Dad had just replaced all of the old water pipes under the house."

"I heard they had termites." Frankie made a face. "They should move into a condo."

She loaned me a pair of jeans and a checkered shirt. They fit like my own name. Frankie's eyelids were red-rimmed. She sat with me in the living room with the television up loud and talked skittishly about the heat.

I had not done much better. I found almost nothing to say about the trip. I didn't bring up quitting my job or burning myself. I told her that I had met some people going to Branson, Missouri.

"I've heard of it," she said. "Ida and her boys saw Mel Tillis there."

We went to our rooms not long after that. I recognized the fringed bedspread, the vanity and the lamp all with a shock of family feeling. I ran my hands over the carved ball legs of the vanity before I slept.

Now Frankie flung the nest far out into the field. She stood in the lane a long time, shaking her broom. There were a few wasps in the sky. The broom straws lost a clot of dust to the breeze.

I came out of the house to meet her near the shed, where she had gone to put away her gloves and broom. Frankie groaned softly as she sat on a rusty lawn chair in the corrugated tin dome of the shed, which was open so she could drive her tractor through. The rope swing still hung from a high rafter. We sipped the peach tea I had brought from the kitchen and watched the bermuda grass move.

Frankie turned to me and grasped the flesh of my upper arm. "Carline," she said, "Ida's funeral wasn't right."

I reached up to pat her fingers. "Why? What happened?"

She let go of my arm and tugged on her tunic, which tended to ride up. "That funeral could have been for anybody. The minister barely knew Ida. Not even her boys spoke." Frankie put her glass down in the dirt. She sounded angry.

I drank some tea, swallowed a shard of ice. "Was her husband there?"

Frankie reached up to settle her hair. Her elbow punctuated the fat of her arm. "Tom passed away a few years ago."

I felt protective. "Maybe you could do something to honor her." The gate behind me was clanging.

Frankie drew a line in the dust on the big old car parked beside us. "I'd like that." She pulled a Kleenex out of her pocket, wiped the dirt off her finger, and looked at me. "The Library Guild is meeting today. Perhaps we can discuss it."

My ice had melted completely. I was a little afraid of the Library Guild. Sometimes as a girl, I had heard shouting or sobbing coming from meetings in the living room. I stalled. "Isn't this car Ida's Mercury?"

Frankie pressed her hand against the door and made a palm print. "She left it to me in her will."

My head was tilting back farther and farther. The sky had hazed over. I looked at the high curved roof of the shed, and saw wasps circling the rafters. Frankie was telling me that she and Ida used to go on drives. Her voice was tense and careful. It seemed as if she didn't want to cry in front of me. I wished she would.

I tried to sit forward, but the legs of the lawn chair folded slowly beneath me. I hit the dust on my back, spilling tea. Frankie stared down at me, startled and worried, her glasses sliding to the tip of her nose.

"Oh god," she said, her bouffant pointing skyward. "I hate it when that happens. Are you okay, Carline?" The tea made a puddle in the dust.

Frankie stood and offered me her hand. As I looked up at the familiar crescent of her belly and the globes of her breasts, I thought of generations of women in my family fighting household insects and observing deaths. There was nothing to do but take my place among them. "Okay," I said. "If you want to plan another service for Ida, I'll help."

Tartar licked me in the face. Her tongue skimmed my teeth. I shut my lips and sat up, covered with dirt. She leaned against me, nuzzling my arm.

"Another service?" Frankie looked surprised. "Do you think we could do that?" She slapped her leg and called, "Tartar, come here. Carline, I hope all that dust doesn't give you asthma."

Wheezing had been a central drama of my childhood summers in Texas. Something in the long moving fields of sorghum, alfalfa and cotton, the dusty lofts full of raccoons, hay and corn cobs, in the horses' glistening coats and clipped manes; something in the house closed up to hold in machine-cooled air, the gray flowered rug, the hard sofa, the den furniture with horseshoes branded into wide pine arms; something in the big pantry with its shortening, cereal and Tabasco, or the rounded refrigerator with its tomatoes, lemon pie, pickle jars of drinking water, peach jam and chicken left from dinner. Something caught in my lungs and kept me up nights struggling to breathe.

Frankie would want to keep me with her all summer, so she'd fight it. Just as she used big bottles of iodine she got from the vet to treat chigger bites and cuts, and paint stinging smiley faces on my skin, she wrangled asthma remedies out of the professionals in town. She brought home a mask for me to wear every time I left the house. It was a thin sheet of yellow foam fitted into a plastic snout. It made my face hot and made me feel like a freak. She talked Mr. Louis at the drug store out of pills that kept me woozy and prone to sleep all day in the cool, darkened den. She brought me sprays that tasted awful and sprays that I never felt enter my mouth, no matter how hard I inhaled. Nothing seemed to work.

She sat up nights with me, running a violet brush through my tangled hair. The rhythm soothed me. Frankie pulled me into her lap in the big rocker with curved arms and told me to think about every breath as a wave of wind washing through the grass. I tried to sleep sitting up, with short dreams of grasses growing matted in my lungs, and long gasping bouts of wanting my mama and my bed at home.

Frankie talked to my parents on the phone about the fact that I was allergic, but we never established to what. I loved the rope in the shed, feeding the horses and watching *All Star Wrestling* while Frankie hooted and peeled apples with a knife. I never told my mother I wanted to go home.

I wasn't wheezing now as I got up and brushed white dust off my jeans, but Frankie coughed a little in the cloud I raised. Tartar backed up against her, pushing for affection. Frankie fingered the dog's dusty hair. "I think another service might be a good thing. Ida believed in trying until you got it right. She was a teacher."

I leaned against the Mercury, already going over my checklist for planning events. "We'll need an estimate of the number of guests, so we can find a suitable location. Not too many stairs for the old people, and plenty of seating. Speakers, food. Maybe a video of Ida or a slide show. Music. Invitations, too, all sorts of questions there. We'd need at least a month of lead time, and that would be pushing it. What do you think we would need for a budget?"

Frankie yanked a full tick off Tartar's neck and threw it to the dirt. "I haven't thought about it." She ground the tick under her saddle shoe. "How long were you planning on staying?"

Tartar sighed as Frankie pulled another tick from between her eyes. I sighed, too. "My plans are kind of open-ended."

Frankie looked up at me anxiously. "When do you have to get back to work?"

I kicked dirt over the blood from the ticks. "I quit. I'm taking a little break before I look for something else."

"A break?" Tartar wagged her tail and wriggled. Frankie let her go. "What about money?"

I looked at the ground, feeling my face turn red. "I'm okay. I've got savings." I didn't want to have to come up with any explanations, so I picked up the empty glasses. "I'll carry these back to the house."

Frankie didn't try to stop me. She said, "That's an awfully good idea about the service, Carline. Would you mind making some potato salad for the Guild luncheon? Potato salad puts them in a productive mood, and I've got mowing to do."

I took a shower, then put on a housedress from Frankie's closet. I found an apron in the pantry and a bag of potatoes in the low cupboard, turned on the water and started to scrub.

Frankie had two candy dishes shaped like chickens on a shelf over her sink. I lifted the lids. Empty. Handling their stubby beaks sent me back to the days when I used to wash them if I were in a leisurely mood when I did the dishes. Eventually, I rinsed the dots of paint from their eyeballs, and Frankie told me dusting would suffice. She had called them her hen and rooster, but looking at them now, I saw that they were both hens.

I wiped the hens with a damp towel, thinking of Ida. All through my last summer at Frankie's, Ida had spent a lot of time at the house. I had distinct memories of how sloppy she was. I had never understood why Frankie put up with it. Ida drank oceans of diet cola poured into Dixie cups. Frankie had given me the tedious job of gathering the many used cups from the counters and side tables to throw away. I felt Ida should have done that herself.

Rubbing each potato's rough skin set my teeth on edge. I tried harder to get a clear picture of Ida. She had been tall, with a leathery face. A teacher. She had been mostly silent with me, although quick to talk about the heated politics of the Library Guild. At fifteen, I hadn't been interested.

She had a couple of lank little boys and a husband, a nice man named Tom who would come over and turn the crank on the freezer until the cream hardened to the texture of Maltomeal. We all sat outside and ate it slowly to avoid headaches from the cold; then Tom would take the boys home. They had to feed the dogs. Ida and Frankie would walk down to the tank. I was left to soak the freezer bucket and wash up.

There was no good explanation for why I had stopped coming to see Frankie after that summer. Asthma was a part of it. That year I had ended up in a hospital back home, wearing oxygen tubes and watching city lights from a high window. But, in my heart, I never believed in asthma as an explanation for anything. Taking a breath seemed inevitable, whether it rasped or not.

I remembered now that Frankie had told me when Ida's husband Tom passed away. That was rough on those boys.

I cooled my wrists under the water running from the tap, then chose a new potato. I stopped, confused, as if the potato I was holding were a mystery in my wet hands. As I scraped off the eyes, the image came to me of Lilian on a hot day, holding her breasts up in front of the fan. Suddenly, it was obvious: Frankie and Ida had been lovers. I shut off the faucet, but kept pushing the scruffy against the potato's disappearing skin. I should have seen.

I put the potato in my mouth, and bit down. For just a moment, a kind of grief matched the gagged feeling and the bitter taste. The potato sucked at my teeth as I took it out of my mouth and set it on the counter. Bite marks cut the peel. I filled a glass from the tap, and drank.

By the time I picked up the scruffy to finish my task, I was shaking my head. My aunt was mourning her lover. Frankie with an erotic life was not part of the story I thought of as home. I felt like a fool.

I finished scrubbing the potatoes and filled a pot with water, but I didn't set it on the stove. Instead, beginning to feel aggrieved, I stored the potatoes in a giant Ziploc bag. I cut the bite marks out of the one on the counter. I should have thrown it away, but, instead, I prepared it for the meal.

Then I left the diligent air conditioning to find Frankie.

She was on the tractor in sunglasses and a bandana, mowing the grass on the edge of the white dirt lane. The wide seat on the old, big-knobbed John Deere held her high above the ground, massed like a cumulous cloud in her blue polyester pants suit. She did a smooth turn at the bottom of the lane and headed back toward me. The sunlight quivered around her. The motor roared.

As I walked down the lane, she shut off the blade and cut the engine. I stood next to the enormous tire, and called up to her. "Frankie."

She took off her sunglasses, squinting at me. She seemed a little dazed from the noise, the fumes and the heat. She had probably been crying. "Carline."

I held up a jar of cold water. As she reached for it, I touched her wrist. "Do you think we could have a talk when you're done?"

She took a deep drink. I looked up at her thick thighs and hips, her sunburn and strong hands as if everything had new meaning, as if it were all a code. I knew the bandana meant that she was trying to protect her hairdo, which wouldn't fare well under a feed cap.

She screwed the lid back on the jar, handed it down to me, then said, "I'm going to mow a path to the tank. I'll meet you at the water."

I went back to the house and finished making the potato salad. I recognized the gaudy label on the mayonnaise jar from childhood. The pleasure of seeing it again embarrassed me. I didn't want my loyalties to be cheap.

There were snakes in the field on the way to the tank, so I found some boots in the closet and put the jeans back on before I went out. The radio sermon I'd heard on the bus came to mind.

Frankie was climbing down from the tractor when I reached the tank. She moved slowly and winced. The tank was a small pond, dug to give livestock a place to drink. Frankie didn't raise cattle anymore, but I could remember her herd sleeping off the day's sun there. Now, the water was green, and there was a ring of cracked mud extending its bank.

"It's low," I said, eyeing Frankie as she leaned against a tractor tire. She seemed composed, but I worried about the back of her pantsuit. Machinery stains were among the most difficult to remove, right up there with mustard and blood.

"We need rain." Frankie glanced at the hazy sky. The smell of cut grass was thick as steam. Tartar stretched out in the shade of the tire, panting.

I spotted the hulk of the old row boat beneath a tarp. Frankie groaned, but squatted down with me to lift it off the blocks. We dragged it into shallow water. I knocked the mud dauber nests from the oars, took off my boots, rolled up my borrowed jeans, and gave Frankie my hand to help her into the boat. Tartar jumped into the bow and put her nose in the air. I pushed the boat into deeper water, then clambered in.

We floated low but well-balanced. I was clumsy at the oars. Tartar stared into the water. Frankie untied her bandana and dunked it over the side, then closed her eyes and draped it across her face. Rivulets ran down her neck. When we got to the middle, I pulled in the oars and let us drift.

I leaned forward and lifted the bandana away from Frankie's eyes. "I've been out to you for years," I said. There was no point in mincing words. "Why didn't you tell me about Ida?"

She didn't say anything. Tartar, scratching, rocked the boat.

I moved the bandana away from Frankie's mouth, too, so it hung damply across the bridge of her nose. She swatted at my hand without opening her eyes. "I talked about her a lot."

"You know that's not what I mean." Something throbbed in my palm. "I think I got a splinter from the oars."

Frankie opened her eyes and reached into her pocket for her knife. The bandana fell into her lap. She traced the closed edge of the blade with her thumb. "Give me your hand."

In a tribute to childhood, I sucked it. "I don't want you to try to get it out. Not in a boat."

She shrugged and opened the blade. "Have you got a match?"

In my purse, which was on the bed table in the guest room back at the house, I had a book of matches from the Angler Courts Motel. I reached in the pocket of the jeans and found a cheap lighter. I handed it over. Frankie clearly loved Ida. There was no use in pressing her to break her habits of discretion. I wanted to hear about it, to know a family history that might reflect my own life, but she had her own standards to tend.

She clicked the lighter on and held it to the blade. I bent forward to see. The boat rocked, and Tartar looked back at us.

"Stay there, girl," said Frankie. "It's okay." We both stared at the metal, waiting for it to turn black under the flame. Frankie had taught me to sterilize a needle by burning it before breaking skin. Still watching, she said, "I told you Ida and I used to go on long drives in the Mercury, looking at crops and making plans. She had a family at home, but she was reckless in that car."

I wondered if she meant reckless like a drunk driver or reckless like a teenage couple at a drive-in. I reached for the knife.

She gave it to me and let the lighter go out. "Ida loved to drive, and she loved to dance."

I stroked the blade across my palm, pressing near the splinter to try to get the end to pop out. It was tender, but I could feel it shifting.

Frankie reached out of the boat and drew circles in the water with her fingers. "Once when we were putting up peaches in freezer boxes, we started dancing in the kitchen to the radio. Patsy Cline."

I spotted the end of the splinter. When I touched it with the knife, it sank deeper into my hand. Wincing, I squeezed the skin, then caught the sliver with the tip of the knife and pulled it free. "Got it."

Frankie looked at me, then back at the water.

I could see Ida in a yellow apron. I remembered slicing scores of peaches with a sticky knife. For a moment, I imagined my aunt wedging her fingers in the knot where Ida's apron was tied low on her hips. It was enough. I flicked the tiny hair of wood over the side, and asked, "Did people know?"

"We ate peaches all that winter." Pulling her hands out of the water, she dried them on her pants. "I can't believe she's gone."

I took my turn staring at the water. It was opaque. The boat cut and muddied the reflections of the trees. I was disturbed. I had always imagined Frankie to be in love with the white rock, the tractor, the grasses and the kitchen cabinets, not reaching for the edges of her friend's clothes.

I pushed again for images of Ida. A long braid and a corded neck. She squeezed the tops of my arms in greeting, making jokes about butter and pies. She sewed and had driven Frankie and me in the Mercury down some dark, curving road to a county talent night, where she played the banjo.

Once, Frankie and Ida had gone to Austin for the weekend when the husband was away on business. I baby-sat. All I remembered were those skinny boys staring at me across a pan full of frozen fish sticks. I couldn't get the oven to light. We ate peanut butter instead.

A frog jumped with a dense splash like a stone. Tartar started and shook, wanting to chase it, but stayed in the boat.

"Lilian ate frog legs once. They tasted like chicken." It felt right to find a reason to say my lover's name. Lilian was a vegetarian, but she had a past. I missed her.

Frankie reached for the oars and handed them to me. "I've got to get changed before the Guild shows up." Her tone was definite, but her face sagged. The tag was sticking out of the neck of her tunic top. I leaned across to tuck it in. She put her hand on my collar and pulled me in so she could kiss my cheek. "Thanks for coming to be with me," she said.

I kissed her back, feeling both joined and far from her. Tartar—a little jealous—tried to stand on my shoulders with her sharp claws. I shrugged her off. She sulked in the bottom of the boat until a perch broke out of the water just as we reached the edge of the tank. Then she barked.

AFTER THE BOAT RIDE, I STOPPED BEHIND THE house to hose mud and stickers from my legs. Frankie's water had always been cloudy, but I grew up believing that because it was full of minerals, it was a source of strength. Its sulfur smell was one of my earliest memories. She had town water inside now, but I knew this was pumped from the well. I sniffed it, getting used to my new conviction that I was the lesbian niece of a lesbian aunt.

I was taking a drink when I heard the slow hum of an engine turning off the farm-to-market road. I wanted to slip in through the back door to change into good clothes before I greeted the Guild, but the only way I could shut off the hose was to walk into full view. I wasn't vain enough to leave water running in this dry part of the world.

As I came around the house, I saw the bus that I used to ride every day on my commute driving slowly up the lane, raising dust. For a moment, I was convinced that the editorial board of *The Modern Homemaker* had sent it to fetch me. That was no more strange than the idea that Tucker and Mel might have stopped by to visit my aunt.

A sedan turned in behind the bus. Gray-haired women leaned out of car windows, coughing and waving. I recognized Mrs. Poll by her fluted cuffs. We hadn't kept in touch, but I always had a soft spot for her.

I pointed the nozzle toward the thinning grass. Frankie came out onto the porch. Wearing a dress covered with a pattern of twining leaves, she raised her arm and waved back. "Who do you suppose that is in the bus?"

I shut off the faucet without hazarding a guess.

The bus took the wide curve of the horseshoe at the top of the lane and parked next to the shed. The car pulled up in front of the house. I gripped the hose.

Women rose from the low sedan, hoisting covered dishes. Their faces hovered on the point of obscurity for me, then cut into features and expressions I knew. They converged on Frankie, calling both of our names. Tucker sauntered down the bus steps, carrying my suitcase. He looked natty in black jeans and a white short sleeved shirt with two thick stripes of red down the front. He must have read the label with Frankie's address dangling from the handle. The yard felt very crowded.

Summoning my manners, I acknowledged the women with a wave of the hose. It dribbled. "Be with you in a minute," I called. Then I turned my full attention to the bus.

Tucker set down the suitcase. Mel appeared in the doorway, bending over the camp box, his face straining. Tucker stepped up to take the box, then Mel spotted me. He let go of his burden to play air guitar, then spread his arms, soaking in alleged applause.

"Mel! You're such a ham!" I felt a surge of welcome for everyone, women and men. "Tucker. Hi."

Frankie was holding the screen door open to urge her friends indoors. She shut it after them and smoothed her dress. "Carline, do you know these men?"

I coiled the hose on its rack. "They're from the bus company."

Frankie cupped her hand over her eyes to block the sun. "Oh, they've brought your things."

Tucker, alert to the amenities, was striding over. He smiled toward the porch. "Hello, ma'am."

Frankie squared her shoulders and gave a hostess smile. Her leafy skirt fluttered over thick calves. "How do you do? I admire your shirt."

"Thank you." Tucker stopped on the other side of the water tower from me. He regarded me carefully and stuck one hand in his pocket. "Hello, Carline."

"You go ahead," I said to Frankie. "I'll be right in."

Frankie looked curiously at Tucker, then back at me. "Well, sir, it was nice of you to come all this way." She patted her hair and whistled for Tartar, who came out of the shed and trotted toward us. Frankie said, "Your friends are welcome," with a little extra pressure on the word "friends," then she went inside.

Tartar stood next to me, leaning on my legs to be scratched. Tucker pointed to the hose. "Do you think I could take a drink?"

I patted Tartar, then turned on the faucet. "Help yourself."

Mel hustled over and gave me a sweaty hug. "Carline! I'm so glad you're okay."

He was wearing a crumpled shirt open so the neck of his undershirt showed, a cap with the logo from Dick's Bar and Grille, and a new pair of boots. He handed me the sewing bag. "This looked important."

"God, yes, Mel." I grinned at him. Hugging the bag, I could feel the soft bulk of the curtains and the hard edges of the photo album. "Thank you."

Mel held onto my hand. "It's good to see you."

Tucker was slurping water as it arced out of the hose. He didn't give any sign of noticing the smell. When he finished, he straightened up and handed the hose to Mel. "Here, partner."

He reached into his shirt pocket and pulled out a small black canister with a gray lid. He held it out to me. "I brought you the film."

That put a damper on my mood. I was grateful that they had gone to the trouble to find me with my suitcase and snapshots, but these men were from another world. I was supposed to be in the living room, offering condolences and making small talk. I had been planning to snub Tucker later, if necessary, on some brief public bus ride back home. It confused me for him to be trying to make amends here in my aunt's front yard.

I kept enough of my wits to take the film.

Tucker smiled tentatively. "I wanted to be sure you made it." He glanced at Mel bent to the mouth of the hose, then leaned toward me and murmured, "I tried your idea."

The look on Tucker's face was concentrated and intense. I didn't know what he meant. Putting the film canister in my pocket, I kept my tone neutral. "I appreciate your concern."

Mel wiped his mouth with the back of his hand, watching us.

I had the curtains back, along with the photo album, Tucker's film, the camp box, my suitcase full of clothes, and most of my dignity. Still, I couldn't shake the feeling that Tucker was getting away with something, and the relentlessly interested part of me wanted to figure out what it was, especially if I was getting credit for some kind of idea. Hoping that I had read Frankie's hospitality correctly, I said, "Would you like to join us for lunch?"

Holding the sewing bag under one arm, I pulled Frankie's boots back on my damp feet while they fetched the suitcase and the camp box, then I held the back door open, gesturing the laden men before me into the house.

As soon as I stepped into the living room, the women hooted and yelled, "Carline!"

I forgot about my muddy jeans and stood there blushing with pleasure. Tucker put the suitcase down and followed close behind me. Mel hovered sheepishly in the hall.

Mrs. Poll struggled to her feet, opened to her arms, and said, "Give me some sugar."

I put down Lilian's curtains, and complied.

Small as she was, Mrs. Poll hugged me fiercely. Behind us, I heard somebody say, "Such a healthy girl," with an emphasis on the word "healthy." It meant fat, with a sweetness that kicked like Frankie's strong iced tea. I jerked a little. Pushing back so she could take a good look, Mrs. Poll shook her head at the fact of me. "You look so much like your mother that it's scary."

All I said was, "Good to see you." It was true.

The skin of her face was threaded with tiny red veins. It looked ready to bunch or tear. Mrs. Poll had persuaded Frankie to let her take me into Dallas and buy me a pair of hot pants when I was thirteen. I had never been so rash as to wear them to junior high, but had loved the theoretical possibility. She had bought herself a wrap-around skirt with shorts to match, in case of breezes. Now in linen pants and a chiffon top, Mrs. Poll gripped my arm for a moment before I turned to the others. "Ida would have been sorry to miss seeing you. You stayed away too long."

What could I do, except kiss her again? "I wish she could be here."

Gwen Watson made loud smacking sounds across the room. "Hey, Carline, save some for us." I bent to her, and smiled while she held both of my cheeks. All of them were due extravagant liberties. When I stood, Kimmie Griggs clapped me on the back, "Have they made a Yankee out of you yet?"

I knew there was no correct answer to that, so I batted my eyes and clasped my hands under my chin like a silent movie star, showing off as if I were still thirteen. Everyone laughed, except Frankie, who was sitting in a chair she had brought in from the kitchen, with a folder full of papers on a TV tray in front of her. There was an empty chair next to her, for me. She looked pointedly at the men.

I knew then that I had misread her when she said to welcome my friends, but compelled by the manners these very women had taught me, I took Tucker by the arm. "Everybody," I said, "this is Tucker, and that's Mel. They drove all the way from the east with me, then made a special trip from Dallas to bring me some things I left on the bus. I've invited them to stay and eat."

Tucker stepped away from me and gave a modest bow. "I hope we're not intruding."

Frankie gave a tiny sigh that let me know I was stretching her patience, then stood up smiling in her bountiful dress. "Of course you're not. We've got plenty." She scanned the faces of her friends, which were all turned to her. "Perhaps we could reverse the order of business: eat first, meeting afterwards."

Kimmie, impatient as always, closed her folder and shrugged. "I expect we'll be hungry even this early, once we see the food."

I closed the door to the back bedroom and buried both hands in the picture curtains for one sweet moment, then stashed the bag, took a two-minute shower, and put on a skirt and a blouse from my suitcase. It was a relief to wear my own clothes. When I went into the kitchen, the extra leaf had been put in the table. Everyone was setting dishes out. There were relishes, okra, cold beets, barbecued chicken, biscuits and my potato salad. I freshened everyone's iced tea.

Frankie sat at the head of the table. "Shall we bow our heads?"

Tucker raised an eyebrow at me. I ignored him and watched Frankie. Everyone else closed their eyes.

"For these gifts which we are about to receive, we are truly thankful." Her voice cracked at the thankful part.

None of us knew what to do for Frankie, so we looked to the food to situate ourselves. I found the old pleasure of dipping a biscuit in gravy, and was transfixed at the sight of Tucker, my bus driver, eating a creamy heap of potato salad off one of Frankie's yellow plates.

Frankie was gracious as she chose chicken from the platter for each of us. I used to chafe at being prevented from serving myself, but now as she selected a breast for me, I felt honored.

The talk started out light. Kimmie, who still drove a bread truck, traded stories with Tucker. Mrs. Poll asked me if I had seen bluebonnets blooming along the highway during the course of my trip. I admitted I hadn't, but told her that even fence posts looked good to me, since I had lived such a long time in the east.

This may have struck her as sad. She pierced a slice of beet, and said, "Frankie tells me you've never been married."

Before I could answer, Frankie was between us with her long fork. She dropped a drumstick next to Mrs. Poll's beets. "I know you love legs, April."

Mrs. Poll flushed and lost the thread of the conversation. All the women perked up when Frankie addressed their plates. The men seemed less at ease. It looked to me as if Mel were considering making a stab at helping himself to a thigh, but he lost his nerve.

Looking around the table, I felt almost satisfied. This was the clatter I had wanted from a distance. Even Mel and Tucker did not disturb me. Their presence strained the conversation a little, but undercurrents were familiar. Emotion and discretion had always been thick as creamed corn at gatherings of the Guild.

I had known most of these women all of my life. Even their smallest gestures, finger taps on arms to alert each other to the arrival of the gravy boat, stirred recognition in me. I could see that they were grieving. Mrs. Poll passed dishes to Frankie with unobtrusive delicacy. Frankie took little and ate less. Kimmie pulled her napkin into lacy shreds.

Mrs. Poll cut the tip off an okra, then turned to Frankie. "Ida would have loved this. All of us together here."

Kimmie bit into a cherry tomato, which squirted her cheek with juice. "I still can't believe she's gone."

Tucker swallowed and paused, very alert. "May I ask, has someone recently passed away?"

Frankie looked down at her lap, her chin shaking. After a moment, she offered Kimmie her napkin. "Use this," she said in an even voice, then she turned to Tucker. "Our good friend Ida Kirk died of a stroke two weeks ago."

It struck me that Frankie had learned to hold her emotions in check by keeping secrets in a small town for a very long time.

Tucker put his hands flat beside his plate, and made eye contact around the table. "I am very sorry to hear that. I can see how much you all miss her. Was she a neighbor?"

Mrs. Poll rolled her pearls against her scalloped collar. "She was a dear friend. We were all very close."

The women, nodding and sighing, were not looking at Frankie. She gazed at her empty lap. I waited for some mention of the bond between Frankie and Ida. These women would know they were intimate, even if they had never suspected a sexual attraction. It was a long moment of strained silence. Mel had to cough. The closest thing to acknowledgment was the fact that nobody started to eat again until Frankie picked up her fork. I could see why Frankie wanted more than that, for Ida and for herself. I hoped the memorial service would give her what she wanted. I could call Lil to get suggestions of poems by lesbians appropriate for a funeral. Or maybe poems by anyone good.

Mel and I did the dishes. Frankie tried to talk me into leaving them and coming to the meeting, but I plunged a fistful of silverware into the water and said that I would get out there as soon as I could.

Tucker, sitting sideways in his chair to watch us, spoke up. "Is the meeting about to start?"

I pulled my hands out of the water and planted them on my hips. "It's women only."

Frankie, frustrated with me, slammed a cupboard door. "Anybody can come to a meeting of the Chalk Library Guild."

Tucker was on his feet. "Well, then I think I might sit in."

As he walked into the living room, Frankie stared after him, dismayed at what she had done. Mel and I exchanged looks. I wanted to support Frankie, but it might be my only chance to ask Mel some questions.

"Go ahead," I said to Frankie, nudging her with a dry elbow. "I'll be there in a few minutes."

Shaking her head, she went.

While I stacked dishes on the counter, Mel went out to the porch where we had left the camp box. He came back with the Venus of Willendorf ashtray and a bottle of beer. He handed the goddess to me. "I thought you might be missing this, too."

I was embarrassed, but glad to see her. I took her down the hall to my bedroom, rubbing a finger across her rises and hollows before I stowed her discreetly in my purse.

When I came back, he had opened the bottle.

I had to ask. "Did you go through drawers of the camp box?"

Mel nodded. "I was looking for a bottle opener. Do you want half of this beer?"

I glanced toward the living room. "They won't like it. This is a dry county."

He held his finger to his lips and pulled two Dixie cups from the dispenser on the wall. "We'll keep it quiet." He filled the cups and hid the bottle under the sink behind the Ajax.

I sipped the warm beer. "What in the world is Tucker up to?"

"He's just interested." Mel shrugged. "He always is."

"Okay, you can rinse." I picked up the rough-backed sponge, thinking that being chronically interested was one thing that Tucker and I had in common. "Mel, what are the two of you doing here?

Why do you still have the bus? I thought it was going to auction."

"Tucker loves that bus. He bought it." Mel dunked the first plate in rinse water. "I went in on it."

I scraped bits of gristle into a bucket for Tartar. "I'd like to hear about it."

Mel settled the plate into the rack and reached for the next, keeping up a steady rhythm as he talked. "I was worried—we both were—about leaving you by the side of the road. I wanted to call the highway patrol to pick you up, but Tucker said they might take his license. We argued about it all the way to Memphis."

He took a quick look at my face. I hated the thought of the two of them driving along discussing me while I was alone on the hot road, but I was glad they hadn't called the police. It was a matter of pride to me that I had gotten the rest of the way to Frankie's without Tucker's help.

"I hate to say it, but once we hit Memphis city limits, I gave up. I had to figure that you could take care of yourself. Tucker found a radio station that was playing blues, and we started seeing pink neon guitars and houses with strands of white lights hanging off their porches like it was Christmas. We could have caught I-40 west, but he went through the city. He had me reading the directions to Elvis Presley Boulevard from the back of the Graceland brochure."

Mel rinsed the butter dish. "I knew a woman once who was crazy about Elvis. She said he poured everything he had into his songs. She could move like he did, too, even in a tollbooth. That's where we worked. You would have liked her."

I ran my finger around the drain. Mel didn't know me well enough to be so sure what I liked. "What happened in Memphis?"

He picked up a dish towel to start drying. "The sign at Graceland said to park across the road, but Tucker pulled up at the gates. The lot was crammed with charters, row after row of big coaches that made our bus look puny and out of place. Tucker took a picture of them from across the street with a cool look on his face, as if he'd just flown in on a private jet more modern than the *Lisa Marie*. The whole strip was depressing, full of souvenir shops and motels advertising twenty-four-hour Elvis movies. I got out and stood on the sidewalk to read what people had written on the stone fence. 'You're still rocking on strong. I love you. We miss you.' Names and dates. They got to me. I told Tucker, 'Put down the camera. These people come from Belgium, Albany, Colombia, Tupelo, wherever, to pay respects to a man who is long dead, but you can't find your way clear to drive back to Kentucky to look for a woman you yourself left by the side of a road?' We were kind of staring at each other, and, at that moment, a lady took off her t-shirt so her husband could snap her picture in a black bra in front of the silhouette of Elvis playing guitar on the gate." Mel seemed to concentrate very hard as he said the words, "black bra." I rolled my eyes.

"Tucker was mad that he missed it, but all he said to me was, 'You're an idealist.' He claimed to be an opportunist, himself, but we got back on the bus and skipped the gold record collection to look for you."

I emptied the standing water from the sink, wiped sludge from the broiler with one of Frankie's paper towels, then picked up a steel wool pad and began to scrape. Listening to Mel talk about their dilemma was satisfying in a greasy, flammable way. Scrubbing harder, I told him, "I got a ride to Poplar Bluff, Missouri, and took a train from there."

He held Mrs. Poll's casserole dish to his chest as he dried it. "I thought you might do something like that. We kept seeing tracks. We were all over western Kentucky and Missouri before we gave up and drove back through Little Rock." He shook his head. "I was pretty concerned for you, Carline."

I chipped at the burnt places with my fingernails. "I'm sorry, Mel. I didn't know what else to do. What about the bus?"

Mel's voice got confidential. "He had a deadline to get to the auction in Dallas. I couldn't figure out why he wasn't mad, but once we started driving around looking for you, he relaxed. He was practically serenading me about repowering an old bus engine with a new transmission and all the advantages of a thirty-five footer and the importance of customer service. Finally, in Arkansas, he spotted a white double-decker bus leaning in a field. It was pretty far off and looked abandoned, half hidden in the grass, but there was no mistaking the double rows of windows. He turned off to search for it. We were near a little town called Judsonia, south of Bald Knob. We found the bus, but couldn't get close to it. It was inside an electrified fence behind an old catfish place. We could barely see the bus, but damned if Tucker didn't jump out and sidle over to it, as if he was about to try to get through that fence, right there in broad daylight, with no telling who was around. There was an orange box for a newspaper near the road, which meant somebody lived there. I climbed down and told him not to do it. He looked at me for a minute, then asked me to give him a little privacy. I was about ready for some of that, myself, so I took a walk down to the river and cooled my feet. When I got back, he was sitting on the bus step with his camera in his lap, waiting for me. He said we were staring opportunity in the face. That's when he told me he needed a stake to set up in the transportation business."

Mel's hands looked very big as he ran the dish towel in the curves of a glass bowl. "I was thinking about all those big coaches in Memphis, and told him we could never compete. He said that a smaller bus could make people more comfortable on a short trip. A niche, he called it, somewhere between motorcoach and a shuttle van. He said he knew how to customize the interior. I got persuaded, called Simone, and talked her into taking a chance with our retirement account. So, we're partners." Mel's shirt was damp. "Carline, I wish you could have seen Tucker bid. He put everything he had into buying his old bus."

I was sponging the counter. It was easy for me to picture Tucker driving satisfied groups on tours. I couldn't imagine what the wife was thinking to turn over that money, but she knew a lot more about Mel's judgment than I did. Still, Tucker's plan didn't seem right. It struck me as incomplete.

He had stopped drying, waiting for a comment. Wiping my hands on my apron, I said, "I hope it works out for you." He obviously wanted more, so I added, "I appreciated the water you put out by the side of the road."

Mel nodded. "Tucker's a good guy, Carline. He just didn't know what to do." He propped the platter in the drying rack, and drank the last swallow of beer from his Dixie cup. "It was his idea to bring your stuff to you."

"Thanks," I said with an edge in my voice. I stacked the leftovers in the refrigerator in plastic bowls and swept the floor. Mel went out the back door to take scraps to Tartar and shake out the tablecloth. We were done.

I peered into the doorway of the living room. All of the women had folders out now. Mrs. Poll was sucking the ear piece of her rhinestone glasses. Tucker was sitting in a wooden chair, his legs crossed at the ankles, his face polite and alert.

Kimmie, looking stern despite her candy-striped pullover, stood next to an easel with a pad of paper propped on it. She glanced toward the doorway and gestured elaborately toward a seat. "Carline. Join us."

I cut through the room, waving. "Be right there." In the bedroom, I pulled out my empty curtain and a picture at random. The needle was waiting, threaded, in the pin cushion. I had been missing the touch of this fabric, and had always loved to sew in meetings where I didn't have a leadership role.

I sat between Frankie and the picture window. She was staring intently at some typed notes. Mrs. Poll smiled and mouthed the word "pretty," happy to see me with sewing in my lap. The picture I slid into the pocket was Lilian's boisterous family, posing on a couch at a reunion. Her mother had her hands on Lil's shoulders, but there had been several people using cameras at the same time, so Lil was looking to the left while her mother smiled straight on. Her sister was holding a nephew and laughing at the baby in her husband's lap. The brother was sitting sideways on the arm of the couch, and his wife had her knees turned sideways to avoid jabbing Lil. Her dad had his hand on the back of the other sister. The oldest niece, a smart kid, had been looking at me when I snapped the picture.

Kimmie wrote the word "possibilities" across the top of the paper. "There are proposals to fund a bookmobile, new computers for the library staff, magazine subscriptions, a CD player for the music library, a lecture, or, of course, books." She made a list as she talked.

Mrs. Poll held up her hand for a nod from Kimmie before she spoke. "The library already has a book budget. We should do something else with the plant sale money."

Feeling contented, I stitched and listened. The air conditioner whirred under everything. I heard Mel clumping through the hall. Frankie spoke every now and then, but for the most part she was silent, glancing at her notes.

An idea came to me swiftly, like a fax. The Guild could publish *How To Ride a Bus*. If they put up the money for a print run of 500, they could sell it for a profit at the next plant sale. It was such a suitable project: literary yet practical. My cheeks heated with the flush of formulating a proposal. It was a feeling I missed from the best days at my old job. On the verge of signaling for Kimmie's attention, I forced myself to finish basting and consider the minuses. Was it wise to cast my lot with the Chalk Library Guild? Did I still have a chance at funding by my old department? Would there be whispers of nepotism if Frankie backed me?

Buzzing with ideas, I gazed at my aunt. She seemed strangely indifferent to the discussion. I noticed that her papers were shaking. Leaning a little closer, I managed to see that they were headed with the word, "Ida."

I sat up straight, dropping my strategies. Frankie had told me that this meeting was about a memorial service for Ida, so why were we talking about a plant sale?

"*Smithsonian*," Frankie sounded nervous. "*National Geographic*." Everyone was calling out names of magazines.

Looking around the room, I felt stirrings of recognition. For an instant, I was certain that they were a bunch of dykes, then I was unsure of everyone, including me. I tapped my knee with the thimble, disappointed with my own self-obsession. These women were concerned with supporting literacy. Sexuality was irrelevant, except that Frankie had her hand to her mouth. She looked miserable. I thought she might be finding it hard to speak to her friends about publicly mourning her lover.

I finished the pocket, then put the curtain aside. It settled onto the broad windowsill in a graceful heap. I bunched a swath of it in my fist and held on to keep from yelling, "Enough!"

Finally, I let go of the curtain. A decision had been reached. Subscriptions and a printer. Still wearing the thimble, I raised my hand.

Kimmie pointed her marker with an comic flourish like a fairy godmother offering her wand. She had known me when I was six. "Carline?"

I didn't hesitate. "When do we talk about the memorial service for Ida?"

Kimmie touched the side of her nose with the marker. It left a red spot in a crease. "It's not on the agenda."

Frankie stood. Her voice caught in her throat. "I'd like to plan a service. I want to ask for your help."

Kimmie looked around the room. "I think we should talk about this now."

Everyone nodded. Mrs. Poll had tears dribbling from underneath her glasses.

I took careful notes. The planning went smoothly. Nobody suggested that it might be one service too many. Nobody questioned whether this was an appropriate use of the Library Guild's time. They all seemed clear that mourning took precedence. We agreed to do a site search. Frankie took a deep breath and offered to say a few words. Gwen took charge of the music. Kimmie said she'd work on the guest list. Mrs. Poll offered to oversee food preparation. I said that I would help Frankie with general coordination.

Tucker cleared his throat. It was startling. He said, "If I'm anywhere in the vicinity, I will happily provide transportation."

There was a silence. He uncrossed his ankles and sat with both feet planted on Frankie's floral carpet. I wondered if he had ideas for the Library Guild plant money, too, but that was such small potatoes that the prospect seemed unlikely.

She looked him up and down. "That's a very kind offer. How long do you plan to be in the area?"

Through the doorway, I could see Mel sitting at the kitchen

table, flipping through a magazine. He smoothed it open to the center page as Tucker answered, "When you ladies pick a date, I'll decide."

That made Frankie blink. Kimmie said, "Let's move on."

I had to wonder. He might be seizing a chance to cultivate Chalk as a market for his bus tours. Maybe he wanted a short practice run. Maybe he had more business in Dallas. Or maybe he just didn't feel like driving back east.

Guild members gave themselves a month until the service. No one asked Tucker again about his plans. The women departed with their empty dishes, refusing leftovers and kissing cheeks.

Mel and Tucker were still standing in the yard as the sedan faded into dust plumes. Frankie patted her hair and said, "Why don't you spend the night at the Chalk-It-Up Motel? It's off the farm-to-market road where it meets the highway."

They took the hint. Tucker offered each of us a firm handshake. Mel gave hugs. Frankie stepped into hers as if it were something she needed.

As they were climbing into the bus, Frankie asked if they wanted some leftovers. Mel winked at her and mimed biting a big sandwich. Tucker propped a foot on the black step and said, "That's very generous of you, ma'am, but I doubt we'll have access to refrigeration."

Frankie threw back her shoulders like a soldier of hospitality. "Drop by tomorrow. We'll give you boys chicken and cobbler to take on the road." It was a suggestion to go away tucked inside an invitation, but she offered it with warmth.

"We'd appreciate that." Tucker took the driver's seat.

Mel grinned through a window. Frankie and I waved. When we caught each other's eye, she shrugged.

THAT NIGHT WHILE FRANKIE WAS EATING A nectarine and staring silently at a wrestling show, I went out to the shed to call Lilian. Frankie had an extension in the shop so she could work on the tractor without missing calls. My interest in it was privacy.

The shop was a corner of the shed Frankie had closed in to make a work and storage room. It smelled dank. I flipped the light switch and stepped inside. There were no windows, but the shop had a concrete floor instead of the hard-packed chalk in the rest of the shed. It was lined with plank counters and shelves full of small boxes heavy with nails, nuts, washers and screws. There was a vise the size of an anvil in the middle of the room, and saws hanging on the wall.

It was a rotary phone. My fingers recognized the hard dial, with its clicks and spins. The ring at the other end sounded distant. Lilian picked up. "Hello."

Her voice was intensely familiar. I felt confused at finding myself so far from our couch. "Hi."

"Carline." She said my name as if it were inevitable. "Where are you? I've been worried."

I picked up Frankie's broom and leaned my chin on the wooden end, missing her so much that I could barely speak. "Didn't you get my message?"

"I got it. I got the note you left clipped to the refrigerator, too." We both waited for the next thing to say. She came up with it. "Are you at Frankie's? What's going on?"

"Frankie's suffering. Did I tell you that her friend Ida died? Well, Frankie's never talked about it, but Ida was her lover." I was sure to the bone.

"Poor Frankie." Lilian took a slow breath. "No, you didn't tell me about Ida. You didn't tell me much." She sounded as if her chest were being pressed under a heavy skillet.

I started crying. "Oh, Lilian. I'm sorry. I could have waited until you came home. Did you win the slam?"

"No." Her voice steadied. "It sounds like Frankie needs you."

She was working hard not to slight my relationship with my aunt. I wiped my nose on a rag. "I'm going to be gone for a while. Frankie's wanting me to help her plan a memorial service. I'm sorry you lost the slam, sweetheart."

Lilian made a noise. "How's your blister?" she asked, abruptly.

"Huh? Oh, that." I tried to sound reassuring. "It's much better. Don't worry. No big deal."

She didn't appreciate my effort. "Carline, you quit your job without even talking to me about it, told me you burned yourself, took off for Texas, and now it's no big deal? I know you're trying to help Frankie, but that's not the whole story. What am I supposed to do, cross my legs at the ankle and sit here waiting for you?"

I didn't have explanations, but thought we needed a decision. "Do you want me to come back right now? I will if you want me to." I tried to mean that.

There was a sensation of motion along the veins in my arms, as if I could physically feel Lilian summoning her patience. She said, "Write me letters. Tell me what you can."

I said I would. I tried, right then. I told her all I knew about Frankie and Ida. I told her about the picture at the pool, the fight with Tucker and my long walk. Talking with Lilian gave me words for things I had forgotten. I told her about the ride to the train station in Poplar Bluff through fruit stands selling melons, peaches, cantaloupes; motels making a point of being American-owned;

and establishments like Meek's Golf Carts, Jesus Loves You Auto Salvage, Tank N Tummy gas station/restaurant, and a jungle-themed gentlemen's club, Call of the Wild. I described what I had seen when we drove into Bluff, where a billboard that said PRAY TO END ABORTION had been bright in the dusk and the streetlights arched like wings. I told her the station had been locked.

Lilian listened intently, not asking many questions.

I said I was sorry I had quit my job and left without considering the strain I was putting on her. I talked until my ear was sore and my tongue was dry. When I propped the broom back against the wall, there was a round red mark on my chin.

Just before we hung up, she said, "Minnaloushe has been curling up on your clothes. I leave them out for him."

It was good to picture that.

When she was gone, I noticed that the receiver was wet. I wiped it with a rust-stained towel, then dried my face. I felt businesslike about it. Tears weren't much different from sweat. I didn't want to have to expound on this to Frankie, so I lingered in the sweltering shop. Maybe she would go to bed.

I walked over to the old china cabinet and unlatched its lopsided doors. The compartments were full of more boxes and tools. There were droppings and scattered mounds of sawdust near chewed places in the wood. I lifted the lid of a cigar box, a relic from Frankie's smoking days, which were faint but pungent memories for me. The first thing I saw in the jumble inside was the dry comb of an ancient wasp nest.

The shop had always been a place to approach things gingerly because animals and insects put everything to use. I shook my head as I fingered through the stuff in the box—jackknife, tweezers, lighter, plastic forks, pennies, bolts. Frankie had more tolerance for disorganization than I did. It was a quality she shared with Lilian.

I closed the cigar box and shut the cabinet door. I had a sense of Lilian near me, but filtered through other presences. Frankie's loss was everywhere, like radio voices from our neighbor's apartment when the volume was up too loud. I wandered over to the big cast-iron vise, and started playing with the lever. I tried to let my mind linger on Frankie's grief, to allow myself to know it as accurately as I could, but as I slid the lever back and forth, what I thought about were evenings during the last summer I had spent here all those years ago.

Ida and Frankie were always lolling on the couch, playing Sinatra and Charlie Rich on the stereo. The needle dragged. They would be doodling on legal pads, telling each other morality tales about the other members of the Library Guild as they prepared some kind of committee report.

I had felt jealous and deserted, although I could not have said anything remotely that clear at the time. I took a lot of walks and was on a secret diet. I had lost dramatic amounts of weight repeatedly since fifth grade, only to gain more back again and again. But this was the summer before my senior year, and I had been stoking unrequited crushes on three girls on the student council. I sent them all funny letters and key chains that spelled out their names. A diet was the only hope I could imagine for my passions. It had the advantage of being physically taxing and socially indirect. So, keeping myself down to my best guess at 500 calories a day, I lost seventeen pounds and strained against hunger pretty much all the time.

One night when I was sweating restlessly out in the shop, emptiness and frustration clutching my gut, I had put the tip of my left index finger in the vise and tightened until it turned white. There had been a bruise, and the nail came off. It calmed me the same way dieting did, with physical evidence of control over my body. Making myself thinner meant that I was strong and good. It was a public achievement. Every adult I knew praised me. Cutting and bruising were private, but the intense focus on altering my body felt much the same.

As I thought about this now with my hand on the vise, I found myself distracted by trying to remember the words to old songs performed by Olivia Newton John. In those days, I had been a tepid fan. The task seemed urgent, but titles were the best I could do: "Have You Never Been Mellow," "Let's Get Physical," "I Honestly Love You," "Let Me Be There." I turned the lever and opened the jaws, trying to clear my head.

I ran a finger along the inner part of one jaw. It was smooth. I forced my mind to focus on what the injury had meant to me. I hadn't hurt myself badly. I had never been suicidal. The pain had not been in a sexual context, although yearning had been as present as breathing in those years. I had been fighting feelings I barely recognized: attraction to other girls and fear that I was too fat for anyone to love, ever. Shunned parts of me had stumbled onto a language of pain. A cut made narrow, explicit pain that felt like relief. Like temporary progress toward my dream of being thin, a cut was physical, measurable, and real.

My crushed finger had hurt for longer than cuts did. Watching it heal, I had thought: enough. That was the last time I deliberately injured myself until I held the match to my wrist. I had given up dieting and cutting in the same shaky breath. I had decided to join my body and face my fears. Standing in Frankie's shed all these years later, I made the same decision again.

I stopped gripping the vise, rubbed my hands. I wanted to write Lilian. She'd work to help me find meaning in this history. I closed the jaws and left the shop.

The bulb hanging from the rafters was generous with light. There was a lot of dust. A night breeze was blowing in from the open side of the shed. I raised my arms to cool. Dust coated the tractor, the Mercury, the trailer and Frankie's pickup. I found it restful. This was dirt that belonged.

I used an empty dog food bag to brush off a bench and sat down, smoothing my skirt. I was staying away from Frankie's lawn chairs. I was aware of my internal fragility, but even that seemed sensible. It was more realistic to know I was vulnerable than to assume I was not.

I caught the end of the rope I used to swing on. It was frayed below the knot. Teased, my thoughts blurred and darted. I got up and switched off the light.

Low, long and wide, the Mercury shone in the angled moonlight. I could see the coat of arms on the headlight covers: a cross surrounded by flames. "Mercury" was written in silver cursive above the right headlight. The bars of the grille shimmered above the big front bumper.

I stood in front of it and saw a shadowy reflection on the

hood. Something skittered along the tin wall of the shed. I got spooked. If Ida had a ghost, I imagined that this was where she would be.

I closed my eyes to wish her quiet rest, then fetched the bench and used it to climb onto the hood. The car bounced a little, but the body held firm. It would have been a shame to dent Ida's Mercury. I sat on the hood, trailing my feet over the bumper. The dust made me sneeze.

I probably should have gone into the house, where Frankie had cool air, good lighting, and a probable need for company. She had paper, stamps and envelopes, too. Or I could have slid off the hood and opened the car door. I could have leaned back in the roomy passenger seat and visited more deeply with the surfaces of Frankie and Ida's passion. If I remembered correctly, it was well-upholstered in there.

What I did, though, was kick off my shoes. In brief socks with fluffy balls on the back like winged sandals, I gathered my feet beneath me, resting one hand on the roof of the car. Slowly, I stood up. After I got my balance, I leaned out to grab the rope.

I caught it by the knot and tucked it between my thighs, just like when I was a kid. The Mercury shook as I jumped.

I flew, trembling. My feet rested on the knot. I worked my body in the air, urging it higher, bumping the Mercury, then arching toward the rafters. I bounced off a post, back to the car, and knocked over a lawn chair, laughing. My skirt bunched. My arms bulged, unexpectedly ready. I was swinging in a rhythm of blurred ground and effort, losing the idea of balance in a feeling of grace. The rope chafed my thighs as it slung me in circles.

My palms were burning so fiercely that I thought I had to drop. Instead, I clenched the rope, held in air by the full grasp of my body, much stronger and more fluent than a vise.

Next morning, Frankie and I sat at the table to list our tasks. My hands were tender from rope burn as I took a pencil from the coffee can I had decorated with wallpaper the summer after second grade. Frankie seemed tired. When I asked how she had slept, she got too busy rinsing our empty cereal bowls to answer.

Back home, I left for work before Lilian got up. I would shower and receive Minnaloushe's attentions, then I'd go kiss Lilian before I hurried to catch the bus. Sometimes she got out of bed early to make tofu pudding so that we would be primed with plant estrogen. Lilian's faith in tofu reminded me of Popeye with his spinach, although, actually, she liked that, too. She even had a tattoo on her upper arm, but instead of an anchor, it was an axe.

I bounced the eraser end of my pencil against the table a couple of times, then tried to give Frankie another opening. "What did Ida like for breakfast?" It sounded foolish, even to me.

"How would I know? She ate at her house." Frankie nodded impatiently at the note pad. "We should hand-address the invitations. I'd like to ask her boys. MJ is back at college, but it would be nice if they both could make it."

"Okay." I wrote down envelopes and stamps, resolved to quit fishing for confessions. "Maybe we should enter all the names on a computer, so we have a central list."

Frankie stared into her teacup. "I hope they come," she said, color rising in her face. "We aren't close."

"We'll make sure to invite them. Maybe we can get those flower stamps." I made a note to buy extra Kleenex. Just as I was about to ask her ideas for the program, we heard the bus rumble up the lane.

Mel and Tucker came to the back door like family, calling hello. They trooped into the kitchen and pulled up chairs. Frankie opened the paper to the crossword puzzle, starting to work it as we talked. Mel was dapper in suit pants and a button-down shirt. Tucker was wearing his cut-offs again. He set his camera on the table. Seeing it there bothered me.

"This sure is a nice place," Tucker said to Frankie. "Any chance of you giving us a tour?"

Frankie had always loved taking people in the pickup across the pasture down the steep road to the creek, then up to the red oak. She also seemed relieved to get away from the task at hand. "I believe I could do that, if you've got the time."

"Oh, we're in no rush." Tucker leaned back in his chair, a study in relaxation. "No hurry at all."

I was annoyed by the interruption, but I couldn't think of any problem with him going on a ride with Frankie to let her show the place off. It was thoughtful of him to take an interest, and might cheer her up. "You all go on," I said. "I'll do a little more work on the list."

Mel peered across the table at Frankie's crossword. "I'll stay here, too, if you don't mind. I've been doing an awful lot of riding around."

Tucker rose and stepped toward Frankie's chair, as if to help her get up. She waved him off. Taking her time, she stood. "Okay, Carline, we'll be back in a while."

After they left, Mel picked up Frankie's pen and bent over the crossword. I hated to work in the presence of idle men. "Excuse me, Mel, would you mind taking that into the living room?"

Mel tucked the paper under his arm and got out of my way with enough alacrity to stay on my good side. "I hope you don't mind if I take a nap," he said, pausing in the doorway.

I shrugged. It didn't matter to me if he stretched out on the couch.

I worked on the list a little longer. Flowers. Speakers. Clean up. It looked scant, but I hoped it would all add up to mourning. My lists were not usually ambitious. They recorded small lacks and inconveniences, such as the fact that I was out of Vaseline. I wasn't sure a list would help with deeper wants.

I gripped the pencil loosely and let it drift. I hadn't worked on my pamphlet since I arrived at Frankie's, but I couldn't think of anything to say at the moment about riding a bus. A cloud of strokes darkened the paper. My arm seemed animated, separate from me. I covered the page until it was soft with pencil lead. When I exerted my will to write, "How to Cope with Death," the words were gray on gray, invisible. It was like writing on water. I could still see blue ruled lines. I had always loved how lines ushered items down a page, loved them in the half-conscious way I loved most things about my life. I decided to ask Frankie if I could use her computer to type my How To notes.

The to do list was gone, but I had it in my head. I thought again of Ida's ghost. If she were hovering to guide my arm, she didn't have much to say. Mindful of Mel in the living room, I spoke softly to her absence. "People miss you, Ida. Frankie's a little lost."

It was definitely time to put away the oat flakes. I took the box into the pantry, faintly surprised to have trouble finding where it belonged. Not much else had changed in Frankie's kitchen. There were two margarine tubs full of catsup packets on the shelf near the door. The one without a lid was overflowing. I thought I recognized the first signs of Saving Disease, which caused a person to clutter storage space. I used to do a crisp half-hour on it near the end of my Good Living course, back when I taught full-time.

I picked up one of the tubs to toss into the trash, then stopped, reminding myself to be careful. For all I knew, Ida had collected these. I could imagine her wrapping them in a napkin and bringing them back from fast-food lunches with the idea that they would come in handy to somebody sometime. Some of the packets were bent in the middle, as if pressed by a finger. Frankie might be keeping them as relics.

I put the tub back on the shelf, closed the trash bag with a twist tie, and took it out the back door. It wasn't full, but I wanted a little air.

I was weighting the garbage can lid with a brick to fend off animals when, through the window, I saw Mel walk into the spare bedroom, the room where I had been sleeping. He passed out of view. Could he possibly think I had given him permission to nap in my bed? I hurried back inside.

The air conditioner hummed, already on high so early in the day. I moved quickly through the house. Finding the door to the bedroom closed, I opened it.

Mel was looking at himself in the vanity mirror with a dress pressed against his shirt. He held it by the hanger at an awkward angle. I could see crescents of sweat on the undersides of his sleeves. As he turned to me with a start, beads flashed with reflected light.

I was shocked. "What are you doing with that?"

Face flushed, he handed the hanger to me. He picked up a plastic bag from the fringed bedspread. "Here, I took this off."

I let him hold it. "Mel, why are you even back here? Where did you get this dress?"

He sat down on the bed, wadding the bag in his fists. "My back is stiff, so I thought I'd stretch out. You said it was okay."

"I expected you to be on the couch." I hung the dress on the chair next to the vanity, then sat down there, too. "It's rude enough for you to come into my bedroom, but there's no excuse for you to be handling Frankie's things. You're a guest."

"You're right. There's no excuse. I'm sorry." He nodded, then looked intently toward the dress. It was impossible to miss the drift of his gaze. "I saw it in the closet. It's so beautiful."

I glanced at the closet. It was a deep walk-in. As a child, I had curled up there for hours, light-headed with heat and closeness, rolling marbles in Frankie's shoes. All I could see now was the shimmer of dry cleaning bags clinging to obscured garments.

Shaking my head, I thought, superballs, cuff links. Bubbles. Mel liked shine and bounce. He was retired, but wore suit pants. He was kicking fringe with his heels, eyes lowered now.

Mel was out of line, but I was getting calmer. It galled me that Mel could toy with women's things without living a woman's life.

I thought of Lilian in the tight aisles of her store, brushing through old suits thick as leaves with one big hip, blouses size 8 to 14 with the other. I'd seen her hug an armful of old trousers on the rack. I thought of myself burying both hands in the fabric of Lil's curtains.

Mel touched a bead. It sparkled. The dress was a sheath, lined with silk and covered with intricate patterns of silver beads. The sewing was meticulous. It had a very long zipper. There was a wrap of pink chiffon to drape over the shoulders, with a rhinestone clasp. It made for displays of joy. It would never fit Frankie. I couldn't imagine her wearing it if it did.

I said the name aloud. "Ida."

Mel stroked the silk with one finger. "The one who died?"

It had only been two weeks. This was an unbearable intrusion. Mel might not have known, but I did. Still, when I unhooked the hanger from the back of the chair, I held the dress in the air between us. Part of the hem draped Mel's leg. With a serious look on his face, he smoothed it over his knee. Feeling complicit, I unsnapped a rhinestone cuff. Mel shifted on the bed, pulling more of the skirt toward him.

I could picture him trying it on. It would be tight at the shoulders and fall straight over his hips. The hem would flutter right around mid-calf. He would have to take off his shoes and socks to pull it off. The idea of his big-knuckled hands tugging the wrap forward to get it to hang straight made me grin. I could see the lines boxer shorts would make under the beads and silk.

"Play dress up if that's what you want, but not with this dress." I touched his rough cheek. "It isn't yours."

He looked at me, nodding slowly.

"I'll put it back in the closet." I tried to sound brisk. It wasn't Ida's presence I was feeling, but Frankie's. Frankie had been lending me clothes, but they were her own. Ida's dress was different.

Mel leaned toward me. "Don't forget this." He opened the edges of the plastic bag, then lifted it slowly over the top of the hanger, careful not to let it rip.

We both jumped as we heard the click of the latch. Frankie came into the house, calling, "Carline?"

"Just a minute," I yelled as I stood up. The fabric slid away from Mel's trousers without resistance, but the bag was clumped around the neck of the dress.

Frankie had already crossed the living room. She stood in the open door, looking at me holding the dress with the plastic hiked up.

"That belongs to Ida." She sounded choked.

I started crying in a useless way. Mel stood and smoothed the bag modestly over the dress. He said, "I'm sorry. I asked to see it."

He and Frankie gazed at each other in silence. Her face was very red. Her jaw was clenched. Her whole body was shaking.

Mel took the dress to the closet, moving carefully, not taking his eyes off Frankie. He widened a gap on the rack and gently slipped it in. "It's a beautiful garment."

Frankie hit the wall hard with her fist. "You don't have any right to be handling Ida's things." She turned to me. "Stop your blubbering."

Mel and I stood still. She stared at us for another minute, and then she left. We watched through the big windows in the living room as her pickup tore down the lane, raising dust.

Mel started to say something about the stages of grief, but when I pointed at the door, he went.

I sat on the bed with the door closed, blowing my nose and wrapping my fingers in the spread's fringe. I had been trying to be good to Frankie, but had lapsed over beads and silk draped across a man's knee. It was ludicrous. I wanted to blame Mel, but, even more than that, I didn't want to face Frankie alone. When Tucker wandered in from the shed with his camera, I came out of the bedroom to ask them to stay to dinner.

Mel caught me in the pantry to say, again, "I'm sorry."

I winced and handed him paper plates. "I should have made you put that dress away the moment I laid eyes on it, and asked questions later."

Tucker had questions of his own. He finished his cobbler, saying, "I still don't understand. Where exactly did Frankie go?"

Mel sighed. Tucker put down his fork and the two of them went outside. From the window, I could see them leaning against the side of the bus, having a talk. At one point, Tucker kicked a tire. Later, Mel patted the hood. When they came back in, Tucker was subdued and a little stiff, but he didn't ask any more questions. We all sat in the living room and stared at the Dallas evening news. I didn't have the heart to do my sewing.

Frankie drove up during the weather. My eyes followed the headlights as they came slowly toward the house. I wondered how the glare in her living room looked to Frankie from the lane.

Mel and Tucker stood when Frankie came into the room. I hit mute on the remote, but left the picture on, as if I couldn't stand not to look.

Frankie walked in front of me and bent to the television to click the power button off. She put a bag from Target down on the coffee table next to her silver teapot, and took a seat alone on the stiff couch. Her eyes were swollen.

She said, "I overreacted. It's a difficult time."

I glanced at Mel and Tucker. Tucker looked attentive, as always. Mel's face was red and his hands were shoved in his pockets. A look passed between him and Frankie that almost seemed to be recognition. I thought about that. They were both of a generation which valued propriety, but I was discovering intricate private lives.

"Ma'am." Mel spoke up. "I do want to apologize for being so insensitive earlier." He pulled his hands out of his pockets and gripped the chair. "I never should have been handling your things."

Frankie opened the teapot lid then closed it again. "Please sit down."

Tucker returned to the recliner and levered it to an upright position. He watched everybody. Mel sat in the rocker, looking every inch his age. His voice was soft but steady. "Yes, ma'am."

I leaned forward. "I'm sorry, too. I never meant to add to your grief."

Frankie picked up the Target bag as if grabbing a throat. The plastic crackled. "Cleaning supplies."

Once she said it, I recognized the contents of the bag by shape. Oven cleaner, sponges, paper towels. My spirits lifted.

"There's a lot to do before the service. Carline and I could use some help. I want you men to stay and work, if you will."

Mel and Tucker glanced at each other. Tucker raised his hand a little before he spoke. "We could do that, I imagine. Neither of us has any place else we have to be right away. We'd need to agree on terms, of course."

Frankie set the bag in her lap and folded her hands. "I'll pay you decently. You'll need a place to stay, so I thought that one of you could take the back bedroom, and one of you could use the sleeping porch. I'm sure Carline won't mind moving to the couch in the den."

WHEN I WOKE IN THE MORNING, THE CROCHETED comforter was in a bunch by my feet, and I was anxious about my purse. It wasn't on the TV tray where I had left it the night before. Immediately, I suspected Mel. For most of the night, I had heard him snoring in the living room. He had refused the bedroom, so Tucker had a queen-sized mattress to himself.

The only way these sleeping arrangements made sense was as a consequence of having failed my aunt. If she considered my nights on the narrow couch fit punishment, I was determined to accept them with grace.

Dangling off the edge, I found my purse tipped over among the dust balls beneath the couch. My wallet, matches, Kleenex packs and the Venus ashtray were spilled on the nubby rug. I slipped onto the floor to gather them back. I was tempted to put Venus on the mantel to keep me company, but she was a little hard to explain. I placed her carefully in a side pocket of my purse.

Frankie and Mel were already in the kitchen when I went in. Frankie was sitting at the table in her denim apron, eating grapefruit. She had the crossword puzzle half filled. Mel was at the stove, stirring hash browned potatoes with a spatula.

"Morning, Carline." Frankie seemed in good spirits. "What's a three-letter word for wing?"

"Ell." Mel set a plate full of hot potatoes before her on the table. He had on the apron I usually used.

I was in a bad mood as I went to the pantry for the oat flakes. While I was in there, Mel reached past me with his long arm and picked up one of the tubs full of catsup packets. I wanted to grab his wrist to stop him from ruining our morning with another transgression, but he was too fast for me.

"Perfect," said Frankie, as I turned to look at her. "I never remember to use those up."

Mel dropped a packet on the floor and mimed stomping on it. "We used to spatter these in the school cafeteria when I was a boy."

I thought that the idea was repulsive, especially at breakfast. Mel was being much too cheerful after his mistakes. His shirt had come untucked.

Frankie took a bite. "Must have looked pretty gory." She put her hand over her mouth and laughed so hard that I had to fetch a Kleenex pack so she could wipe her eyes. The only explanation I could think of was strained nerves.

I poured my cereal. "Do you feel like going over our list of things to do?"

"Later. I've got errands in town this morning."

I waited until Mel went down the hall to take a shower before I spoke to Frankie with an urgency that surprised me. "I've got a full roll of pictures. Will you drop it off to get developed for me?" That was when I knew I wanted to see Tucker's pictures more than I wanted to make sure that no one else ever would. Frankie took the film without asking questions.

When I heard the pickup pull out, I looked out the window and saw Tucker sauntering across the yard. He let Tartar out of her pen and scooped dry food into her bowl as if he had done it every morning of his life, then sat down on one of the low beams of the water tower, yawning and watching her eat. He leaned back against a big, rusty pipe like someone who might be there all day.

I spilled a little salt, and threw a pinch over my left shoulder to ward off bad luck. Frankie had taught me that.

The days preceding the service were full of work. I took charge of desserts. I made pecan fudge, dense and sweet. I worked raw crust into balls, then rolled it out lightly for pecan, chocolate and lemon meringue pie. I made peach cobbler and apple crunch. I put everything in the freezer before baking, so the crusts would be crisp on the big day.

I got on the phone to the Library Guild to follow up on their tasks. This gave me a buzz of accomplishment, as if I were back at my old job, keeping up with the board. Mrs. Poll gave me a list of who was bringing salads and meat. The menu seemed overly starchy, so I wished I could pass on a copy of "Meal Planning for Large Groups," one of the most popular brochures in the *Modern Homemaker* series, but all I did was suggest a raw vegetable plate. Kimmie Griggs offered to sing, but Gwen held her off, warning that Kimmie did only passable impressions of the late, great Kitty Wells. We wanted someone good.

Frankie was diligent in addressing invitations. I watched her put a typed notice in an envelope to take down to the newspaper office.

"Is that wise, do you think, Frankie, in view of the nature of your relationship with Ida?" I was taking all the books off the shelves in the hall to dust.

She sealed the envelope without looking up. "A lot of people had relationships with Ida. They should have the chance to come."

I blew a spider off the Condensed Classics version of *Jane Eyre* and pursed my lips to keep from saying the word, "lover." Frankie knew a lot more about Chalk etiquette than I did. If she wasn't worried about attracting the attention of bigots, I wouldn't bring it up. She touched her hair with a round brush before she went into town.

Mornings, Frankie shut the door of the back bedroom and sat at her desk working on her computer. She didn't have a modem, but used an old PC for word processing. I got glimpses of her through the blinds. I thought she must be working on her talk for the service. She used a lot of paper and emptied her own trash.

Afternoons, she cleaned, alone or with me. I loved watching her complicated face as we moved the couches to vacuum underneath them, or I handed her jelly glasses from high shelves as I stood on newspaper on her counter in my stocking feet. I wanted to leave them where they were, but she insisted on putting them in boxes, which we stacked in a corner of the porch. The cupboards were clean and surprisingly empty. She gave these tasks a sharp attention I appreciated. We talked very little, but I felt us falling back into ease.

When we ran across a cache of scarves in a dresser drawer, Frankie gathered them into her hand. "These were Ida's."

They rustled in the air conditioner wind, giving off a faint, sweet scent. "Sometimes she left clothes here. Things she could spare. She knew I liked that"

I stiffened, waiting for Frankie to speak of Mel with Ida's dress, angry again. Instead, she pulled out a big one with blue flowers and black trim. "I want you to have this."

I folded it into a triangle and knotted it loosely at my neck. It was a pure polyester gift of Frankie's good graces. She shook out the other scarves. Reaching beneath a stack of nylon slips, my hand closed around a familiar shape. It was the gardenia Venus of Willendorf soap that Lil and I had given to Frankie, still tied with string in its net bag.

Frankie blushed when I held it up. "It has a nice fragrance," she said, taking the soap out of my hands and tucking it in with the scarves at the back of the drawer.

Tucker and Mel painted all the door and window frames, since there wasn't time to do the whole house. They patched the fence. They hosed off the shed and trimmed weeds around the water tower. Mel left a thatch of tall grass around the outside faucet, where a toad lived. He said visiting the toad would be something to do with kids, if any came to the service.

I glanced nervously at Frankie when Mel mentioned this over a barbecued beef sandwich at the midday meal. I didn't know how she would take to him making suggestions about Ida's service. She didn't show any reaction, but just gazed at him steadily until he turned a little red. When he picked up the plate of sweet gherkins and offered them to her, she speared one.

Tucker also drove. He would borrow the pickup, since the bus was too long to be navigating around Chalk. He took Mrs. Poll to the Elks Club to see about renting a hall. She found it too stuffy and too dear. We finally decided to hold the service in the shed.

Most evenings, Frankie got out the blender and made yogurt banana smoothies fortified with malt to keep up our strength. We played dominoes. Frankie and Tucker were standing partners against Mel and me in Forty-two. I kept expecting my competitive streak to rise, but found myself more eager to shuffle than to bid. Mel adapted his poker attitudes with ease. He teased Frankie fluently. She let him. We set Frankie and Tucker a little more often than they set us. The dominoes slid and clacked under our hands.

After a few rounds, we would watch the television news, then go to bed.

I worked on the curtain at night in the quiet of the den. I took my time picking over snapshots and sewed slowly, trying to make the project last. I used a picture of Lil grinning and clutching a sheaf of poems before a reading at a bookstore, ankles crossed in her striped silk pants. I put in one of her youngest niece and nephew playing with wooden trucks on a gold carpet, and one of rocks in a river where we had had a picnic a few years ago, and another one of Lil running in low waves on a beach near Gloucester, breasts lifting like the cresting water beneath her long-sleeved shirt. It had been cold.

I wrote to Lilian every night after everyone was asleep. I trimmed the edges of the pages with my sewing shears after I tore them out of the notepad. I neglected the How To project to tell Lilian how the taste of fudge seemed to compliment love and grief. I described the layers of feeling I could see in Frankie's face. I sent Lilian an invitation to the memorial service. I promised to tell her in person the story of Mel and Ida's dress, and kept the curtains secret for a surprise. I thanked her for looking after Minnaloushe.

In every letter, I told her I loved her. I barely mentioned how much I wished I could touch her; my absence was my own fault. I didn't allow myself Xs and Os before I signed, but once when I was writing in pencil, I stroked the tip sideways so that it left a wide gray curve under the last "love."

Each night I would walk to the end of the lane so I could leave my letter in Frankie's box. Usually, the flag was already up.

Mel sent out small envelopes with angel stamps, addressed to his wife. I felt curious about her.

One night less than a week before the service, I couldn't get a clear breath. Something in the air had gotten to me. My spray was useless. Propped up and half asleep, I tried to concentrate on the wheezing—its rhythms and whistles, its deep, false pulls.

At three-thirty, I got up off the couch and went to the kitchen to make some coffee. People said it helped.

I sat at the table, my heart pounding with caffeine and albuterol. Moths fluttered over the cabinets until I went after them with the broom. I killed one against the wall with a sharp whisk. The others dispersed.

The small exertion left me gasping. As I sponged away the smudge that the moth's body had made on the paint, I thought I heard someone in the hall. I shut off the light with an irritated click. When asthma kept me awake at home, I rubbed my chest with Vicks and roamed the house naked, breathing in medicated fumes. I watched late night television. I sent email and gave myself foot massages. I listened—through headphones out of consideration for Lilian—to female vocalists, both country and pop. Sometimes, less thoughtfully, I was able to persuade her to distract me with sex. But with other people sleeping throughout Frankie's house, I felt trapped.

I had finished my sewing project the night before, so I pulled the curtains out of the bag and spread them on the rug to admire for a while.

In the last picture, I held up a quilt I had made from scraps of clothes from Lilian's store, a project that had taken many months. My arms were stretched wide to give the full maple leaf effect. All that could be seen of me behind the quilt were my nose, glasses and hair, but it was a good portrait for my lover, just the same.

After I put the curtains away, I was restless on the couch, tucking my hands under my breasts for comfort. My nose was streaming. My lungs were failing to swell with air. I wanted to go home.

Quiet after a long bout of coughing, I heard the rattle of the tags on Tartar's collar through the open window. She whined a little. I looked out the window and saw that someone had shut her in the pen. Tartar was usually free at night. I thought it was a mistake.

I got up and dressed in the dark room with exhausted relief. It felt better to be moving than to slump under the covers, sleepless and short of breath.

Tartar jumped up to lick me when I let her out. The moon was low, dimmed a little with the first hints of morning, but stars were still out. I leaned on the gate to watch Tartar's joy at being released. She ran a wide circle around the water tower, then went under the fence and streaked down the hill toward the guest house. She was soon out of sight without giving me a second glance.

Annoyed, I watched her go. Tartar usually stuck close to the house, at least when people were around. I didn't want to call her back and wake up the whole house, but I didn't want her to chase wild animals all over the county and come home stinking with a muzzle full of quills.

I patted my pocket to be sure I had my asthma spray, then went after her, following the barking.

I opened the gate and started down the hill, breathing steadily, taking it slow. The Johnson grass was tall. It stirred as I moved through it. The moon settled into a haze of faint light. The night sky was fading like denim. I headed toward the decrepit guest house.

It had been empty for years, since before I could remember. Frankie had told me that a black family had lived here before she moved in, but they didn't own it. They had left when she bought the land. There was no story about where they went.

I could see the tarpaper nailed in a diamond pattern across the buckled roof. Old bottles littered the porch. Grasshoppers made scuffling sounds. There was no door.

I saw a shape circling the guest house, yipping. I was about to whistle when I heard, "Tartar, stop." It had to be Frankie, but her voice was oddly strained.

Tartar plunged towards the far side of the house, wagging her tail. As I came closer, I heard a man laugh.

Under the cover of Tartar's excited barks, I pressed through the weeds to the corner of the house. Stickers scratched my arms, but I stood with my back to the tarpaper, concentrating, willing my conspicuous lungs to let me breathe in silence. Tartar barked a little more, then settled down.

Frankie murmured to her. "Now, how did you get out? Crawl under the fence? Anyone would think you were a tomcat."

As the man laughed again, I peered around the corner into the open field.

Frankie propped herself up on one elbow on a musty old army blanket stretched out on the grass. She was looking at Tartar. The dog curled at the edge of the blanket as if she'd been there all night. Frankie gave Tartar's head a stroke with her foot, then turned on her side and reached out to the man on his knees beside her.

It was Mel. "Good dog," he said in a drowsy, perfunctory way. He was folding something shimmery and diaphanous. His shirt was loose and open. Frankie cupped his belly. As I watched her trace the hair below his navel, I all but held my breath—easing air out slowly, pulling in a thin stream. Mel sighed. Frankie's blouse was covered with grass. There was familiarity in the way her palm scooped the soft belly.

He held his hand over hers for a moment, then moved to find his jacket. He slipped the folded bundle into his pocket.

I pulled my head back and leaned on the wall. The guest house groaned. Peepers and crickets practiced rhythms. I felt unbearably lonely, immersed in pulsing insects, weeds and full air, as if the pasture itself were more carnal than any sexual heat Frankie and Mel could raise between them. My wheezing was getting worse. I felt sick of my own breath.

Slowly, I started back up the hill. The insects stopped trilling as I passed. I didn't look back, but fastened the gate behind me. It clanked in a businesslike way. I walked across the white dirt to the shed.

I stopped next to the tractor, resting my hand on a headlight. My fingers found a rim of grease. I could have climbed up for the knobbed steering wheel, the high view. Instead, I leaned against the edge of the tractor seat, down to jealousy and confusion. Frankie was seeking comfort. Sour responses came over me hard. I found her greedy, my fat aunt, taking a married lover while she was supposed to be mourning. I felt tricked. Wasn't she a lesbian? Frankie's sexual life was no kind of attack on me, but I was fighting a sense of insult.

My reactions were as ugly as a girl crushing her finger in a vise. I was a grown woman with all my limbs in the grip of phantom pain. No wound, but it hurt. I rested my face against my arm.

I was wheezing and the sun was coming up. I didn't want to be there when Mel and Frankie climbed the hill. I couldn't imagine facing them over eggs and biscuits. I checked under the floor mat in the pickup for the key. When I didn't find one, I walked across the shed, brushed under the dangling rope, and opened the door of the Mercury.

It was a mess inside, as if Ida had just been driving around town waving out the window and throwing her wadded tissues and diet cola empties on the floor. I bent down and felt in the cluttered darkness under the seat until I found the spare keys.

I adjusted the driver's seat, which was pulled back too far for me. I hadn't driven since the time last year I had borrowed Lil's Toyota to go to the National Home Extension Agents convention in Maine. I had a current license. It was in my purse on the TV tray beside the couch in the den. I pulled out gingerly.

Many times after that morning, I tried to piece together what I had been thinking when I took the Mercury. I wanted to be gone. That was the strongest feeling. It seemed like a necessity. I was struggling with breath. I was angry. I had strayed too close to Mel and Frankie's intimacy. My mind replayed the way Frankie turned to him. I felt abandoned and deceived. Later, that seemed crazy. I didn't believe Frankie owed me an explanation for her sexual choices or the ways she carried Ida's loss. I read a lot when my mother died, spent whole days pinning myself down to feeble mysteries. I hadn't planned on telling anyone else how to grieve.

But when I was backing out past the bus in the drive, I didn't worry about Frankie. I told myself she was too busy with Mel to notice that I'd taken the car out for a spin. I noted how quickly she seemed to have gotten over Mel's part in toying with Ida's dress. I felt clear-headed and justified above a throb of undifferentiated anguish as familiar as my pulse.

I made it past the bus without hitting it. I took a stately horseshoe turn, then headed down the lane.

The road was slender and empty. I remembered to turn on the headlights. The moon was down. The Mercury felt sluggish. That seemed appropriate to me for a dead woman's car, but when I was accelerating on the other side of Chalk, I realized that I had been driving with the emergency brake on.

I went all the way to Lake Merle. By the time I got to the broad, empty parking lot, there was a pervasive gray light. I pulled over next to a rusty trash barrel and rested my head on the steering wheel. Straightening up, I took a puff of asthma spray. My asthma had subsided, but I wanted to be sure of my breath.

There was a lime green pickup with a flag decal in one corner of the lot, but I felt alone in the world in a car filled with trash. Beyond the picnic shelters, the lake lapped at a red mud beach. I recognized this variation on the color of dirt from my childhood, but now it was almost lurid. I climbed out of the car, but bent back into it to clean.

I found a plastic bag from a shoe store and dragged mounds of old tissues and advertising circulars into its mouth with a cheap wooden snow brush, which Ida had surely never used. I started by putting the crushed cans aside for recycling, but a bitter impatience overcame me, and I dumped them into the barrel. I dug bottle caps from the musty carpet, and gathered old receipts that fluttered like moths when I tossed them into the trash.

I found three pencils, a cat's-eye marble, a cloth-covered button, and two twenty-three cent stamps, which I kept. I piled gritty coins on the asphalt by the back tire. As I worked, I had the feeling that I was burrowing closer to Ida. I got down to details, prying up the floor mats and shaking them out above the sparse grass at the edge of the lot. I picked dirt from the carpet with my fingertips. I knelt to run my hands between the seats.

Finally, I shut the door and leaned against the Mercury, grimy and spent. Feeling as if I needed a cleansing myself, I got up and headed toward the lake.

Lake Merle was so big that I couldn't see its opposite shore. There was a line of light at the horizon, throwing clouds into relief. The morning kept coming slowly, but it was already hot. I was tempted to go into the water, but down the beach I could see a fisherman making slow casts. I couldn't very well strip down to my underwear in front of him, and if I got my clothes wet, they would take a long time to dry.

I tried to protect my khaki pants from the red mud by sitting in the grass, but the chigger bites made me give that up. I took off my shoes and socks, tucked my asthma spray into one shoe for safekeeping, and dug my toes into the mud. The dark water pinked, then grayed. I watched the shifts in color with exhaustion, as if looking at tenderness with a cold eye. I thought of Lilian running at the ocean. Mel and Frankie on the grass.

There was a beer tab near me, sharp edge up. I did the dangerous thing, and buried it.

I was so tired, finally, that I simply lay back and let my head rest in the mud. The sky was scrolling into higher light. I blinked and saw Mel folding lace again, his belly white and textured like the cratered moon. I didn't know exactly what he had been doing, but it made me want to cry. Frankie had driven me out to Ida's grave in Chalk Memory Gardens last week—turned earth and a flat plaque, next to her husband. Very well tended, just off the interstate. Only artificial flowers were allowed. Frankie brought convincing violets to crowd into the holder. She had spared some for the husband. Her eyes had looked raw.

I closed my own eyes and knew myself to be full of errors, unredeemed by the cleaning I had given the Mercury. A note, I thought. I should have left Frankie a note about borrowing the car. I should have stayed at the house and made everyone waffles. I dug my elbows into the mud, and let mistakes strain out of me: callow self-obsession, prudishness, theft, intolerance, and meanness. The mud softened, holding my shape. I sank into it, feeling deeply eased. I thought of the lake waiting for me, as if water waits.

My hand rested on the slightly damp, stretched cotton of my underpants under the waistband of my khakis. I had one knee bent, and one leg stretched toward the lake. I could hear it lapping. Then I heard the slap of footsteps coming toward me at a brisk pace.

I opened my eyes, but didn't turn. My bowels clenched. I was afraid to be stretched out in such a vulnerable position, so easy to see on the nearly empty beach. I crossed my legs at the ankles.

The footsteps came closer. It could be anyone, I thought: boys who hate fat women, with handfuls of rocks. A lady on her morning walk, seeing me as a thick pile of sloth. Someone without any interest in me, or else staring with fascination. It could be the Venus of Willendorf, stumping through mud on stone legs. It could be the fisherman on his way home. It could be a large dog.

It would have been easy and wise to turn my head to see who was coming, but I still didn't look. Instead, I settled my hips more deeply into the wet red dirt to let fear drain from me, too. I stretched my legs. My arms drifted up to rest on my breasts. My fingers were flat along the inner slopes. I lowered my eyes toward them, not craning to see. I was in the Venus position without the hollow to hold ashes. I had a belly, like the original. Nothing was missing.

The steps approached at a close distance. They slowed. I was observed. I sensed it like heat, but it didn't draw my attention. I was resting deeply. My lungs were quiet as I breathed into my shape. I curved both ways, toward sky and dirt. My flesh fell loosely over its scaffolding of bones. I met myself in mud. There was nothing more holy. The footsteps passed on.

After a time, I got to my feet and ran across the mud into the lake. The water was sultry. My feet sank into the soft, chunky bottom, so I kicked my legs out behind me, dropped my head, and swam hard away from the shore. When I got deep enough to tread water, I unfastened the zipper and worked out of my khakis. After I tied them around my hips, I looked back at the beach.

There was a single figure walking, blocking the sun from his or her eyes, looking my way. I was too far out to see more.

I stretched back and floated, staring again at the sky. The water was murky and lukewarm. Lake weeds brushed my legs. My hair streamed away from my head in strands and clumps. My t-shirt billowed, stretched by the water. My underpants clung under my belly's crease. I was bathed by the lake's shifting hold. I could see my belly rising in the water like Lil's in the bathtub or Mel's in the field.

I dove backwards and surfaced again. This, finally, was what I wanted: to be drenched. I had thought I wanted stasis, old bonds, a place where I would be so familiar as to be unrecognizable, so had come to Chalk to be the homely niece of a maiden aunt. I thought Lilian and sex would wait while I found my place in the natural order of an inherited landscape. Instead, I found sexuality as present as breath, and nothing simple about breathing. Fears and marvels rippled through me like swimming snakes.

Out there, my body listing with the current, I drifted from a grassy image of the memory gardens to the dead possum on cracked asphalt by the side of the road. Describing circles in the water with cupped hands, I thought that most fears came down to fear of death. Doing frog kicks, I knew I should be getting back with the Mercury. It was the way to help Frankie or at least do no harm. But my mind caught on the fact that boys screamed out of cars at me in response to an abundance of flesh. Fear of fat was fear of death. People who turned away at the sight of me could not turn from their own bodies, their own mortal softness, from the approach of their own sure deaths. I could not drive away from it, either. I arched, kicking lazily. We were all so scared of the flesh.

Lake Merle lulled me past the point of articulate thought. Water lapped at my neck. When I got out I would be a mess, I knew – muddy, dripping and facing complicated duties I had scrambled to avoid – but for now I was in the belly of the world. I floated and almost slept.

I waded out slowly. The clay turned mushy at the water's edge. I held my hands out for balance. My fingertips had wrinkled like raisins. The air was dense and hot. My pants dripped around my hips.

I looked up and down the beach. There was no one in sight. Somebody, though, had dropped a candy wrapper not far from my shoes. I took it with me to the parking lot and threw it in the trash barrel before I squeezed myself into my khakis, put a bag down on the seat to protect the upholstery, gathered up the pile of change, and drove away.

Other cars pushed past the Mercury on the highway. It was full morning. I was parched. I had to get the car back, but didn't want to arrive at Frankie's with a need that couldn't wait. A fancy realtor's sign with brick columns read: "Chalk, your dream hometown." I pulled up in an ample parking space in front of the drugstore.

I spread the quarters, dimes, nickels and pennies out on the wide dash. Ida had left three dollars and sixty-three cents, all told. I dropped a dime in the parking meter and took the rest into the store to buy a drink.

My t-shirt was plastered to me with lake water, but the woman behind the counter acted thrilled when I set down a Squirt. "Why, you must be Frankie's niece. I'd know that chin anywhere. I'm coming to the service. We all miss Ida so much."

"It'll be good to have you with us," I said, trying not to drip on her floor.

She dug in a box, then slid an envelope across the counter. "Your aunt had some film developed."

Tucker's pictures. Patting my wet pockets, I said, "I forgot my purse."

She rippled fingernails at me. "Take them. I'll put it on Frankie's tab."

I turned on the engine and the air conditioning in the Mercury, then tore open the envelope. I had to take a quick look. Most of the pictures had been taken in our town back east. Sometimes, there were several slightly different views of the same scene. Turning them over one by one, I saw broken steps, dangling rain gutters and untidy lawns. The mud on my feet itched as I recognized a car buried in sand under a bridge. The whole place seemed shabby. Still, as I glanced at them, I felt myself leaning closer, yearning for home as I used to yearn for Chalk.

There weren't many that included people, but there was a good one of Mel. I paused to take a look. He was standing at our morning bus stop in his usual suit coat and crisp shirt, holding a coke can. His hair bristled. There wasn't much sun. The mortuary that used to be a bank was behind him. I knew it well enough to recognize the former drive up window, which had been boarded over and painted gray. Mel's tie clip was bright on his somber tie. His face was still.

I thought what a suitable partner for Frankie he would have seemed if she had sent me this picture of a stranger a month ago. But, of course, Mel and I had our years of silence at the bus stop between us. We had our own relationship.

It was startling to hit pictures from our trip, but I barely glanced at them. A parking lot full of charter buses with clustered high-rises behind them, sound barriers, pylons. Further west, he took more: a heavy canopy built to shelter gas pumps, with nothing but posts and dirt left underneath. The rusted dumpster beside the motel, and the swing set out back, with a view.

I flipped to the next picture. It was me, lying naked beside the motel pool. I set the rest of the pictures on the passenger seat, lifted this one in both hands, and stared.

I remembered that I had felt invisible when Tucker caught me, but in the picture I seemed arranged to be the object of attention. The difference made me aware of seeing myself through his perceptions. My body was silhouetted against chain link by light from the cabins behind it. Hanging on the fence, my jeans were a dark shape.

I was on my side. One hand rested on my hip. My knees were bent. One foot stretched behind me. My breasts, falling sideways, curved toward the camera. My side swelled and ebbed before the steady line of leg. My eloquent belly spread and flattened on the concrete.

Tucker had found things to look at on me that were actual and interesting, but what he caught was different from what I usually believed myself to be. I knew my body was opulent, but that was not what I felt most mornings as I bent over to center my breasts in the cups of my bra. The physical tensions of that act alone—in my shoulders, ribs and in the balls of my fingers as I pulled to catch the hooks – made a story of compression and resistance.

I didn't see that in Tucker's snapshot. I saw disorienting beauty, much more like what I had just felt at the lake. Looking at it tapped the sense of profound possibility that was a fresh, almost physical, memory. Like looking at my lover, it made me catch my breath.

I stared a little while longer. I wished I could show it to Lilian. I counted on her to be generally unimpressed, but to give an important thing its due. Still, even without her steadying gaze, the picture didn't make me feel vulnerable. I had the negative and the only set of prints. I wondered what Tucker had intended to do with it. It didn't seem right for any of the uses I had imagined.

The rest of the pictures looked different after I had seen mine. Even Graceland with its rock-n-roll gate and insistent graffiti was poignant: "Elvis is my daddy! Branden, 2000." As I flipped back through shots of bulging dry wall and cracked, weedy sidewalks, a sense of family rose in me. I saw Tucker looking to the world of ugly things. He found Mel and me to belong there. The idea hurt, but the images moved me. I wanted to trust him, not to clean things up.

Getting back to Frankie's was becoming more pressing as the minutes passed, but I got out of the car again. I stopped at the curb to run my fingers through my hair and tuck my shirt in, but it was hopeless. People carrying grocery bags or strolling with their dogs shot quick glances at me. A little girl carrying a clarinet case stopped in the middle of the sidewalk to stare. She had long hair pulled back with butterfly barrettes, and her eyes were blue. A full-grown woman, I smiled and said, "Hello."

She didn't speak or look away. I paused for a moment in the frame of her gaze, then went back into the drugstore and used Frankie's credit to buy more film.

I took the turn carefully. The Mercury moved with a wide dispassion that was some comfort to my nerves as I came slowly up the lane. When I saw Mel standing on the scrubby lawn spraying Raid on the nests of fire ants, my stomach seized up and sent an echo of Squirt into my throat.

He lowered the spray can and watched me drive up in Ida's old car. I felt the front tire leave dirt for grass. I did a quick correction with the steering wheel. I hoped it didn't look like an anxious swerve.

He put the can on one of the front steps, and wiped his hands on a rag. I turned away from him and parked near the shed.

Mel came across the drive in a saunter, with Tartar crowding his heels. When I met him at the water tower, he murmured,

"What did you do, Carline, cross the county line and spend all night in a bar? We've been worried sick about you."

His face was exhausted. My resentment had faded. What I felt was guilt. Trying to brazen it out, I said, "I went for a swim."

"A swim?" Mel's glance flicked over my muddy pants and damp, tangled hair. His clothes were immaculate. There was no evidence that he had been rolling in the pasture until all hours of the morning.

My own exhaustion caught up with me. I leaned against one of the water tower's rusty pipes. I intended to offer an explanation, but, instead, blurted out, "Mel, did you know I'm a lesbian?"

He stared at me for a perfectly timed beat, then did a pratfall. He sprawled on the ground, legs waving in their gray suit pants, and gasped, "No!"

It was quite a performance. Tartar started barking. I had to laugh. Frankie appeared on the porch. She shaded her eyes to look toward us.

He raised his head to wave at Frankie, shouting, "She's okay!" He spoke to me more softly. "Of course I knew. I've seen you kiss your girlfriend at the bus stop."

Offering him my hand, I said, "Get up, you idiot." I felt like an idiot myself. Had there been someone I was trying to fool?

Mel dusted off his pants, but I hurried toward the house when Frankie turned and went back inside without even speaking to me.

I took my shoes off on the porch, but my feet were muddy, too. When I stepped inside, Frankie stared at me. "You're not hurt?"

I lost bits of dirt when I shook my head. "Frankie, I'm…"

She looked out the picture window. "Wash up. Then we'll talk."

I cleaned the tub after my bath. I straightened Frankie's stack of *Reader's Digests* and put out matching towels. I played with the shampoo bottle, watching slow bubbles through the plastic. Then, I walked down the hall to the kitchen.

Mel got up when I came in. The look on his face was almost timid as he touched Frankie's napkin and said, "I better get busy."

I poured myself a glass of juice and started out badly. "How did everyone sleep?"

Mel retreated to the hall. "See you later."

Frankie was sitting across from me, way too still. Her mouth was tight, but she was loose around the eyes. The skin over her collarbone crinkled like a tissue. "Your mother was fond of Ida," she said. "The times she met her, she liked her."

I couldn't stand the tension. Planting my elbows on the table, I tried to explain. "I was having an asthma attack last night. I thought going to the lake might help. I didn't think you would be worried. I expected to be back before anyone noticed I was gone."

Frankie wiped her hands, patted her hair, and said nothing.

"I'm sorry," I offered uneasily. "I cleaned out the Mercury."

Frankie lay her head on the tablecloth and started to cry. Harsh sobs shook her whole body.

I came over to kneel on the floor next to her and put my hand on her arm. We stayed that way long after my knees began to ache, but when I moved to rub her back, she shrugged my hand away. She was still gasping and crying. I got up, fetched the Kleenex and pulled a chair around the table to sit next to her, my fingers barely touching her wrist.

Eventually, she lifted her head. She wiped her eyes, blew her nose, and said, "Ida gave me that car. In her will, right in front of her boys and the lawyer, she said it was for me. You just disappeared with it, as if you didn't care about anyone and everything belongs to you."

I nodded, ashamed. I had known that car was precious to Frankie. I closed my eyes and saw an image of Ida driving up the lane in the Mercury's prime, coming to take Frankie for a spin. She pulled up beside the house and got out, her long legs unfolding in peach stretch pants. She cradled an empty casserole dish. It was tomato red with a glass lid, and Frankie stood on the edge of the lawn exclaiming over it. I had seen yearning on Frankie's face, seen Ida leaning forward to meet her. When they got into the car, they had kissed.

Even then, the Mercury had been too big. It drank gas as if this were a limitless world. But Frankie loved it. I thought she experienced being seated on the leatherette upholstery as being cushioned by core truths.

"Forgive me," I said to Frankie.

"What possessed you?" She was crying again.

Frankie loved Ida very much. I had known that for years, although I'd never thought of it as romantic love. Struggling with what to say now, the best I could come up with was the truth. "I was upset when I took the car. I saw you in the pasture. With Mel."

There was a drop of juice on the table. Frankie rubbed it and repeated, "Mel."

I sat back in my chair. Frankie stopped crying. She shook her head, looking at me. "Carline, you should go."

"What do you mean?" My voice scratched like a bad match. I knew.

Frankie held up empty, trembling hands. "Go home."

BUS TIP

Pack light

IN A STATE OF DESOLATE NUMBNESS, I CALLED THE airlines. I despised flying, but that was not a good enough reason to keep Lil waiting if I was no longer welcome in Chalk. Frankie offered to give me money for the ticket, but I used my credit card. Things would be tight at home, but I figured I could always get work as a housecleaner. My earlier economies were irrelevant: this was a trip I had to pay for myself.

Restless on hold with ads murmuring in my ear, I tried out arguments to get Frankie to let me stay. I felt pinned by my own selfishness. My aunt had taught me young that actions had consequences, but I hadn't thought for a second that she might send me away. The taped voice on the phone urged me to dream of Europe. I was repulsed by the romantic music tinkling in the background, the names of cities being dangled like lures, but I sat through it until an operator helped me arrange to fly standby.

I folded my clothes neatly into the suitcase, stuffing the sewing gear in a couple of socks. I placed the photo album flat on top, but kept the curtains in the bag. I didn't want to crease the fabric or bend the pictures. When I finished packing, I went outside.

The heavy air made me stop and feel my pocket for the shape of my asthma spray. Sprawled in the shade under the porch, Tartar lifted her tail, but didn't get up.

Tucker was standing on an old sheet spread on the ground, painting the side of the garage with small, quick strokes. He wore a feed cap high on his head. His arms were sunburned and peeling, and the back of his t-shirt was dark with sweat. The radio was broadcasting a baseball game from inside the garage. He turned it down when he saw me. "Mel told me you were leaving. Do you need a ride?"

Mel was holed up in the den, watching a Three Stooges movie and eating lunch. He must have slipped out to alert Tucker. I thought, for a crazed moment, about marrying Tucker. He looked good in his soft jeans, with his t-shirt loose at his waist. He was a hard-working, cheerful man with outside interests. I could set up housekeeping and make cornbread. It was an ineffective fantasy. "To the airport," I said. "Please."

He slid his brush along the spongy wood. "No problem."

Taking the scraper, I left him to clean the brushes and wash up. Tartar followed me, tongue hanging. We went into the shed. The wasps pursued their business in the rafters, uninterested in me. I found that reassuring. The Mercury had red mud on its fenders. I brushed some into a baggie I had brought from the kitchen. Scraping the ground, I filled the baggie with white dirt and rocks to bring home to Lilian.

Tartar scratched herself. I turned her ears inside out, then smoothed them flat again, urging myself to be more attentive and true to the fidgeting grace of bodies on earth. Banished from Chalk, I would have to do more than wait it out. Tartar rested her head on the ground.

"She's a good dog."

I turned to see Mel standing at the opening to the shed, the sun bright on the lane behind him. He had his duffel bag slung casually over his shoulder, like a soldier on leave. Tartar rolled on her back, hoping for a rub on her belly.

I hid the rocks in my purse and stood up. "Where are you going?" If he was taking off on Frankie, Tucker was sure to offer him a ride.

"Nowhere, right now. Your aunt asked me to stay a while." He eased his way closer, and put the bag down on the hood of the Mercury. "Carline, I feel terrible that she…"

"What's the duffel bag for, then?" Disturbed, Tartar got up and padded out of the shed.

Mel raised empty hands. "I just want to show you something. Okay?"

I shrugged. I had just urged myself to be more attentive, after all. When Mel reached into his bag, I half expected toy snakes coiled in cans to pop out. He leaned on dumb jokes. Instead, he brought out a soft bundle of cream-colored fabric. I had seen him holding it this morning in the pasture. Lingerie. I should have guessed.

He must have noticed my discomfort, but began to unfold the cloth tenderly. I was transfixed by his air of concentration. It had been the same with Ida's dress. This was a silk camisole edged with lace. He held it up by wide straps, then handed it to me.

I took it by a bow at the tip of its V neck. It smelled a little musty. It occurred to me that he would be very happy digging through the bargain bin at Lilian's store. "Shouldn't you be showing this to Frankie?"

"I have." He let me dangle the fabric for a moment, then took it back. He held it loosely mounded in his hands. "Someone I loved gave that to me when she left me for a woman, almost thirty years ago. It was hers."

He slipped a hand inside the garment. Part of his palm showed through the lace at the hem. He smoothed it from the inside, then matched the seams to refold it. "I wish I could find her." He tied the camisole into a bundle with the straps.

I shook my head. Mel had romantic dreams I found dangerous. "What about Frankie? What about your wife?"

He put the bundle back in his duffel bag. "They're both remarkable, too." He took a step towards me, looking sincere. "I wanted to tell you that you're not the first lesbian I've known."

"Okay. Thanks a bunch." I stared at him, thinking that Mel might love the camisole nearly as much as the memory of a woman. It would be easy enough for him to slip it over his head and get a slinky feeling under crisp shirts. For all I knew, he did, or maybe he just loved the drama of silk unfolding when he opened the bundle. I didn't ask if he knew about Frankie.

Instead, I said something too obvious for me to let it go unspoken. "Mel, don't you think it's time to get your own lace? I'm sure somebody in your life would take a shopping trip with you. Or try catalogues with large sizes. The fashions have gotten much better over the past ten years. They're easy to find on the Internet."

By the time Tucker came out of the house with my suitcase, Mel had borrowed a pen and was scribbling down Web addresses on a sheet from my note pad. I was always willing to be a resource, but it was time to go.

Frankie had said she would keep the camp box until I needed it. Now she came into the yard to hand me a big jar of iced tea and the bag with the curtains. I had told her they were for Lilian. "That's a nice color," she said. "I hope your friend likes it." She tucked the facing into the neckline of my dress. I pulled her in for a hug, which she allowed.

"Thank you for all your help," she said, formally. "Have a safe trip home."

I shook Mel's hand and wished him luck. When I looked back from the door of the bus, he had his arm around Frankie.

I sat close to Tucker, crying. The rows of empty seats were repetitive and bleak. He hit the button on his cassette player. It was the King himself, singing "Love Me Tender."

"A classic," I said thickly as we turned onto the farm-to-market road. I was making an effort. We had a two-hour drive to Dallas.

Tucker's gaze was temperate. "That's okay, Carline. We don't have to talk." I was relieved.

I didn't have eyes for the outskirts of Chalk as we left the Taco Bell, the Dairy Queen and the new outlet mall. I hid my face in my arm, sobbing against the window as quietly as I could. I got a cramp in my neck and left streaks on the glass. The road signs were made illegible by my grief.

As I wept, my mind played sluggishly over the fact that my aunt had sent me away. I had eased nothing for Frankie. It was a harsh failure. My breath was ragged but deep. I cried until the skin of my face seemed swollen away from its supporting bones.

My arm fell asleep against the window. For the first time in weeks, I noticed the burn. It had healed red and smooth. I held my finger on it, touching one of my mistakes. Frankie was fat, but I had not told her anything about my troubles with hate and pain. I had dug down to the gravel between the tufts of the Mercury's carpet, but had not managed to get that said. Frankie had left the rope hanging in her shed for decades, for no purpose I could see. Did she use it for work? Did she swing there herself? Was she waiting for more children to appear? Why couldn't I have asked what she did, what she wanted? Even silent, I could have been a witness as she made her way through isolation and the aftermath of death. It would have been little enough. Now, the chance was gone.

As I dug for Kleenex, I felt an envelope in my purse. I wiped my face and looked over at Tucker, uncharacteristically quiet behind the wheel. Perhaps he was showing respect, or else was absorbed in thoughts of his own. His chin bobbed faintly with the music. It occurred to me that there was no more time to waste.

"I have the pictures," I said, moving my purse into my lap.

He glanced at me, then back at the road. We passed a stretch of barbed wire fence with silver hubcaps on it. Tucker's heavy foot on the gas pedal made them blur. He spoke casually, but with an undercurrent of excitement. "If you're up to it, I'd like to see them."

The last time I had been on this bus with Tucker, I had tried for his camera and keys. Looking at the pictures with him would complete unfinished business between us. I wanted that with him, at least. And I was grateful for the distraction. I unsnapped my purse, dug for the envelope, and handed it across the passenger line.

He opened the flap with one hand. His steering wavered. I got up and, steadying myself against the fare box, took the stack of photos. "I'll give them to you one at a time."

He checked my face. "Are you okay standing there?"

I braced one foot against the box and wrapped my arm around a pole. "Fine."

He rested his wrists on the wheel and held the pictures against the windshield with his fingertips. He looked at each one intently. I thought of the way Lilian made patterns with the used prom gowns she hung on the walls of her store, spreading the skirts wide. She would get just that expression of distracted concentration as she tacked the hems in place.

He held up an abandoned factory, a place we used to pass on the bus. In the photograph, the many windows were full of mystery. I had no idea how it was done. The rectangle of the photo was edged by a gas station and a sign for Cold Beer, Chilled Wine streaming past.

"These are pretty good," Tucker said, motioning to me for the next.

A gutter draped off the side of a house like a ribbon of icing falling from a cake. We passed an exit sign riddled with bullet holes. Tucker drove regular routes of beauty that I had seen only in flickers on my commute.

A grain elevator bellied closer. A tractor mowing the shoulder jutted into our lane. I gasped, but Tucker adjusted. He turned his neck, "Where's the picture of you?"

I had thought to skip that, but chose not to hold back. I braced myself and gave it to him as we started up a hill. The engine downshifted. We passed an industrial park. There I was, heaped and naked, framed by a prefabricated building with no windows beside the highway. I was one more shape in the riveting world. The picture made me feel both diminished and released. Insects left marks on the glass.

We passed scatterings from a blown tire. He looked at me with his head tilted. "What do you think of it?"

There was a silence. He checked his gauges, steered. I gave him another picture. It was a sidewalk buckling as if the ground breathed. We drove past a fairgrounds. One ride had blue lights.

I held the photo of me, looking down at it with only my hand and the ridged floor of the bus as a background. I let myself remember my anger, all of it, and continue to look. I thought of thousands of women's bodies used to sell magazines, diets and auto parts. I remembered the locker room after the fat women's water aerobics class I had taken last fall, and how, covertly, I used to glance at each naked body, scanning for beauty or a history of mortification. Or both. The picture was taking me places. I thought of Frankie, with a body so much like my own, as furious at me now as I had been at Tucker, and not without cause. I stared at the picture—my body, his image. Finally, I said, "You were wrong to take it, but it's good."

He nodded. I started flashing pictures of our trip at him, moving faster. New York City was a railroad bridge with decorative plants hanging down over the road. There were rear views of squat buildings at the Vince Lombardi rest area. I tried to say more about his picture of me. "I usually get seen as ugly." I started crying again. It wasn't news, but it was raw. "That shouldn't matter, but it does." I waited with my eyes on the picture, then said, "You did something different. I look like I belong there."

I wanted more. I wanted to be recognized as specific, myself. Tucker's picture didn't give me that, but it was an exercise in presence to look at the things he had snapped. Still, I had to speak again. "You should have asked me."

If he had asked, the answer would have been no. I would have kept more control over my likeness, and lost the view of my body as a sloped and lovely form pouring over the concrete deck of the pool.

"I know. You're right. I'm sorry." Tucker gazed at a shot of a low building with both a picture of a catfish and the word "catfish" painted on its wall. All business appeared to have stopped. Metal was flaking off an old Greyhound sign. It had been painted white, but the logo showed through the paint. There was an electrified fence, tied with small strips of faded plastic. He held his stare for a long time, then said slowly, "The other thing is speculation."

I went back to my seat, almost reconciled. "What are you talking about?"

He passed a tanker. We didn't swerve. "Real estate. I have to be practical. If I see a property I'm interested in, I take pictures of anything that might bring the value down. Warped floors. Busted fixtures. The hound on that bus stop sign looks just like a ghost." He laughed. "The whole place is a relic. I got on the computer at the Chalk library and found that catfish place listed on a HUD site. It has water damage, mold, problems with the roof, and they still want $30,000 for it. I might get it for less if I have pictures of it looking like a dump heap."

I felt more and more insulted as I took in what he was saying. Tucker saw it in my face. "Carline, don't get me wrong. I'm a serious photographer. Even if I never own a motel, it would have been a crime to miss you by that pool. Well, except that it was worse to make you feel the way you did when I took it. So sorry."

He stretched back to hand me the photo. "I would take pictures all day long if I could, but everybody's got to make a living. I keep an eye out for opportunities."

I put most of the photos back into the envelope, leaving only the one of me on the seat, then picked up the jar of iced tea. I wanted him to stop talking. "Would you like something to drink?"

"Thanks. That would be nice." He paused as if he had something else to tell me, but, taking the hint, he said no more.

I unscrewed the lid and shut my eyes, trying to catch any coolness that rose from the remaining slivers of ice. There wasn't much. I opened my eyes, in too deep to quit. "Tucker, are you telling me that you took my picture at that motel hoping that a fat nude by the pool would bring down the price if you ever made an offer?"

He looked uncomfortable. "I might have been thinking something like that before I lifted the camera, but by the time I shot, I was caught by the image. That picture of you wouldn't help me buy the motel. It would only be distracting. The dumpster, now, there's one that works on a lot of levels. It's expressive, but, in terms of market value of the motel, rust is in the buyer's favor."

I poured with a steady hand. Sending a stream of cold liquid down a driver's collar would be dangerous. I had once read the story of a woman who had scalded her arm with hot tea at a moment of inexpressible loss. There was poetry and effectiveness to such gestures, but I was done with them.

Besides, I had never been naïve when it came to Tucker's motives. What he was telling me now didn't approach the worst that I had imagined. Looking at the picture was a private experience, separate from anything he might say. It was almost like being in the pool again, straining and resting in flickers of light.

His words, though, were irritating. "Tucker, I just told you what the picture meant to me. Why would you want to wreck that?"

He took a drink, then put the cup between his legs to free his hands for the wheel. "I'm trying to tell you the truth, Carline. I owe it to you."

I glimpsed a sign for the airport as it floated past. We were getting close. I thought about the pictures in our album, how they piled up effortlessly: the shots we took, the ones our friends wanted us to have. Everybody posed, then went on talking, pledged to each other in countless small ways. Tucker's pictures were less social, more of a struggle, but they had touched me deeply enough to make me feel a little bit accountable to him, too. I drained my cup. "I accept your apology. I'm not asking for anything else."

When he pulled up at the curb, I gave him the envelope. I put the print of my picture into the zipper compartment of my purse, but let him have the negatives. All of them.

He bowed slightly from his seat behind the wheel. "I'll send you copies."

"I'd like that." I got up and stood behind the white passenger line with my purse over one wrist. "Are you going back to Frankie's?"

He nodded. "I'm sorry you had to leave, Carline."

"Thank you for the ride." I burrowed in my purse to find the film I had bought at the drugstore in Chalk to give to him. "Take pictures at the service."

He took the film and pushed the knob to swing open the door. "It would be an honor."

I wedged the paper bag overflowing with rose curtains beside a burgundy leather bag in the overhead compartment, and looked down at the well coifed woman who was staring up at me, appalled.

"Hi." I was resigned to being unpopular here. Flying standby, I had come late to claim a middle seat. This lady fingering her necklace and the old guy next to the window were going to have to spend some hours with my hips. "I'm sorry to disturb you."

"Oh," she said, gathering her sweater into her lap. I waited a moment to see if she was going to move to let me in. As I started to push past her, she jumped up.

"Thank you." I hit the button for the stewardess and tried to get my purse under the seat. The bulging sides didn't quite fit. Hurrying, I snapped it open and reached inside. My hand closed around something bulky. I pulled out the Venus of Willendorf ashtray, flecked with napkin lint. I pushed the purse under the seat and squeezed between the armrests. It was tight. The guy next to the window kept staring out over the wing. He shifted when I dug for my seat belt buckle, but that was all.

The lady sat down again, her face grim as she picked up her magazine. She was very thin. If I held onto the top of my arm, our sleeves didn't touch.

A brisk stewardess hit the call light. "Yes?"

Before I could answer, the lady said, "Are there any more aisle seats free?"

The stewardess looked impatient. "Sorry, it's a full flight."

I spoke up. "Could I have a seat belt extension, please?" The belt wouldn't fasten without it. Lilian, who hated flying, would blouse her shirt out so nobody noticed that she couldn't buckle up. I wanted to be safe from turbulence, so I always asked.

The stewardess nodded and hurried away. The lady beside me sighed, but didn't comment. The stewardess brought the extension, slipping it to me discreetly, like a tampon. Then we sat back to enjoy our flight.

I settled Venus against my belly and thigh, covering her with my hand. It was awkward to be clutching a fat goddess ashtray, but I didn't want to disturb my whole row by leaning forward to place her in the seat pocket. Besides, she was a comfort to me.

I was exhausted from strong feelings and lack of sleep. It hurt to breathe the dry air. I stared at the fabric of the seat in front of me, filling the hollow in the ashtray with my thumb. My credit card had taken a big hit to buy this ticket. When I got home, I would have to make a list and a timeline, decide what I wanted or at least what the story should be, then call my home economist friends to look for work. I would add up my savings and make a budget, something I should have done the night I quit instead of leaning on credit cards and the kindness of relatives the way I had been.

The armrests were gouging into my hips. Still fingering Venus, I thought of the extravagance of wide seats in Tucker's bus, which had looked so desolate to me this morning. Taking notes was out of the question because I had no room to move my arms, but it came to me that a key point for *How to Ride a Bus* might boil down to: Don't take a plane.

Lilian had an airplane strategy that involved carrying a book of poetry. She preferred poems that were at least twenty years old—complicated lyrics about the inner lives of lovers, their halts and secret places; or rambling epics about cities, suffering, marvels, and seas. She would immerse herself in a poem and push its meaning to the surface. Sometimes the effort made her pant like a runner, but it cut the flight short.

I had called Lilian from the airport and told her I was coming home. I caught her in the middle of a sale at her shop. She said, "Thank god. Are you all right?"

"Shook up," I told her. "Lonely. Ready to be home." I could hear a customer asking about tutus when she said, "I have to go."

I said no to drinks and peanuts when the cart came around. I was hungry, but the tray table hit my belly, so there was no place to rest a cup. The lady in the aisle got a diet cola. She was drinking Ida's brand. The guy said he wanted water. He looked gray and miserable. I thought he might be ill.

He drained his water quickly, then said, "Excuse me," as soon as the cart had passed. He wanted out to go to the bathroom. I had no place to go, and the lady beside me flipped her tray table up, but otherwise didn't budge. I gathered nerve to start negotiations with her, but the guy didn't wait. Maybe he couldn't. He climbed over my legs, knocking Venus out of my lap.

She hit the base of a seat and broke into big, chunky pieces. The guy didn't stop. He was untangling himself from the lady's legs and hurrying down the aisle. She looked at me once, twice, then turned back to her magazine, sipping her drink.

I was hit by a sickening wave of regret. I unbuckled my extended seatbelt, lifted the armrest on the empty window seat side, and leaned to try to gather the pieces. It was not easy in this sliver of space. I heard the lady suck her tongue to the back of her teeth in disapproval. I didn't look up, but drew one of my knees onto the seat so I could get my hands to the carpet to search for fragments. My rear end was in the air, but there was nothing to do about that.

The shards were sharp. When I was sure I had gotten them all, I came up with my hands full. The lady and the guy were both standing in the aisle, looking at me. So was a stewardess. "Trash?" she said, holding out a garbage bag.

I looked back at all of them. "Actually, I need these."

The stewardess, a trained problem solver, leaned past me and pulled the air sickness bag out of the seat pocket. "Put them in here."

I filled the bag and rolled it up tight. I put it in my purse, which now compressed to fit back under the seat. I got up to let the guy reach his spot by the window. I couldn't blame him for breaking Venus. We were trapped.

My temples were pounding; my cheeks were flushed; and my hips had tender grooves in them where the arm rests pressed. Out the window, I could see blue and clouds. I had always considered it tacky to turn an image of one of the first known sculpted human figures into an ashtray, but I missed her now that she was gone. I had had nothing but bad luck with crazy glue. There wasn't much hope.

After I changed planes in Atlanta, I was next to a couple who spoke to each other in a language I didn't understand. They huddled together and left the armrests up. As we were taking off, the man held out his arms to mime wings. All three of us giggled. They were sweet, but I was too wiped out to make friends. It had been a very long day.

I WAS SO TIRED BY THE TIME I GOT TO THE APARTMENT that I put my suitcase down at the bottom of the stairs and waited for strength to climb. There were dust clouds in the corners of the steps. I noticed the delicate patterns they made before I thought of sweeping. It was a change in me.

Lilian opened the door in a t-shirt like Marlon Brando wore in *A Street Car Named Desire*, brushing crumbs from her breasts. Unbelievably beautiful. I took the stairs. We kissed on the landing, across the suitcase. Blood rose to my face. She smelled of lemongrass soap. I was home.

A fan pointed at the door, stirring a breeze to greet me. Minnaloushe rushed past it towards my feet. "Good kitty," I said as he rubbed my legs. "Brave kitty." He hated fans. His fur ruffled in the wind of the blades.

Lilian sat on a kitchen chair, propping her feet on my suitcase. The posture was cocky. Her toenails were red. "God damn it, Carline. I've missed you."

I put the bag on the table and pulled up a chair. "Here," I said. "Bedroom curtains. They're for you."

"Thank you." Lilian pulled one gently out of the bag and held it up in front of her. I watched her face through the rustling fabric as she pointed at the photos, saying each name with unmistakable pleasure. "You've been thinking of home."

I meant to start talking or take her in my arms, but my mind left a gap. My chin dropped. I fell asleep still trying to speak.

I didn't hear the phone ring the next day. What woke me was Mel's voice on the answering machine. Lilian had gone to work. The curtains were hung neatly on a rod in the window, coloring the light in the room.

"Carline, we've been worrying about you. Tucker said he got you to the airport, but you didn't have a definite flight. Your aunt thinks you left a pair of slacks here. We can send those, but we'd like to know how you..."

I rushed to pick up the phone. "Mel, I'm so glad you called. Did Frankie give you my number? Can I talk to her?"

"Oh, good, you made it home." He sounded relieved and slightly furtive. "You've got a spot on her speed dial. She's out in the yard, messing with Tartar. She's not ready to talk right now, but she couldn't sleep for being anxious about you."

I draped myself with the scratchy throw from the couch. "I feel awful about how I left things with Frankie. And I feel responsible for bringing you into her life."

There was a silence. Mel cleared his throat. "Frankie can make her own decisions. I think you should try to talk to her."

Minnaloushe was sharpening his claws on the couch throw. I scratched his head. "Did you tell Frankie that you're a married man?"

He laughed, unflappable. "That's not your business."

I pictured Mel getting Frankie through a hard night on the sleeping porch, playing polkas on the clock radio and juggling pillows wearing a crocheted angel from her nightstand on his head. He was right. It was none of my business. I wondered how many times I was going to have to realize that before it stuck. "Mel, don't hurt my aunt."

He didn't tell me that I had nerve to say that, but it might have crossed his mind. All he said was, "The service is day after tomorrow. Don't forget."

"There's no chance of me forgetting that."

Lilian and I were strolling in the cemetery before supper when she said, "I read your letters, but you haven't told me anything since you've been home."

I was thinking about how quiet our walk had been. There were no stares or insults on the street, nothing but friendly nods. Once or twice, Lilian had brushed against me, rustling our clothes. Now she stopped beside a thin stone to look at me.

The dead here were unobtrusive. I moved close to a familiar tree. "Frankie kicked me out."

A bird cried like a car alarm. Lilian shook her head. "How could that happen?"

I sat down among the tree roots. No one was buried there. Lilian sat, too.

"I got angry because she had sex with the guy from the bus. Mel. I wrote you about him. It was as if she was trying to prove she wasn't a lesbian. Anyway, that's how I felt. I couldn't stand it. I took off in Ida's car and didn't come back all night." I brushed an ant off my foot. "Frankie told me to leave."

Branches were hanging low around us. Lilian snapped a twig. "Maybe she's not a lesbian. Why is that the point?"

I pushed to explain. "I don't care who Frankie sleeps with or how she thinks about it." I had felt jealous disappointment, but it was past. "She's torn up about Ida. Mel's no help."

"How do you know?" She was sitting cross-legged, belly resting on her thighs. Her anger was unmistakable. "Sounds to me like you were looking for an excuse for another abrupt departure. Like the way you left me."

I concentrated on Lilian. "Are you still wondering why I took off in the first place?"

She gave a slight nod, fingering the ground.

We had hours of daylight left. I picked at a piece of bark.

"Before I left for Chalk, I would come here on the way home from work to avoid hassles from the kids hanging out downtown. It was sensible, but terrible. I'd feel contempt for my body. Nobody had to say a word. Sometimes, they did, though. I told you about those boys throwing cigarettes."

Lilian wrapped her arms tightly around her legs and looked at her knees. Everything I said about my own body had implications for her. I knew that in the deepest places knowledge can go, in my lungs, gut, heart.

I touched her foot, and started to quote her. "'Dieting is a wheel of losing and gaining and losing and gaining that grinds up years, money, and joy.'" I was giving a workshop to the buried. Lilian already knew, and no one else was listening. Still, I wanted her to hear how well I remembered the things she had said. I held onto her ankle. "I was well-informed, but still burned myself over the distaste of strangers."

Birds poured out unrelated music. Lilian was crying. I made pits in the ground with my heels. "It was like driving and trying to stay awake." Lilian had seen me drive. "I kept going under, shaking myself out of it, then falling again into fear and self-hate. The worse part was that it seemed so ordinary. I needed to stop."

Past a stubby family tomb, a styrofoam wreath full of carnations tipped over in the breeze. Lilian stretched her legs away from my hand. "How could you hide all that? Why didn't you tell me?"

Looking at brick and clapboard houses outside the iron fence, I thought of Frankie's discretion about Ida. Her habits of concealment were so deep that she could scarcely break them to mourn. My feelings about being fat in this world were a din inside me, but I didn't know how to speak of them. With Lilian, I had to try. "I didn't have words for it. It was more like numbness. And I guess I thought it would hurt you. I didn't want you to see me lapse into hating my body, wondering what I felt about yours."

Lilian nodded slowly. "It does hurt."

For a moment, I couldn't bear to look at her. I read the name Sarai with two dots above the i. She had died a little girl. The sorrow of that for her long-dead parents married the pain in Lilian's voice. It washed through me then parted into separate griefs. Frankie might be feeling something too raw to call sorrow. Trying to imagine it was like stepping barefoot on broken glass. I turned to Lilian's reddened eyes.

"I keep making a mess of things, Lil. But I've always wanted you. I never made that mistake." The few times I forgot the beauty of Lilian's fat body, it had been like forgetting the force of gravity: over in seconds.

She leaned back against a big root, reserved. "Then why did you leave?"

"Frankie needed me." That didn't begin to cover it. "And I wanted very badly to see her. I wanted to see Chalk, to think about things that happened there when I was a girl. I wanted a change in my life so concrete that it couldn't be ignored."

A small plane flew over, engines shaking the air. I took an essential turn of mind. "What do you want, Lilian?"

She stretched flat on the ground, getting dirt on her tank top and boxers. "I don't want to talk now," she said, looking up at the leaves, her face dappled in the shifting light.

I fumbled in my purse, pushing the bag with the broken ashtray aside to find my baggie full of dirt. "Here. White dirt from Chalk. That red is from Lake Merle." I had been swimming in the lake yesterday morning. It seemed like years ago.

She rolled over and took the baggie. Pulling apart the seamed top, she held her face to it. When she looked up, she said, "Not much to smell." She kneaded the dirt through the plastic, then opened the bag, licked her fist and stuck it inside. It was something Minnaloushe would do. Her hand came out coated with dust.

"It's a good present." She rubbed her fist over her thighs, leaving white streaks on her shorts. Opening her hand, she brushed her mouth, then swept slowly from shoulder to hip, lingering over her breasts.

It moved me to watch. Her gestures always had. She meant to get through everything with me. I could see it in her dirty hands.

Wiping her lips on her arm, she leaned toward me. "I can taste where you've been."

I lay down with her against the root. She pressed close. Our bodies filled that piece of ground.

Before we went home, we cut across the Burger King drive-thru to the supermarket parking lot. We needed to pick up a few things.

It was too hot to hold hands. Lilian's shoulders bobbed as we trudged along. I thought about the air conditioning in the Mercury, but didn't wish for a ride. I wanted exactly what I had. Driving would go too fast.

I decided to make Frankie's pimento cheese sandwiches and spinach salad for supper. Lilian liked a drink with soy milk and frozen orange juice. I wanted strawberries. We didn't have a list.

At the corner of the building, near the video place, boys were gathered on their bikes like a flock of birds. One at a time, they clunked over the curb, trying to jump it. A boy without his shirt stubbed his front wheel. The bikes were small. The boys leaned over their handle bars. Their concentration struck me as fierce.

Lilian hesitated, giving me a tense glance. We were unfamiliar fat women approaching boys. Walking toward them, I saw the danger: It would hurt all of us if I were afraid.

A boy with a buzz cut hit the curb flying. Both thick tires spun above the sidewalk. He slid into a turn when he met asphalt on the other side. Slowing, he raised his hands in the air. The other kids put their feet down, impressed.

From a near distance, I raised my hands to celebrate with him. It felt exquisite. I clapped and shouted, "Wow!"

They looked at me, laughed.

I yelled, "Whoo-hoo!" Lilian grinned.

The boys started to circle again, gaining speed. As the automatic doors swept open in front of Lil and me, I popped a wheelie with an empty shopping cart.

On the way home from the store, I showed her Tucker's picture. We talked all through supper about fury, jealousy, vulnerability, nakedness, beauty, and forgiveness, the picture flat on the table between us. Finally, she took the pin cushion into the bedroom and found a place for the photo on the curtain. "We'll need a new pocket," she told me, sliding pins through the corners, "but I think it works."

That night, Lilian read me poems. I sat cross-legged beside her, rubbing her back while she fished among books scattered on both sides of the bed, naming poets with an intimacy I loved. "Hopkins, Clifton, Rich, Yeats, Dickinson, Stein, Poe." She had taken over my nightstand while I was gone. "Keats."

I followed the shifts along her shoulder blades as she started "Ode to A Nightingale." A faint breeze stirred the curtains. Her voice slowed, lingering among the dense sounds.

In some melodious plot
Of beechen green, and shadows numberless,
Singest of summer in full-throated ease.

Lilian was stretched on her belly. Her muscles, bones and fat made more poems beneath my hands. I was attentive to them, following the rills of her body, letting her voice take me under as it had from the first.

But here there is no light,
Save what from heaven is with the breezes blown
Through verdurous glooms and winding mossy ways.

Desire broke surface. Hands slipping lower, I pressed sweet spots I knew would make her hips lift, voice quicken, thighs part. She loosened slowly and did not neglect the poem. She kept melancholy awake in the words, but song was strongest. Wet with sound, I stroked her. She spoke the final question. *Do I wake or sleep?* I brushed her slick cleft with my breasts. She dropped the book. For a time, distinctions were lost.

I made oatmeal with toasted walnuts and brown sugar for breakfast. Lilian beamed as she ate, playing with my feet under the table. Minnaloushe, keeping us company, crunched dry food in his bowl. I reached across the table and kissed Lil's hands. "Would you come back to Chalk with me? If we're welcome?"

"Yes." She didn't mention ticket prices or cramped seats, but watched me closely.

I told her what I was thinking. "The first time I made a pie after my mother's death, the meringue wept down the sides of the pan. Crust had been my mother's specialty. The slices fell apart, but Frankie ate the filling with a spoon, praising the taste. It meant a lot."

Lil nodded. "You want to be there, cooking for Frankie."

It seemed so obvious and simple. "For the service. With you."

She slipped a white rock into her pocket as she left for work. "I can get the tickets. Don't worry about the money. Jen showed me a Web site. Let me know."

It was an hour earlier out west. I spent time with the want ads, circling jobs and teasing Minnaloushe with the pen, before I went to the phone.

I dialed my father. He picked up, sounding gruff. "Hello."

"Daddy. It's Carline."

He called happily to his wife. "Nanette, Carline's on the phone!" Then, "How are you, Petunia?"

"Petunia" always pleased me. I was sorry to say, "I'm between jobs."

He fell into silence. Frank Sinatra was on his stereo. He asked, "Do you need some help?"

I appreciated the offer, but I had plans to set up a housecleaning service or get a job as a cook if I couldn't find a one as a home economist. "We're okay, Dad. Thanks. That's not why I called. I've been to see Frankie."

"You have?" He sounded surprised, and maybe a little hurt. I hadn't visited him at the condo in a couple of years. "How is she? We heard from her at Christmas."

"Her good friend Ida died. Lil and I might go to the service. I thought you'd want to know."

"Of course. I'll send a card." There was another pause. I thought he might be remembering my mother's death, sorting through the piles of notes. I had answered them with a leaky pen. My fingers were stained for weeks. He was thinking of something else, though. "I remember Ida. She had a gigantic car."

I dialed the next number. "Frankie, it's Carline."

"Well, hi." She sounded uncommitted.

I had a memory of pink plastic frames resting on her cheeks. "After Mama died, you took me to the Gulf. You had flamingo sunglasses?"

"You were home from college."

"I remember you shaking sand from a towel, squinting behind those green lenses. You looked silly but invincible."

"You had lost your mother. I had lost my sister."

"Let me come to the service, Frankie. It would mean a lot to be there."

"It's tomorrow. The tickets would be expensive. You don't have a job."

"We might get them cheap on the Internet. Can we come, Lilian and I?"

She hesitated. "I need you to be respectful."

"I'll do that every way I know how."

"Mel will be here. I'm very fond of him."

"I'm glad for you. I'm sorry I messed up before."

She allowed time for my apology to settle in between us, then said, "Okay. You two come on."

WHEN WE WERE LEAVING THAT NIGHT TO TAKE the red-eye, Lilian almost tripped over a Tupperware bowl full of chocolate cookies on the landing outside our door. On top of it, taped to two odd bracelets, was a note.

I hauled Lil back into the apartment by her belt. "What's it say?"

Peering at the loopy handwriting, she read:

Dear Carline,

Deepest sympathies on the recent loss in your family. At the suggestion of my husband, Mel, I took the liberty of looking you up in the phone book. We live a couple of blocks away, but you know that from the bus. Mel mentioned that you were planning to attend the memorial service this weekend. I have received an invitation from your aunt, but am not able to attend. Would you be so kind as to bring these cookies to Frankie? She might not feel like cooking. The bracelets are for you girls.

Sincerely, Simone Tudro

PS I'd be happy to check on your cat while you're gone. Mel said you have a cat.

Lilian handed the note to me, along with a bracelet of hammered pennies, pierced and strung together. "I put out a huge bowl of dry food for Minnaloushe, and Sarah said she'd stop by. He'll be fine for a couple of days. Nice lady, though. She seems to know a lot about you. Do you think she knows about Frankie and Mel?"

I left my bracelet on the table. "I wouldn't venture a guess. When did you get to be so open minded?"

Lil slipped her own pennies over her wrist and shrugged. "After I changed my mind about a few things I had been absolutely sure of. When did you?"

We got in too late to take the shuttle, so Tucker met us at the gate. "I've got the Mercury," he said after we shook hands. "We would have been squeezed in the pickup, and it's a bit more sensible for a group this size than the bus."

I smiled, thinking of our less-than-sensible trip together across the country. I thought it was generous of Frankie to trust me in the Mercury again. As Tucker unlocked the doors in the parking lot, Lil said, "Roomy."

"It stalls if the engine gets too hot," said Tucker, "but at this time of night, we should be fine. It's a smooth ride for such an old car."

I settled into the capacious back seat, still tidy from the cleaning at the lake. "It was Ida's. Now it's Frankie's."

"You told me." Lil turned around in her seat to see if I was okay. I nodded, grateful for her loving eye.

"Lil's a poet." Once we were on the highway, I leaned forward and spoke above the a/c. "Tucker's a photographer."

Lil glanced at him and said blandly. "Yes. I've seen an example of your work."

Tucker looked nervous. "Oh. Of course." None of us had anything to say for a few minutes, then he cleared his throat. "So, did Carline ever give you an idea for a poem?"

Lil blushed. "Carline is an idea for a poem."

Tucker met her eyes, and they both laughed. Lil reached back to touch my shoulder and said, "Among many other things."

The traffic was sparse except for fast-moving trucks. I watched reflectors catching headlights along the shoulder, content to be praised. It occurred to me that Tucker was as far from home as we were. "Are you getting homesick at all?"

"Me?" He shrugged. "I've got some drinking buddies and housemates that I've been fighting with about paying their bills, but, no, I'm not dying to get back." We passed a well-lit sign for the Highway Church of Christ. Nobody spoke again until Tucker said, "Do you mind if I turn on the radio?" We were treated to a crackling tribute to the music of George Jones, otherwise known as the Possum, almost all the way to Frankie's.

Moon was bright on the chalk as we turned into the lane. I held onto Lil's shoulders from behind until I had to let go to get out of the car. When Tucker and I went to the trunk for the bags, he murmured, "Carline, I need to talk with you."

The front door opened, spilling glare. I shrugged at Tucker. As far as I was concerned, the two of us had pretty much talked ourselves out. Frankie came outside, groping in her purse. The family resemblance was strong. I went toward her. She crossed the porch and leaned down, holding out a roll of candy. "Want a wintergreen?"

I sliced the wrapper with my fingernail and lifted a LifeSaver off the roll. It had more bite than sweetness, but I felt forgiven. Lilian and Tucker each took one, too. We went inside with Frankie, sucking hard.

I woke in the morning in Frankie's bedroom with Lilian asleep beside me. Her legs were tangled in the fringed spread. Tucker had been bumped to the couch. Mel slept with Frankie on the porch.

I had turned over the cookies from Simone the night before. Frankie said, "How thoughtful." She must have known about the wife. The mild look on her face was a masterpiece. I was reminded again of how well Frankie had hidden her feelings for so many years.

I sat up, tucking the sheet around Lil. Because I didn't want to wake her, I resisted the urge to let my hand linger along her hip. I thought of how Ida used to trail crumpled Dixie cups sticky with diet cola all over the house. It was my most vivid memory of her. The liberties she took in Frankie's home had made me jealous, but that was our link. That and love for Frankie. I took a sip of water from my bedside cup in salute.

I had dressy clothes for later, but now I pulled on a pair of jeans and a rugby shirt. I was sitting on the bed tying my shoes when I spotted Tucker through a gap in the curtains. Up early, he was bending over to hose off the ridged steps into the bus, a last minute touch before the service. He dried the steps with paper towels, then washed each wheel. I could see his tenderness for the old bus as he delicately pointed the hose.

Tucker was full of quirky affinities that yielded to more ordinary ambitions. I was familiar with that kind of compromise, myself. I had always admired the engaged way he talked to people while he drove. Now I watched him pull the bus over to the concrete steps Frankie used to make it easier for her to mount a horse. He bounded up them to squeegee the windshield free of dust and bugs. The glass gleamed under his industry. If there had been an Instamatic handy, I might have been tempted to take a snap. Instead, I kissed the air above Lilian's neck and folded neat cuffs in my socks.

Mel was standing in the kitchen wrapping a couple of cookies in a paper towel when I came in. "Welcome back, Carline," he said. "Did you get to meet Simone?"

Frankie picked up a white-handled knife and cut a grapefruit in half.

Feeling edgy, I helped myself to sausage from the skillet, then sat down at the table. "No, she dropped the stuff off. Her note was nice, though."

Mel beamed. "She's a special lady." He put his hand on Frankie's shoulder. "I better get to work." They kissed.

The back door slammed behind him. I hoped it wouldn't wake Lilian.

Frankie slid fruit onto my plate. "So."

There were hollows under her eyes. Her cheeks were slack. She looked as if she had shrunk overnight. She was wearing a pantsuit under her apron. I resisted the urge to tell her it was a nice outfit. If we started down the road of polite evasions, we might not ever make it back. Instead, I took a bite of sausage. "So."

"I'm frightened." She scraped sections from the rind. "I'm not ready for any of this. I barely believe she's gone. I smell her every time I open the bureau. She had her own drawer. Mel's sweet, but we're not serious. Neither of us wants that." She wiped her hands on a napkin. "I gave him one of Ida's scarves."

She's told me about Ida now, I thought. This is telling me.

"Ida was always scared for her boys." Her voice got thicker. "Scared of losing them, terrified of disappointing them." She steadied herself, picked up a spoon, ate a bite of grapefruit. "Mel is carrying a torch for his first love. He loves his wife, too. They have an understanding."

I looked at my plate, imagining Ida's fear. I thought Frankie was making a mistake with Mel, but she was a full-grown woman. I might have said the same about Ida, if anybody had asked. She had been married, too. From what Frankie said, Mel was treating her well. For once in my life, I wasn't interested in my own opinions. "So, you're scared?"

"I've got all these people coming today with nothing to say to them." She looked lost and tired. "But what I'm scared of is what I'm going to do when they're gone."

Hearing Lilian in the hall, I took Frankie's hand. "You'll be all right."

She gripped my fingers. "I've made a decision."

"Good morning." Lilian walked in and turned the stove on under the teapot. "I must have slept late."

Frankie let go of my hand, and assumed her manners. "Oh, good morning, Lilian. Let me find a cup for you."

This was my lover's first few moments in daylight at Frankie's house. I didn't want to make it harder for either of them, so I didn't press Frankie to explain. Instead, I grinned at Lilian, and said, "Good morning, Morning Glory." It was a family endearment. My mother used to say it to me. Lilian puckered her lips from across the room. Frankie sighed, smiled.

When the three of us were settled at the table, Frankie took a small box out of her apron pocket and handed it to me. "I want you to have these."

Lilian made a sound of appreciation as I lifted the earrings by their posts and watched them dangle. They were elegant silver triangles with black enamel and tiny purple stones.

Frankie watched me. "They were Ida's. Do you like them?"

I did. "I love them. I wish I had pierced ears."

Lil leaned on one elbow, the better to admire them. "We can get them altered so they screw on in the back."

"I pierced your mother's ears." Frankie made it sound like an offer. "When we were girls."

I was touched. "Would you do that for me?"

Both of them answered, "Yes."

Those moments at breakfast seemed to exhaust Frankie. She asked if we were through in the bedroom. After we gathered our clothes, she shut herself in with the air conditioner, the closet, the bed, the desk, and the vanity. I heard her crying, but didn't knock. Tucker drove off in the bus. Mel stayed outside. Lil and I cleaned the kitchen, then took showers and got dressed. I left the earrings in a box in the medicine cabinet, but put on a navy dress and taupe hose. My Rockports matched. Lilian was elegant in gold pants and a black shirt. She did make-up for me: mascara, color. She skipped the eyeliner because I was trembling. This could be a hard day. "It's okay," she whispered. I had said the same to Frankie, with less cause.

We heard the bus in the lane. Frankie opened the bedroom door, looking haggard. "It's them."

She hurried out the front door and down the steps. Tucker pulled the bus to a showcase stop in front of the picture window. The women of the Library Guild emerged, calling out to Frankie as the wind excited their skirts. The sight of them here early, eager to help, made me miss the more energetic members of my old board. Lilian retreated to the bathroom to do her own make-up.

Mel, who had been hovering, joined me in the living room. "Show time," he said, looking forlorn.

I picked a piece of lint off his shirt, thinking that I owed him an apology. I got an inspiration. "Wait here. I've got a present for you."

After I fetched my purse and asked him to hold out his hands, I poured the remains of my Venus of Willendorf into his palms.

Her head was in one piece. She had broken in fairly big chunks. He cleared his throat awkwardly. "Isn't that your goddess?"

"Right." I didn't mention her double life as an ashtray. "I thought your wife, since she's so handy, might be able to put her together again."

His face lit up. He was so proud of his wife. "She could make these into a hanging. She does beautiful things with wire and macramé."

Mel bent toward me with his hands cupped, as if he were offering the Venus back to me. He said, "Thanks for the advice you gave me the other day. You know, about going shopping. My wife loves to shop."

I couldn't help but be pleased.

By the time we got to the porch, Tucker was bringing folding chairs off the bus and leaning them against the shed. The chairs were on loan from the Methodist church. Frankie, Mrs. Poll, and Gwen were peering into sacks of food the Guild had brought. Kimmie was in the middle of a story, her hand circling Frankie's shoulder. They were all laughing and crying. Frankie shook her head, denying it all.

Mel and I came down the steps. He slid a little in his wingtips. Tucker handed me a chair. I handed it to Mel. Soon Lilian joined us. We unfolded long rows in the dark hollow of the shed, which had been emptied of trucks and tractors while I was gone. The flatbed wagon was set up across the back as a stage.

I hurried to open the gate so Tucker could park the bus out of the way. Frankie herself pulled the Mercury out of the freshly-painted garage. The lines of the hood emerged slowly from the shadows. She made an event of it, beeping the horn, turning on windshield wipers, flashing lights. Lilian, resting one foot on the gate beside me, murmured, "A little hysterical."

None of the others seemed to find her actions odd. Catching on that Frankie was trying to be a spectacle, Mrs. Poll stopped taping butcher paper to card tables, and clapped. "That's Ida's car," she announced. "The Mercury."

Frankie did a loop around the water tower. Kimmie trotted up with a bunch of daisies from a grocery sack. Frankie braked to let her tie them to the antenna. Both of their faces were red and overexcited. Mrs. Poll, wearing the masking tape on her wrist like a bracelet, sang half a line of "Miss America."

Frankie gave a little wave, looking as sure of love as she was of grief; then she missed the open gate and drove the Mercury into the back corner of the shed.

Mel sprinted across the yard, but Lil and I were there first. Frankie looked up at us, a little dazed. She had a cut on her chin where it had hit the steering wheel. "Humiliation," is what she said.

"No," I gave her a tissue to wipe the blood off her chin. "It's nothing. As long as you're okay."

"How do you feel?" asked Lilian. "What hurts?"

"My chin. I have a headache." Frankie gave an embarrassed smile. "I'd like to get up."

Mel and I helped her out of the car. She was a little shaky, but stood without wincing.

Mrs. Poll replaced the tissue with a decorator napkin. "I'll call the doctor. He's coming, anyway."

"Do you have to?" Frankie asked.

"Just to check," I said.

"What about the car?" She looked distraught.

"The bumper," Mel told her. "One headlight. I don't think you bent the fender. That is a durable automobile."

"We could cancel." Mrs. Poll put her peach fingernails lightly on my arm. "I could make a few more calls."

Frankie stepped away from me and Mel with erect posture. "Absolutely not."

So she lay on the stiff couch in the living room, where she could look out the picture window as preparations continued. Tucker raked the rock, erasing tread marks and stirring up clouds of dust.

The doctor covered the cut on Frankie's chin with gauze and told her to take ibuprofen. He told her to stay awake. Frankie wanted only a few moments of rest.

Mel bent over her with his knee on the couch cushion. He kissed her on the forehead. "The car started. Tucker can fix it. We drove it out back." In the hall, I turned away, toward the guests.

They weren't acting like guests, though. They were Frankie's old friends. Relieved that her injuries were minor, the women filled the kitchen. The sight of them swarming around the table, shoving wooden spoons into salads, pulling the plastic wrap off platters and putting pans of rolls into the oven gave me both joy and pause. I considered chasing down Tucker to make him chop something to keep the gender roles a little bit fluid, but I needed to toast walnuts to sprinkle on a cheese ball, and couldn't be bothered.

The excitement in the kitchen—the smell of onions and cold baked hams, the vision of Lilian, swathed in one of Frankie's aprons, breaking open heads of lettuce with her bare hands—gave me strength. After I made patterns with crackers and carrots around the cheese ball, I went back to my aunt on the couch.

She was staring at the rug instead of the window. "The air conditioner's straining," she said. "Too many people in and out."

I pulled up a chair. "A tough time to have an accident."

Her face pushed against its own surface. "I feel so stupid. Ida's car."

It was the wrong moment, but I told her. "I've done things more stupid. Like hurt myself on purpose for the most puerile reasons. Boys calling me names."

I paused. She blinked at me. "Oh, Sugar."

It was another family endearment, and it shot straight to my blood. Feeling dizzy, I stated the obvious. "You're not stupid. Someone dying makes things hard."

Frankie nodded. She was working to get air. I offered asthma spray, but that was not what she needed. I sat with her a few more moments, until she said, "Okay."

I didn't ask any questions, and neither did she. We would have years to talk. She wanted to be alone, but held my fingers loosely before she let me go.

The people gathered decorously and in good numbers, taking their seats with a minimum of fuss. They parked on the side of the lane, with overflow on both shoulders of the farm-to-market road. Some turned chairs toward each other to speak in small groups. Mel, in a bow tie, ushered as needed. Mrs. Poll and Kimmie greeted. Gwen stayed in the kitchen, minding the rolls.

With blood on her tunic, Frankie had changed into a shirt with a button-down collar that wouldn't brush against her bandage. My staunch aunt looked almost delicate as she walked among her friends. They reached from their seats to touch her gently. Some of the men stood. Frankie was at her most gracious when she was most tense. I saw her pat the doctor's shoulders as if he needed comfort. Perhaps he did.

Lilian and I, sitting toward the back, said hello to people who remembered me as a girl. Some confused the two of us, the way fat women stand in for each other in the memories of acquaintances, but they were closer to recognizing me than I would have come with most of them. I knew Ida's boys, though, as soon as I saw them with their long faces and rawboned strides coming up the lane. They were beautiful young men. As they sat down, Tucker knelt at the end of their aisle and snapped a picture. Before he took it, I saw him mouth, "Okay?" One of them gave a slight nod.

A short woman stood beside the flatbed and started playing a flute. Frankie made her way to the front with Mrs. Poll. She greeted a minister in a collar, too. I stiffened when I saw him. I thought the preaching had already been done.

The minister climbed steps of concrete blocks to stand on the wagon. The flute-player came to a stop. The minister said he wanted to welcome us with what he understood was Ida Kirk's favorite Bible verse. He read in a polished voice, "The chariots shall rage in the streets, they shall justle one against another in the broad ways: they shall seem like torches, they shall run like the lightnings."

I glanced at Lilian, who raised her eyebrows. It sounded automotive, like something Tucker might make up. Lilian could probably tell me the whole story. She had been known to describe my belly as a heap of wheat set about with lilies, quoting the Old Testament chapter and verse. She was fearless when she read. She ranged anywhere.

I couldn't stay with the minister's professional voice as he described the chariot ride of life. My mind couldn't settle on anything he said. When I found myself thinking about my job prospects, I took a deep breath. I wanted to be present to pay Ida last respects. I doubted it mattered to her, but it mattered to Frankie. I closed my eyes to concentrate.

I saw Ida smiling with luminous beneficence against the wavy tin wall of the shed. Looking straight at me, she lifted a Dixie cup full of diet cola and poured it on her head. It cascaded over her, sticky, dark and strong enough to accomplish the transformation promised in a thousand commercials: through the veil of cola, she was light.

The minister stopped speaking. There was a rustling among the people. Ida flared and vanished. I opened my eyes, ready for other illuminations. Frankie climbed onto the wagon and planted her feet.

"I love Ida and I miss her every day. She played a fierce game of Forty-two, with variations she learned from her husband, Tom, who practiced with other members of the Chalk police force at the back of the station house until he passed away. She was the only woman I know who could make the work of putting up peaches unforgettable. Her peaches came out of the freezer sweet as the day they were picked. That's a comfort in winter. She was willing to dance when she cooked. There was always something on the radio that could make her move. I know that there are people here who have scruples about dancing. The minister will tell you that Methodists once took a hard line against it. No card playing was allowed either, which might be why people around here got so interested in dominoes. Ida could make a wild bid look pretty. Just about everything she did was pretty, and that's no small accomplishment."

My aunt went on like that, her skin so red as to become transparent, listing skills and pleasures in her lover's life. Frankie was burning with feeling. It was visible. Lilian was shaking her knee, giving herself over to the details. Frankie didn't stop.

"Ida had a big car. I made a dent in it this morning, ran into this shed. I am struggling without her. She loved to drive. You knew her. She loved her boys, Kyle and MJ, as much as life. I'm not saying anything new."

I watched the boys give each other ambivalent looks as everyone turned to see their serious faces, their ears exposed by conservative haircuts, and the Ida-like way they sat. Frankie had told me that MJ came home from work at the Yellow Front to find Ida on the kitchen floor. He thought she'd been trying to get to the phone. He picked her up and drove her to the hospital, wondering if he should have called an ambulance, if he were doing something wrong. Frankie had asked the boys if they would speak, but she hadn't even been sure that they would come.

I wondered if they liked to read. I could send them paperbacks. They would be lonely without their mother, even if they saw her in visions. I watched the back of their necks. They were so young.

Frankie had sweat dripping down her temples. She said, "I can see Ida sitting on the tailgate of this wagon eating watermelon, leaning forward to keep the juice from her clothes. She could spit a seed from here to the water tower, although she'd never do it in mixed company." People laughed.

Frankie bent toward us, nodding slowly, gathering strength from response. "I miss her." She took a sharp breath. I breathed with her, and, all around me, others did, too. Frankie let grief settle in her face. "I love her. She is with me every day. Speaking of her to you means so much." They were simple declarations, but I saw the release in my aunt's eyes as she stood before friends and neighbors gathered in her shed and said, "That's enough."

Lilian kept her hand on the back of my chair while one of Ida's former students sang and played "Crazy" on the guitar. I had always loved that song. Her voice strained, but she tapped the vein of feeling Frankie had opened. Mrs. Poll spoke about the way Ida had championed the library. The principal of Ida's school gave rote remarks, but behind even them, I felt traces of life, lost. My eyes blurred with tears. The people on their chairs in front of me became a single shape, fragrant in the heat of the shed. Pain was nothing to set me apart from them. I was blinking and indistinct, a mourner. The Methodist choir sang a hymn. The service was done.

The boys left so quickly that the gritty plume their truck raised in the lane was settling over the rest of us as we began to stir from our seats.

Lilian asked if I was okay, brushed dust from my cheeks, then hurried to the house to help Gwen and Kimmie bring out food. I didn't feel the pull of hospitality. I wanted to tell Frankie I loved her, to hug her hard as I could.

She was in the middle of a small crowd near a card table that already had flowers and a bowl of fruit. Mel saw me coming before she did. He picked three apples out of the bowl and started juggling. "Heads up," he said, tossing an apple to Frankie.

She stopped in the middle of a sentence and gave him a look. The apple hit the ground. He nodded toward me, then added an orange. A little girl in tights fetched the errant apple. Mel worked it in. Other kids gathered to watch.

Frankie was too surrounded for a hug, but she smiled at me. The minister said, "We sure will miss you." I didn't know what he meant.

People were clustered in small groups along the horseshoe drive. Lilian came down the back steps with a huge jar of tea. The screen door was swinging open again behind her. Mrs. Poll crouched near the garage to help a little boy with his shoe. Tartar watched from the shade with her chin resting in a groove worn by years of tires eroding the hard, white ground. Small puffs of dust rose from our feet. Mel threw the orange so high that half the children around him looked up. I craned my neck to follow its flight past dark water tower pipes to the chalky sky.

Everything stopped there, caught on film. Even as Tucker took the picture, straddling a pipe, my mind floated up past him to look over everything. Acquaintance with Tucker and his camera had taught me this trick: reverse the angle and pull back. I slid tender vision over Lil and jar, Mel's arm reaching after the orange, Frankie's dear bouffant among the other heads. The rutted, heavily peopled ground stretched like a second sky beneath us.

Drifting toward it, I saw my own part. Tucker said he was driving to Texas. I asked to go. Frankie said Ida's funeral hadn't been right. I said, try again. I walked all the way into Lil's poems. Mel showed lace and I saw. Tucker snapped a picture. I looked. Boys made gestures toward setting me alight. I burned, but found water. I swam and made phone calls. I rode the bus. These were common adventures, but I found myself grateful to have arrived where I was. This showed in my rapt face in the picture, looking up.

The orange fell past Tucker, who had already snapped those of us on the ground. Mel scuffled sideways to catch it. Dust rose like fresh smoke. Tucker lowered his camera. He had climbed the water tower to sit on a rusty pipe in good khakis. He waved at me and called, "I'm coming down."

The girl in tights was shushed by her mother for yelling, "Jump!"

Tucker leaned off the pipe and dangled the camera by its strap. I took it so he could more easily descend.

The minister grabbed Frankie's elbow. She nodded politely, and he led her to greet the choir.

Tucker watched them go, then asked, "Did she tell you?"

"Tell me what?" I handed over his camera, not sure that I wanted to know.

"I'm in negotiations with Frankie about buying this place," he said softly, watching my face. "That big old shed is a good garage for a start-up charter bus company."

The first thing I thought was, this is a memorial service. It would be the single worst place to behave badly. With that in mind, I found a folding chair, and sat down.

Frankie selling her land to Tucker. I couldn't believe it was true. He would buy it if he could, but why hadn't she told me? I thought about our conversation at breakfast, and supposed that she had tried. Slumped in the folding chair, I had a vivid memory of shooting arrows into bales through dusty shafts of light in the barn. I didn't try to sink back into those moments lush with pollen and string-cut fingers. I put my hands on the hot metal chair, and held on. I loved this place from various distances, but it was Frankie's home. She might want to let it go.

Tucker, still talking, pulled up a chair beside me. "I think it might go through, but there are a lot of complications. Frankie should talk to you about all that. It's not my place."

"Why are you telling me at all?" An awful thought struck me. "Does Mel have anything to do with it?" I couldn't stand the possibility that he was trading on Frankie's affections.

"He didn't even know about my interest until Frankie and I made the deal. He's strictly a silent partner in the bus." Tucker put his hands on his knees. "He cares about her, though."

I still couldn't believe it. "Where on earth will you get the money?"

"First time buyer programs. They give micro loans to promote rural business in this state. I've been doing research." Tucker worried his shoe in the dirt. Meeting my eyes, he said, "The reason I'm telling you is to find out if it's okay. Taking that picture of you taught me to ask, so I'm asking."

I rubbed mascara from one eye with my fist. If Tucker took a picture now, he wouldn't see my belly reflected in a pool, but pressed up tight under taupe hose and a navy blue dress. I rested my hand on the flattened curve of it, struggling to loosen something in my mind and heart.

I didn't want Frankie's land myself. Lil had her store, and neither of us would be happy in Chalk, with its small-town sense of protocol. The question wasn't whether Frankie had a right to sell her home, but what she would do afterwards. Did she have plans? I had once edited a financial pamphlet for widows and the recently divorced. Rule one was: No major decisions until one year after the loss. I realized for the first time that this was impossible advice. Frankie had to decide how to live without Ida. I wanted to offer what help I could.

Tucker was still sitting there in rust-stained khakis, waiting for me to speak. I didn't bring up the fact that he had photographed the crowd without asking permission. Any obligation between Tucker and me was not based on impossible rules, but on his need to trust the way he saw the world. I had to trust what I saw, too. There was no reason for me to take his fate in my hands. Neither of us was a child, or naked. I said, "Tucker, you decide."

He kept looking at me. "It's what your aunt wants. I want it, too. I was thinking about opening an ice cream stand, but guess that won't work with the zoning." He gave a lopsided grin. "Still, I'll run tours to Dallas, Fort Worth and San Antonio. I'm turning the garage into a darkroom. I might volunteer to drive a bookmobile." He stood and folded his chair, leaning it against his thigh. "You and Lil could visit any time you wanted."

I stood and folded my chair, too. It couldn't hurt to do a little cleaning up. "Maybe, Tucker. We'll see."

I handed over my chair to him, and went to find Frankie. She was still talking with the choir. I heard someone say that they could see I was her niece; then I was hugging her tightly with my eyes closed. When I opened my eyes, people had moved away, chatting with each other, looking for their children. We had a moment alone.

"You moved me," I told her. "Ida was with us."

I felt grief passing through her. She spoke close to my ear. "I've been wanting to tell you, Carline. I'm going to travel for a while. I'm selling the farmstead to Tucker, but I want what they call an easement on the land."

I opened my eyes and looked at her. "He just told me. I'm glad you know what you want. What's an easement?"

She seemed relieved. "A conservation easement keeps the land from being turned over to developers. Mrs. Poll's daughter at the community college told us about it. I don't know if we can make it fit with Tucker's bus company on the part that's already got buildings, but he's not getting the place if we can't. Kimmie's on the zoning committee, Gwen's on the water board, and Mrs. Poll knows everybody, so they're going to work on it for me. Tucker will have to answer to them."

I had to smile. That shed new light on the bookmobile. He would have his hands full, and so would they. "Well, he did seem to want to be a part of the Library Guild."

Frankie touched my hair. "I want it to be the Ida Kirk Community Land Trust. She loved walking here with me. There are a lot of legal issues to be worked out, so I couldn't announce it at the service." She glanced around, then whispered, "Ida's boys didn't say a word to me. MJ spoke to me the night she died, but nothing since. It breaks my heart."

"Oh, Frankie, I'm sorry." Maybe they couldn't, I thought. They might want to later, but not now.

Frankie and I stepped back from each other, but I reached to touch her shoulder. "The land trust is a beautiful idea. I'm sure it would make Ida happy. And if you want to keep the camp box, it's very useful for traveling."

Frankie was crying, but she gave a tough shake of her shoulders that made her pantsuit shiver like water. "I just might take you up on that, Carline."

Mrs. Poll and the flutist arrived with a brimming plate of food and a Coke for Frankie. I headed for the drinks table to serve tea with Lilian. I had a lot to tell her. I loved the way she was seizing tasks, as if she had never been a stranger here.

THE NEXT AFTERNOON, BEFORE TUCKER DROVE US to the airport, I sat at the desk in the bedroom, printing out my notes for *How To Ride A Bus*. I still had the handwritten pages, of course, but had forgotten the typed version on Frankie's hard disk the last time I left Chalk. This time, I copied the file onto a floppy and cleaned it off the C drive, keeping things tidy. I fooled around a little with different fonts for the title page, too.

The bus was visible out the window, parked in the drive. Through partings in the lace curtains, it seemed inviting. Pledging to myself to finish the pamphlet, I wondered if Frankie would like me to sew pockets on her curtains, too. It was startling to remember that she would not be living here.

Tucker knocked on the door, sticking his head in. "When do you want to leave?" He had offered to show me his business plan, but I was in no position to invest.

"Soon." I had a few versions of the title page scattered on the bed, but I wasn't satisfied with any of them. "Come on in."

He was wearing his denim cut-offs. He glanced over the sheets scattered on the bed. "What's all this?"

It wasn't a secret. "I've been working on a pamphlet."

"I wondered what you were always writing." He said the title out loud, raising his eyebrows in speculation. "'How to ride a bus.'"

I tensed, half expecting him to ask why anyone needed a pamphlet to do something as easy as that. Instead, he said, "Are you interested in any visuals?"

I wasn't sure if I was or not, but told him to fetch the pictures.

We spread them out on the bed. Multiple shots were scotch-taped jaggedly together, their edges lined up to make a panoramic view. Tucker talked to himself as he tried out photos on my pages: stretches of road, white lines, double yellows, the trashed bus, the swing set, the dumpster, the pool. Some were too wide for the paper, but he played with everything. He sat with his ankles crossed, one toe pressed to the carpet, the soles of his shoes in the air.

Tucker slapped a picture of a drainage ditch beside the words: "Bring plenty of water in plastic bottles." I took in the beer cans and broken glass scattered in clumps of bristling grasses that filled the ditch. Shockingly delicate globes of dandelion seeds glistened on slender stems. A hunk of rubber from a blow-out rocked on the flat lip of asphalt outside the ditch. The tire had ripped into a black crescent. I caught a whiff of dead possum again, even though there were no bodies in sight. The ditch was dry. There was beauty in the hollow tangled with weeds and trash, but a traveler might suffer for miles alongside it if she or he were thirsty.

Such a charged juxtaposition of words and images made me wonder what we were doing. Was this still *Modern Homemaker* material, or were we lighting out for new territory? Whatever the answer, I was moved to see that the revealed eloquence of cracked sidewalks, skies and ditches brought new depth and urgency to my sincere advice.

"Tucker," I said, "about that business plan of yours."

He looked up, all attention. "Yes?"

"Do what you need to do to make a living, but emphasize the darkroom. Taking pictures should be central to your long-term plans."

He stared at the photo of the ditch. "Do you remember what you said after I took your picture by the pool?"

"I said you were acting like a jerk." I shuffled through the pictures, entering each one.

"You told me to take pictures inside the bus. I've already started a series. I did some parked at the catfish place in Arkansas. This place." He pointed to a photo I remembered seeing before. "The bus pictures are on another roll. Taking them made me see that I had to buy the bus. I don't have any interiors good enough to show you yet, but I will. I'm thinking of doing some in the shed and the house, too."

The door was wide open, so Frankie and Lilian came in without knocking. "Sorry to interrupt, but there's no time to waste." Frankie put her hand on my shoulder. "Tucker, may we have Carline to ourselves?"

Tucker, as polite as ever, quickly gathered his pictures. He took a couple of copies of the title page, too. "You have good ideas, Carline. You bring them out in other people, too."

"Thanks." I touched his hand. "I'm glad that you've been working. We'll keep in touch." I got up from the bed, then surprised myself by asking, "Could I keep the one of the ditch?"

He didn't hesitate, but smiled at me. "Of course."

I took Tucker's gift and slipped it into my purse. I wanted to spend time looking at it.

Lilian led me to the vanity. "Take a seat." It was hard to change gears, but I did what I was told.

"I'm sorry you can't stay longer." Frankie pulled on a pair of latex gloves and took a new needle from its package.

Lilian ripped open a foil envelope and handed Frankie a wipe. "We'll try to get back to help you move, or Carline will, if we can only manage one ticket. What are you going to do after that?"

Frankie washed my ear lobes with alcohol and heated the needle with a match. "I'm going to drive across the country. I've been dreaming of this for a while, cleaning out the cupboards to be ready when the time came. There are places I've always wanted to see. I read in *National Geographic* that the canyon lands are beautiful. I want to spill a glass of water on the Continental Divide, and spend time at both oceans. I might go to some cities, although I've already seen tall buildings. I might take Mrs. Poll to Alabama to look for her family graves. Before that I think I'll go west into New

Mexico, take I-25, and head north as far as it goes. I wanted to take Mel along for a while, but he needs to get home. Guess he'll have to fly, too."

Her voice shook a little, but she said it right in front of Lilian. Distracted as I was, I was impressed by her candor. I said, "Is that hard for you?"

She was terse. "I'll be okay."

Frankie took another wipe from Lilian and cleaned the needle again. I had been wondering what her plans were with Mel, but knew better than to ask. I spotted him out the window, coming out of the shed to greet Tucker, a bandana tied under his battered cap. "I want to see Yellowstone, and I hear there are some great hot springs in the Canadian Rockies. I've been looking at the atlas."

Lilian held the needle. Frankie pinched my ears to numb them. I sat still. I wanted to warn her about the kind of dreams that rest on too much motion. She was sure to get desperate somewhere. I expected her to drive crying. Frankie had the sense to pull over if it got too bad, but I thought of how she had smashed into the back of the shed. "Are you sure you'll be okay? After the crash?"

She stretched both lobes, pinching harder. I jumped. "Don't move," she said. "Mel and Tucker are fixing the Mercury. It's worth the extra gas to take Ida's car. Tucker says I can park the truck here."

I turned to check with Lilian. She nodded. "Come visit us, or come to stay. We'll take care of Tartar, if you want." I was confident we could work it out with Minnaloushe.

Frankie's face in the mirror looked shocked. "Tartar's going with me. I'll spend a couple of weeks with you, maybe this spring." She took an ice cube from a bag left over from the service, and held it to my ear.

Ice water dripped on my shirt. Frankie said, "Lilian, will you come here with the needle?"

At the mall, this took scant seconds, but I had heard needle guns were not sterile. Lilian pulled my lobe tight across the ice. I closed my eyes and didn't flinch when Frankie jabbed the needle through. The pain was brief. With the other ear, I felt even less.

We should have used gold studs until my ears healed, but there wasn't much blood when Frankie put Ida's earrings in. She dabbed it away with a cotton ball dipped in alcohol.

"How do you like them?" she asked, peeling off her gloves.

She and Lilian were standing so near that their bellies pressed against my arms from each side. Soon, I would need more room, but for the moment it felt good to be tight with the women I loved. To be pierced so carefully was worlds away from cutting in despair. The earrings glinted in my ears. Ready to flourish, I hugged Lil and Frankie by their hips.

EPILOGUE

The oven timer goes off as I finish telling the story. I shake my head from side to side to show off the earrings. Our friends start hooting as if to celebrate Emily Dickinson's betrothal to Mae West. Sarah asks for another poem from Lil, but Jen yells for more food. Lilian fans her crinoline and ripples it in the air, blushing and laughing. The smell of cherry pie fills the room.

I hurry into the kitchen, grateful for a task. I open the oven door to be swept by the heat and aroma of cinnamon, sugar, apples and crust. Grabbing a hand towel, I get ready to make an entrance. I come out snapping the towel and waving the pie pan, the most reckless home economist on the face of the earth. Hungry again, they are calling my name. Everyone except Lilian, who looks me in the eye and says, "Venus."